GIFTED

G. WALTER BUSH

GIFTED

A TRACK AND FIELD NOVEL

AMBASSADOR INTERNATIONAL
GREENVILLE, SOUTH CAROLINA & BELFAST, NORTHERN IRELAND

www.ambassador-international.com

GIFTED

ISBN: 978-1-64960-201-5
eISBN: 978-1-64960-263-3
Library of Congress Control Number: 2022931005

Cover Design by Hannah Linder Designs
Interior Typesetting by Dentelle Design
Edited by Daphne Self

AMBASSADOR INTERNATIONAL
Emerald House
411 University Ridge, Suite B14
Greenville, SC 29601
United States
www.ambassador-international.com

AMBASSADOR BOOKS
The Mount
2 Woodstock Link
Belfast, BT6 8DD
Northern Ireland, United Kingdom
www.ambassadormedia.co.uk

The colophon is a trademark of Ambassador, a Christian publishing company.

For my mom, who walked close beside me on this journey.

ACKNOWLEDGMENTS

Foremost, I'd like to thank Kristen, my wife, who offered the cyber support and expertise this project has required in so many ways when not serving as an enthusiastic cheerleader. Also, this novel would not have been written were it not for my two running children, Kendall and Ryan, whose training and competitive experiences I have shared over the last decade and helped to shape the plot. They contributed to the technical and stylistic elements of the narrative as well.

Finally, many thanks go out to the small corps of readers who took the time to read and comment on the various drafts. Their valuable feedback was crucial to the novel's evolution: Tricia Coblentz, Bill and Noelle Smith, Larry Wheeland, Vikki Vosbigian, Jodie Wicker, Mike Davis, Terri and Bill Smith, Sr., Debbie Martin, and Cindy Smeltzer.

CHAPTER 1

Ben Turner tossed three scoops of dark roast into the coffeemaker and slapped the lid shut. The more bitter the coffee, the better. He winced at the irony. This was sure to be a bitter day.

With the push of a button, Ben set the pot brewing and left the kitchen, the early morning stillness broken only by the tread of his low-cut boots across the laminate floor. Neither tall nor short, he wore an embroidered Montevallo Christian Academy polo that hung loosely over his wrestler's build. The dark blue shirt, tucked behind a belt in his black jeans, needed a good ironing.

Ben stopped in the hallway at a beveled white door and gave it a couple of firm knocks. Drawing no response, he slowly swung it open to reveal a disheveled bedroom half-hidden in darkness. The room sprang to light with the flip of a switch, causing a small cluster of medals hanging on the wall to gleam above the head of his still-slumbering teenage daughter. Steering his way through piles of rumpled clothing, Ben reached the bed and sat next to her motionless figure, wrapped in the comforter like a caterpillar in its cocoon. Speaking softly, he rubbed her back.

"Sarah, Sarah . . . Sarah!"

Despite the prodding, Sarah's response took the form of little more than a moan. "Whaaat?"

"Time to get up. Remember, I'm leaving early for school today to set up a lab. Tiffany's mom will be picking you up at eight." Sarah didn't budge. Opting for a more direct approach, Ben gently shook her as his patience wore thin. "Come on, get up!"

Sarah's lanky frame, draped in an over-sized track meet tee, stirred at last. She sat up, though her eyes remained glued shut beneath a cascade of hair that reached the middle of her back.

"Don't forget your lunch in the fridge, or your running gear for practice."

"OK." Sarah's voice remained little more than a whisper.

"I'm not leaving until you open your eyes and your feet hit the floor." With a groan, Sarah pulled aside her brunette strands to reveal a pair of matching dark brown eyes and untangled her almost gangly legs from the sheets. When her toes finally touched the carpet, Ben added, "I'm going to stop by and visit Mom on the way to school."

For the first time, Sarah managed a clearly audible response. "Oh, yeah," she muttered. "Today is her birthday."

Ben simply nodded. After almost four years, there really wasn't anything new to say. Or feel, for that matter. He stood and bent down to kiss her on the forehead. "I'll see you later at school, sweetie."

"Bye, Dad."

He returned to the kitchen and found the pot had not finished brewing. Sighing over the delay, he ran a hand through his dark, full head of hair, left longer on top and cut closer on the sides. At thirty-seven, he still retained both his natural color and a youthful appearance.

His frustration soon turned to relief. He had almost forgotten. Striding over to the refrigerator, Ben retrieved a long-stemmed rose that had sustained its bloom through the night before placing it carefully in the satchel, already stuffed with graded papers, resting on the dining room table. Then he put on the light jacket hanging over one of the table's chairs. The coffee finally done, he poured the steaming brew up to the brim of his thermos, grabbed the satchel, and headed for the front door, locking it behind him.

Ben, glad for the jacket on the crisp winter morning, made his way through a dappling of shadows and light to a weathered Ford pickup in the driveway. Stashing the thermos and bag, he proceeded to disturb the calm of the neighborhood by turning over the reluctant engine and backing out of the driveway.

Out of habit, he turned on the radio, which promptly blared the top-of-the-hour newscast. He lunged forward to turn down the volume. "Good morning. It's Wednesday, February twenty-sixth, and these are the top stories this morning . . . " The droning voice soon retreated from Ben's mind, replaced by his mulling over the date as he cruised through the labyrinth of tract houses. She would have been thirty-eight today.

Emerging from the neighborhood, Ben found traffic still sparse and the road empty of pedestrians, save for a pair of women running towards him against the flow on the shoulder. Bundled in sleek running tights, hoodies, head bands, and gloves, their reflective neon orange shoes flashed as they bounded closer. Ben gave them a wider berth while noting their impressive pace with a couple of nods of the head. The distance between them swiftly narrowed, and after they flicked by, their images receded just as quickly in the rearview mirror.

The suburban landscape slowly morphed into a more rural part of town, and Ben's mood turned somber again. With the familiar entrance of the cemetery looming ahead, he slowed to negotiate the turn and avoid a gardener, who had just opened the massive wrought iron gates. Ben followed the narrow access road until his truck groaned to a stop at the base of a large, grassy knoll. All at once irritated by the droning, Ben punched the radio off and sat in silence, his knee beginning to shake. Eventually, he removed the flower from the satchel, opened the door, and stepped down onto the crumbling asphalt. The door shut behind him with a clang.

Picking his way through a maze of markers, Ben trudged uphill until arriving at a still-unworn gravestone just beyond its crest, visible from the highway in the distance. Only an occasional car whispered by at this hour. He stepped forward and freed a withered rose from the cobwebs of the plastic holder in order to replace it with his fresh offering. The gesture complete, he stepped back and read the inscription for what seemed like the hundredth time:

Joy Turner
February 26, 1978 – May 21, 2012
Loving Wife & Mother
"For by grace you have been saved through faith. And this is not your own doing; it is the gift of God." Ephesians 2:8

Ben closed his eyes. A few moments later he bowed his head, his hands clasped in front. When he finally reopened his eyes, he gave them a quick wipe and started his trek back down the hill. It was time to get to work.

CHAPTER 2

Ben eyed the microscopes, beakers, eye droppers, glass slides, and nitrile gloves stacked on the tables around him. Then he checked the clock above the whiteboard. Half an hour remained before the start of class, still enough time to get the job done.

Criss-crossing the classroom, Ben began the process of stocking over a dozen lab stations. Barely a minute into the task, the door swung open, and in stepped a trim, six-footer in his forties. His mustache would have matched his thick, dirty blond hair if not for the gray frosting that ran along the edge of his lip. Jack Sutherland, Ben's colleague and best friend, never knocked when entering Ben's classroom.

"Hey, Ben, you got a couple of minutes?"

"Sure," he replied, continuing with his project as Jack walked over to a workstation and leaned back against it in a familiar manner. His arms folded themselves over a school track team tee, complemented by pressed khakis and casual loafers, one crossed over the other. Usually light-hearted, for the moment Jack wore a serious expression.

"Tough morning?" he asked, soberly. "Cathy reminded me on the way out the door."

Without looking at Jack, Ben paused from his work just long enough to answer. "Gets a little better each year, I guess."

A silence ensued, during which Jack smoothed his mustache. After a few nods of his head, he pivoted to a decidedly more upbeat tone. "Well, I wanted to drop by to let you know I may have found a possible prospect."

The statement caused Ben to stop and face his friend, his tone a bit sarcastic. "Are you now playing matchmaker for a poor, pitiful widower?"

Jack laughed before assuming a wide smile. "No, though Cathy might really enjoy that. You and I talked about this last month, remember? Sarah's natural talent will never be adequately served here. We're a K-12 school; we don't have the facilities or, honestly, a coach to match her potential. We don't even have enough athletes to race a league dual track meet schedule." Ben pulled up a nearby stool and sat, deciding to give the conversation his full attention. "Look, you know I'm just a glorified intra-mural coordinator," Jack continued, "and Sarah, with only a few regular season races, still managed to place at the small schools regional last year as a freshman. She ran tough against the large school divisions at the State qualifying meet, too. With quality training, she could be the first in school history to not only win the small schools regional but maybe even qualify for the State meet."

"And exactly what other options are there?" Ben asked, shrugging his shoulders.

Jack seemed excited to present one. "Cathy knows a former college middle-distance runner who works at the gym as a personal trainer but still runs competitively herself. She approached this gal with the idea of taking Sarah on as her personal track coach. Cathy admits the trainer had reservations about the idea, given it's outside her normal gym routine and clientele. But she gave her a business card after Cathy noted it might be worth her time and that Sarah was a really gifted runner." Jack fished his wallet out from a back pocket and handed it over.

Ben glanced at the card for a moment. "What does she charge, and how would it work?"

Now it was Jack's turn to shrug. "The only way to know is to call and find out. I could make you an assistant coach, at least on paper, which would meet rule and insurance requirements. That would also allow you to take Sarah to higher quality invitationals apart from the rest of the team." Sensing Ben's hesitancy, Jack good-naturedly raised his hands. "Whatever you want to do is fine. I just thought I'd throw it out there if you were interested. There's no harm in looking into it." His mission complete, Jack strode back toward the door. He had his own classes to prepare for.

"Thanks, Jack!" Ben called after him. "I appreciate it. I'll think about it." Jack turned and gave Ben a thumbs-up before exiting.

Alone again, Ben tapped the card against his palm as he mused over the news, his knee shaking. Then he looked at the clock once more. He rose and grabbed another microscope.

CHAPTER 3

The final school bell had rung over an hour ago before Ben, armed with his jacket and bulging satchel, stepped out from the school building into the sunny but cool afternoon. He strolled over to the adjacent athletic field filled with gopher holes and sat on a small, dilapidated bleacher. Track practice was nearing its end. Though a Wednesday, it was just the first practice of the week. It had still been too muddy to use the field Tuesday after Monday's downpour. Conditions still looked a little slick.

Jack, blowing a whistle, directed a ragtag group of twenty kids dressed in PE clothes and sneakers, a mixture of girls and boys. As they lined up parallel to an orange cone, Sarah, taller than most of her peers, was easy to pick out—her long hair, pulled back in a ponytail, blowing in the breeze. The crabgrass had been strewn with roughly a dozen additional cones to create a makeshift two-hundred-meter track loop.

"On your marks! Get set! Go!"

When the last command was given, the pack sprinted off to complete four laps around the oval. After the first lap, a couple of boys led everyone, with Sarah loping a few meters behind. By the end of the second lap, she had almost caught them, and near the beginning of the third lap, Sarah took the lead, stretching it to over ten meters by the finish. In fact, she almost lapped a pair of stragglers who preferred to walk while talking the rest of the way.

Following a token stretching session, the practice broke up. Sarah grabbed her belongings, and, with a wave to Jack, Ben stood up and walked with her out to the truck. Depositing her gear bag and backpack into the bed, they climbed into the cab and joined the afternoon commute back home.

Ben spoke first. "How was your day?"

"Same old," she replied cheerlessly, staring out the window as suburbia passed by. A moment later, she added, "Except I kept remembering it was Mom's birthday, and it ruined everything . . . I really miss her, you know?"

Ben nodded. "I know exactly what you mean." He reached across the seat and briefly squeezed Sarah's hand before continuing. "How was practice?"

"OK, I guess." Her voice was tinged with concern. "But I don't know how I'm going to get any better than last year."

Ben frowned and looked over at her. "Why not?"

"Well, for like a million reasons." She laughed before starting to count earnestly on her fingers. "Let's see. One, we don't have practice half the time because rain makes the field too muddy. Two, we don't have a real track. I'm probably going to break my ankle in one of those gopher holes someday, or while slipping around a curve! Three, there's only one coach for everybody on the team, and no matter what event you run we all do the same thing every day! Four, there's no one on the team fast enough to challenge me beyond a sprint, guys or girls."

As Sarah spoke, the truck passed Saddleback Canyon High School, one of several large public schools dotting the valley. Through gaps in the vast visitor's bleachers, they caught glimpses of a track practice in full swing inside the sprawling stadium. Several individual event coaches directed a couple of hundred athletes through a variety of drills and workouts on the modern synthetic track.

Sarah pointed. "How am I supposed to compete with that?" Ben didn't need to follow her finger. He had noted the impressive display of resources and facilities each day on the way home from school for the last two track seasons. "I bet they've got a weight room, too."

Ben took in a deep breath. "What would you think about having a personal coach this season?"

"Are you serious?"

Seeing Sarah's face light up, Ben quickly followed up with a caution. "You wouldn't have any friends or fellow students around."

A burst of air escaped Sarah's lips as she dismissed the concern. "That's not a big deal! Tiffany and Marcie aren't even on the team, and half the kids don't even care; they only come because their parents are still at work."

Ben found himself a little surprised at the intensity of his daughter's reaction. It made the next decision less difficult. "Today Coach Sutherland gave me the contact information for a personal trainer who works with Mrs. Sutherland at the gym. Evidently, she ran middle distance in college and still competes. Do you think I should give her a call?"

"Yes, Dad! Please!" Sarah squealed with a pair of pleading eyes.

Ben nodded. "OK, then. I'll give her a call tonight."

"Thank you!"

Ben wasn't sure just what he had gotten himself into, but given Sarah's reaction, he knew the possibility worth investigating. Her smile the rest of the ride home already served as payment enough.

CHAPTER 4

Sarah had no idea he watched her. Barefoot in black leggings and one of Ben's old college sweatshirts, she sat cross-legged in the middle of her unmade bed, her fingers tapping the keyboard of her laptop and ear buds plugging her ears. Whether she listened to an online streaming channel or a Spanish lesson, Ben didn't know and, truthfully, didn't really care. Sarah kept better than a B average while pursuing co-curricular activities, so he followed the adage 'If it's not broken, don't fix it.'

Moving away from her door, Ben walked down the hall to the study. Sitting down at the heavy walnut desk inherited from his father, he moved the mouse on the pad to stir the desktop computer from its slumber. Amid logging onto his financial accounts, a pair of framed photographs standing to the side of the screen drew his attention. One captured Ben and Joy sitting at a school banquet table with Jack and Cathy Sutherland. Each with a glass in hand, the four clinked them in a toast, smiles filling their faces. He remembered the evening fondly. They had done a lot of laughing that night. How many years ago was it now? Five? Six? He wasn't sure. The only certainty was that evening, that life, now seemed like a world away.

Next to it stood a shot of Sarah as a freshman on the medalist podium at the small school's regional meet. Ben picked the picture up and studied it. A smile stretched from ear to ear on Sarah's face, a large medal hanging around her neck at the end of a thick, green ribbon. His heart warmed. That day had been the first time he saw Sarah smile like that since Joy's passing.

He replaced the photo and pulled out a pad of paper, a pencil, and a calculator. For the next ten minutes he crunched a series of numbers that ended with him circling '$400/month.' He retrieved the personal trainer's business card from his wallet and stared at it. Then his eyes returned to the photograph of Sarah on the podium.

He grabbed his phone and dialed the number. After enduring several rings, the call went to voicemail. The message offered a confident, measured voice: "Hello, you've reached Amber Jones. I'm not available right now, so please leave me a message and I'll get back to you."

Following an abrupt beep, Ben spoke. "Hi, my name is Ben Turner . . . Cathy Sutherland spoke with you about the possibility of training my daughter, Sarah, for track . . . and she gave me your card. I'd like to meet with you at your earliest convenience to discuss the idea further. I look forward to hearing from you."

After leaving his number and saying goodbye, he punched the end call button and looked over his shoulder to find Sarah spying on him at the door. He chuckled to himself. "Well, I guess two can play that game."

"What do you mean?"

"Nothing, Sweetie." Smiling, Ben motioned with his hand. "Come here."

Sarah shuffled over and draped her arms over him from behind, resting her chin on one shoulder. Her face bore a sincere expression. "Thanks for calling, Dad. I appreciate it."

The words found Ben's heart. "Think we should pray about it?" Sarah nodded, and Ben obliged. "Lord, please guide us through this decision, and we ask that You would already be at work in the heart of this trainer. We ask this in Jesus' name, Amen."

"Amen!" echoed Sarah.

Ben kissed her forehead. "OK, back to your homework."

"It's basically done already," she assured him. "Then I'm going to watch the end of *The Bachelorette*."

Sarah stood up and bounced back to her room; Ben's gaze followed her long after her exit.

CHAPTER 5

"Objective, Data, Analysis: all three sections need to be complete and clearly labeled, or you will be marked down." Ben's overview barely beat the bell, and the students quickly packed up and dispersed. All except one straggler who approached Ben on his way to the teacher's desk.

"Mr. Turner, when did you say the lab report was due?"

Resisting the urge to laugh, Ben pointed to the board. "Joey, I repeated the due date twice today, and it's been posted on the board all week."

Joey quickly found the answer before hurrying to join his peers in the chaotic hallway. "OK. Thanks, Mr. Turner," he shouted over his shoulder.

Shaking his head, Ben looked down on his desk to find a notification on his phone. He had received a voice message from Amber and played it. After listening for a few moments, he checked his watch and pocketed the phone prior to grabbing his jacket and keys and locking up his room. On his way to the parking lot, he stopped by the desk of the principal's secretary in the front office, occupied by a grandmotherly woman with a taste for scarves. She looked up from her computer screen with glasses halfway down her nose.

"Hi, Debbie. I'm going to be off campus during my prep period today. I should be back by lunch."

"OK, Ben. Thanks for letting me know." By the time she had found her place on the screen again, Ben was already out the door.

Minutes later, Ben pulled into a busy commercial center and parked outside a coffee shop. Stepping in, he found the store moderately full, with half a dozen customers waiting to order and only a few empty seats. Opting not to join the line, he scanned the room. His eyes soon spotted a slender woman in her late twenties sporting a light-blonde, blunt haircut that fell just past her shoulders. Perched on a tall chair at the end of a barista bar, a familiar pair of neon orange trainers dangled from the end of her toned legs, thinly veiled by black compression leggings that reached her ankles. However, it was a fitted University of Arkansas tee, residing beneath the light, quilted ski jacket she wore unzipped, that confirmed her identity to Ben.

Suddenly a little nervous, Ben willed himself over to stand behind the open seat opposite her. While she cradled a coffee cup with one hand, the other floated above a cell screen. He waited for a moment, hoping for her to sense his presence, but when she failed to look up from her phone, he found himself forced to interrupt her.

"Excuse me, are you Amber Jones?"

Ben noted the pair of green eyes that glanced up warily. "Yes . . . "

"I'm Ben Turner. I got your message," he assured her in his best 'I'm-not-a-stalker' voice. He seemed to have at least some success.

"Oh, hello," she replied, her guard lowered a notch.

Ben decided against offering a hand and slid up on the chair. A hand was not offered either, though Amber did attempt a smile before putting down the phone and clutching the coffee cup with both hands, partially covering her face. Her clear skin required minimal make-up, mostly mascara accenting her oval eyes.

Ben attempted to lighten the mood with a joke. "I didn't need the Arkansas shirt to find the personal trainer in this crowd." When Amber's half-smile served as her only reply, he promptly continued. "Were you one of the runners I saw on Broadway yesterday during my morning commute?"

"Probably. My training partner and I take a weekly long run."

Ben filled the ensuing silence. "Well, thanks for returning my call and agreeing to meet. I'm glad I was able to catch you during your break."

"You're welcome," she replied evenly. "But I want to be up front with you that I gave Cathy my card largely as a favor to a co-worker. I'm not really sure what you're looking for and have my doubts it will work with what I do."

He took his cue to explain. "OK, well, my daughter, Sarah, is a sophomore at Montevallo Christian Academy, where I also teach. Based on her freshman year, she seems to have a gift for running, and the coach, Cathy's husband, thinks she can't reach her potential without some help."

"What's her best event and PR, or personal record?"

"The eight hundred meters. She ran a two-seventeen."

Amber's blank expression remained unchanged. "Did she have any experience before last year?"

"No," said Ben, shaking his head.

"Has she run since last season?"

"Not before starting practice last month."

Before proceeding, Amber seemed to make a mental note. "OK. Go on."

Ben affably complied. "The school doesn't have adequate athletic facilities, and the coach doesn't have much expertise. Honestly, I don't really know how it would all work, though I'm open to suggestions, or what it would cost. Do you even feel capable of training a high school runner?"

Appearing to smother a look of irritation, Amber took a deep breath. "Given my fifteen years of experience in track, I assure you I'm well familiar with female-oriented training at every level of middle-distance, ranging from junior high to post-graduate competition . . . Your daughter's potential seems legit given her PR and lack of experience, but February is a bit late to start serious training for a track season." Amber paused to think a moment further before proceeding even more firmly than before. "For me to have any interest in taking this on, we'd have to be clear about a few things from the outset."

"OK," Ben answered tentatively.

"I have a rigid schedule that doesn't allow for holding a separate practice. So, we would have to use a shadowing style of training, in which she would mirror the workouts I run with my training partner, with modifications, of course. And there would be no flexibility on workout times. Does she have a school schedule that will allow track workouts between six and seven-thirty in the morning as well as afternoon weight and conditioning sessions at the gym? I'm not able to provide any transportation."

" . . . I think we could make that work with some imagination."

"My involvement would also be limited to training; I can't attend her meets given my own competition schedule."

" . . . Understood."

"Well, if those are not issues, this type of training would require a commitment level beyond that of the typical teenager. I have no desire to be a babysitter or a motivational coach. And other activities will need to be scheduled around her workouts."

Ben shifted on his chair and assumed a more confident tone that matched Amber's caution. "Sarah seems reasonably mature for her age and very motivated. She's actually the one who asked me to make the call. But I can certainly make sure she understands the expectations, including making workouts a priority."

Amber wasn't ready to commit yet. "OK. But still, and I'm afraid there's no polite way to say this, you also need to understand that sharing my personal workouts would be an intrusion of sorts into my private life. I wouldn't stand for parental hovering and second-guessing unless there's a serious issue that needs to be resolved."

Ben nearly laughed. "I don't see that as being a problem at all. I'm happy to give Sarah—and you—all the space in the world, and I'm certainly no expert when it comes to running." The conversation stalled, and Ben grew solemn before continuing. "Look, you seem to have really thought this through, and I appreciate that for both our sakes."

Amber's expression relaxed another notch, and her tone softened. "All that being said, your daughter's primary event actually is a good fit, since I'm also an eight-hundred-meter runner. I guarantee she would receive the highest level of running and weight training, not to mention diet and tactics coaching, available to a high school runner anywhere."

"What facilities do you use?"

"El Rancho Community College has a certified synthetic track, and the weight room at the gym is fully equipped."

"So," said Ben amicably, trying to wrap things up, "if we can meet your conditions, how much money are we talking about?"

For a moment, Amber's face looked almost apologetic. "I'd give a steep discount from my normal hourly rate, but at roughly fifteen hours a week, it still won't be cheap: eight hundred dollars a month, payable at the start of each month. And as a safeguard for both of us, I'd want the option to renew on a monthly basis."

Ben succeeded in masking his dismay at the price tag before landing the conversation. "OK . . . I will seriously discuss all this with Sarah." He stood before adding, "Thank you for your time and candor. I'll be in touch with you soon."

Finally releasing her grip on the coffee cup, Amber offered her hand with a more genuine smile. "Look forward to hearing from you."

Ben nodded and headed for the door, leaving Amber the very embodiment of conflict.

CHAPTER 6

It was an hour after sunset when Amber reached her apartment door, her gear bag slung heavily upon her shoulder. She let it slide to the entryway floor with a thud and walked towards the sound of chicken sizzling in the kitchen. There, a woman a couple of years younger than Amber stood fanning herself over a wok on the stove. Her bright orange tights, almost matching her trainers, clung to a figure a few inches taller than Amber and slightly thinner and contrasted sharply with her dark skin. Tight curls framed her face, below which shone a bright gold necklace and earrings.

"Hey, Kiana," Amber greeted on the way to the sink to wash her hands. "That smells good!" Not the most skilled cook, Amber usually set and cleared the table and washed the dishes afterward.

Kiana turned briefly from her stirring to offer a bright smile. "Oh, hey! Did you meet with the dad of the high school girl today?"

Amber frowned. "Yes, and I don't feel great about how I handled it."

"Why not?" asked Kiana with a surprised expression.

"I'm afraid I came off a bit rude, essentially 'my way or the highway.'"

"What was the guy like?"

Her hands dry, Amber started with the plates and silverware. "Maybe a little younger than I imagined. He seemed nice enough, though, not creepy like some guys at the gym who try to hit on me. But what will his wife and daughter be like? I didn't see a ring, but what does that really mean in today's world?"

That comment seemed to renew Kiana's interest. "Was he cute?"

"Man, you don't mess around! I wasn't exactly checking him out." Amber grinned. "I wouldn't say he was ugly." After a pause, her earnestness returned. "Evidently, the girl is a legitimate raw talent. She's run a two-seventeen eight hundred meter with almost no training. But I'm still worried that by adding her into our routine it may hurt our workout dynamic and become a big distraction." Amber's eyes began to water, and her voice grew strained. "I've worked too hard for too long to make my comeback, and this season will probably be my last chance to finally reach the Trials."

"I know," sympathized Kiana, pushing out her lower lip. While keeping one hand stirring, she reached out with the other and touched Amber's shoulder. "On the other hand, adding someone new into the mix, even a teenager, might freshen things up. It might actually be fun. I mean, is it really that ideal now with just the two of us training? Perhaps we could use a change."

"That may depend entirely on the girl . . . and her parents," replied Amber, regaining her composure.

Then Kiana introduced a different angle. "I mean, you could really use the money for the rest of the season. Neither one of us has had a corporate sponsor, but my graphic design work is more consistent and pays better than personal training."

"True." Amber searched the ceiling as she considered the matter. "With all the travel expenses and entry fees, not to mention a temperamental car and the rent increase, finances are getting complicated for me." She sighed heavily. "I guess I'm not as opposed to the idea the more I think about it. I'm fine with it either way. If it's meant to be, it's meant to be."

"Well, I'm glad to hear it, 'cause it's time to eat," announced Kiana, turning off the stove and carrying the pan over to a hot pad on the table.

Before they could sit, however, Amber's phone vibrated. She pulled it from the side pocket of her leggings and read a text message that raised her eyebrows. Then she looked up at Kiana. "Well, I guess it's meant to be."

CHAPTER 7

The no-knocking rule was a reciprocal agreement, and today Ben was glad for it. He charged into Jack's room in a hurry, with the day's opening bell just ten minutes away. In the middle of writing the day's lesson plan on the white board, Jack glanced briefly at him while completing his scrawl.

"I'm stopping by to inform you that today will be Sarah's last day at practice." Ben perched on the edge of the nearest desk in the front row as Jack stopped his task and faced Ben, smiling.

"So, you called her!"

"I did, and we made a deal—an expensive one at that." At the raising of Jack's eyebrows, Ben explained. "Ms. Jones is an intensely focused and extraordinarily thorough woman. She leaves little doubt that she knows what she's doing, whether it's the detailed workout regimen, suggested diet supplements, or the recommended training gear. The shopping list she texted me alone will cost a small fortune!"

"I guess that's good," Jack commented almost as if asking a question.

Ben couldn't help smirking as he confirmed his friend's notion. "Yes, it's good. But she had so many contractual demands I felt like I needed a lawyer."

"What do you mean?" Jack looked confused.

"Let's see," Ben began, now chuckling. "Non-negotiable practice times; no parental hovering; no providing transportation; no babysitting; no expectation of her coming to Sarah's meets; monthly renewal option for both parties." Ben stared at Jack with wide eyes. "I think I'm still missing a few."

Jack joined in on the laughter. "Did she put all that in writing?"

"No, but it did require a no-nonsense sit-down with Sarah to make sure all the effort and expense will be worth it." Ben quickly dropped the humor, and his knee started jiggling up and down. "This will be nothing like we've ever done before, with track workouts in the early morning before school at the community college and weight sessions after school at the gym." He took in a deep breath. "I practically need a crane to get her out of bed as it is. So, I got her to make some commitments about time management, bedtimes, and her attitude when reality sets in . . . as well as concessions on future birthday and Christmas presents. The more I think about it, that monthly renewal option may be just the thing I need to keep Sarah accountable."

"Do you mind telling me how much she's charging?" Jack smoothed his mustache.

Ben had not quite recovered from the sticker shock. "Eight hundred a month." Jack stopped his smoothing and whistled. "But when you calculate both track and weight workouts," Ben added, "that's only around thirteen dollars an hour, which seems more than reasonable given what she's providing. Still the sheer number of hours per month adds up."

"Maybe Cathy can get Sarah a free gym membership."

"That would help," Ben admitted, "but it's only for three months. Maybe I can do some extra tutoring. Though I'd prefer not to tap into

G. WALTER BUSH   33

Sarah's college fund for part of it, Sarah did make a really good point. A couple of thousand dollars is a small investment to make if she can land a college scholarship worth fifty times that or more."

"That puts things in perspective," noted Jack.

"Anyway, thanks for the tip, Jack." Ben stood up and prepared to leave as Jack stepped forward and patted him on the shoulder.

"I'm glad it's working out. I'm sure it will all be for the best. I wish you guys well, and I'm excited to see what happens." Ben took several strides towards the door, and just as he reached it, Jack remembered one last detail with another smile. "Oh, Ben! I understand Ms. Jones is not too hard on the eyes, either."

His hand already on the handle, Ben swung around with a grin. "No comment."

CHAPTER 8

Their hands full of shopping bags, Ben and Sarah wedged their way through the front door as they escaped the rain. Most of their Saturday afternoon had been spent getting drenched while crossing off items on the list of gear Amber requested before Monday's first practice. Her jacket dripping and her hair matted down, Sarah attempted to deposit the bags on the living room couch before Ben redirected her.

"Don't leave those there! Pick them up and continue right into your room. You're going to put these things away right now, not leave a mess out here." With a huff, Sarah picked them back up and carried them down the hall, with Ben in close pursuit.

They removed their jackets and hung them to dry before they unpacked a cornucopia of purchases. Alongside trainers and racing spikes grew a mountain of spandex in every color: compression leggings, shorts, racer tops, and sports bras, with gloves, a rain slicker, a beanie, and a head band thrown in. Ben stored the nutritional supplements in the kitchen while Sarah cut off the tags and put her new track clothes away. When Ben returned, he picked up a small box that contained the most expensive and, according to Amber, indispensable item: the GPS watch. Not merely a recorder of time, distance, pace, heart rate, and calories burned, it could be set to goal paces and, if necessary, even measure elevation change. Once set up, all the information would upload automatically to an online log, where Amber would access and review it.

"Happy Birthday and Merry Christmas!" Ben smiled at his daughter. Sarah merely crawled on to her bed and sat cross-legged in her socks and sweatpants. Assuming a sober expression, she remained silent.

"You're being presented with a rare opportunity," Ben firmly reminded her. "I hope you're ready for it. Remember, either Amber or I can cancel this arrangement each month if it goes sideways. It will take sacrifices. Like getting out of bed when you don't want to. Like doing your laundry mid-week; not waiting for Grandma to do all of it on the weekend. Like maybe starting your homework at lunch during the week . . . "

Sarah didn't wait for Ben to continue the list. "I get it, Dad! I'd be an idiot to blow this!" She looked down while playing with the tassel of the pillow on her lap. Her voice grew quiet. "I won't let you down . . . I won't let myself down."

Worried that he'd come on too strong, Ben switched gears. Grabbing the little-used chair at Sarah's desk, he picked it up, swiveled it around, and straddled it next to her by the bed, his arms resting on the back. "I told Amber we'd have to use some imagination to make this work. So, let's walk through this together and come up with a clear plan to help you succeed." Sarah's dark brown eyes looked up from the pillow. "We need to arrive at the track by five fifty-five a.m. The college is ten minutes away at that time of day, so if we pull out of the driveway by five forty-five we're good. If you have everything ready to go for the next day before bedtime, how long would it take you to get in the car by five forty-five? Remember, you'll shower after practice."

After running the scenario through her mind, Sarah estimated, "Fifteen minutes. Maybe less if I sleep in my workout clothes. Besides dressing—if I even have to—all I need to do is brush my teeth, get my water jug, and walk to the car. Maybe grab a granola bar, too," she added on second thought.

"Excellent! That means you can sleep until five-thirty, but only if you've done all the following the night before: laid out your morning workout clothes, unless you sleep in them; laid out your school clothes for when you get back from the track; and have your afternoon workout clothes ready in a bag, too. You'll change at the gym when you get there. That leaves having your water jug full, and all your school stuff already packed in your backpack. Is that doable?"

"Totally," assured Sarah, her tone rising a few notes. "I should be able to get all that done in fifteen to twenty minutes before bed."

"Great! Now let's talk about the turn-around between the track practice and getting to school. Amber knows we have to leave the track by seven-thirty, which gets us home no later than seven forty-five. Can you shower in ten minutes?"

Sarah gave the matter some thought while sitting up and dangling her legs over the edge of the bed. "Yes . . . but only if I'm quick."

"You'll have to be. And if your school clothes are already laid out, can you get dressed in another ten minutes?"

"Only if I do a rush job on my make-up," she decided with a tentative nod.

"Rush job it is. So, we're at eight oh-five. I will have the lunches made the night before. While you're showering and getting dressed, I'll put your lunch in your backpack, put your bike in the truck for your ride to the gym after your last class, and make your protein shake, which you can drink on the way in the car."

"Maybe eat a bagel, too."

"Sounds good. So, if we leave by eight ten at the latest, we'll reach school by eight twenty-five at the latest." Ben laughed. "That leaves all of five minutes to spare. You'll have to take care of locking your bike at the racks on the way to class. I don't want you to be late, but I really can't be late. I'll have almost thirty students waiting outside my classroom door." Ben's tone suddenly grew firm again. "Believe me, I'll be cracking the whip if you fall behind schedule."

Taking it all in, Sarah shook her head and let out a big breath. "This is gonna be crazy! But I think it's worth taking a chance. I'm so nervous."

"It is going to be a little crazy. For both of us." Ben tilted the chair forward and kissed Sarah on the forehead. "But I believe you're going to rise to the occasion."

CHAPTER 9

Parked outside the stadium, Ben and Sarah observed the surrounding foothills turn slowly from black to purple through the fogged-up windows as the first rays peeked over a high ridge still dusted with snow. The news droned softly on the radio as Ben took a sip of coffee from his thermos.

"Well, so far you're one for one on getting up on time," he said. "You're batting a thousand percent!"

"I was so scared I'd sleep though my alarm," a bundled Sarah confessed, the hood of her sweatshirt falling over the back collar of her letterman's jacket. "I don't think I went back to sleep after five a.m. What will you be doing while I'm at practice? Going home or to school?"

"Neither. Not only would that waste time, but I think I should stick around in case there's a problem, at least for a week or two." He patted the satchel resting on the seat between them. "I need to use my time efficiently, just like you, so I'll be grading papers in the car."

"How are you going to do that? There's no desk in here."

Ben smiled, pleased at his own cleverness. "That's why I brought this." He reached into the satchel and pulled out a clipboard. "With this and my coffee, I'll get along just fine."

As he finished speaking, a pair of headlights appeared at the entrance to the empty lot and gradually grew larger. Ben wiped the fog from his window to watch a silver two-door sedan navigate its way into a spot a couple of spaces away.

Sarah's voice quivered. "My stomach hurts. I'm scared to meet them."

"It may be awkward for a few minutes," he allowed, "but I'm sure you'll feel comfortable with them in no time. They're here to help you."

Still, Ben said a quick prayer under his breath while clicking off the radio, the sound of the sedan doors opening and closing magnified by the sudden silence. Amber and Kiana emerged, both with bags slung over their shoulders and their hands warming in their hoodie pockets, cuing Ben and Sarah to exit into the crisp morning as well. Sarah rounded the truck to join her father and stood stiffly with both hands on the handle of her water jug. Ben broke the ice.

"Good morning, Amber. This is Sarah."

Amber, her hair pulled back in a ponytail beneath a wide headband, squinted into the glare on the horizon and smiled. "Hello. Nice to meet you, Sarah." She gestured with a gloved hand. "This is my roommate and training partner, Kiana. We've been friends since our days running together at Arkansas."

"Hello!" Kiana smiled from beneath her hood while giving a little wave.

"Good morning," echoed Ben and Sarah, waving in return.

Ben looked at his watch. "So, you'll have Sarah back here by seven-thirty? It'll be a tight squeeze for us to get to school, but I think we can make it."

"Yes," Amber nodded. "I'll be sure to let her go by then. That means we better get started. You ready, Sarah?"

"Yes, ma'am."

Amber grinned. "Well, that's a first for me. Sarah, you may call me Amber, and I'm sure Kiana feels the same way."

"Speak for yourself!" joked Kiana. "I kind of like this 'ma'am' stuff! Just kidding, Sarah!" She flashed another bright smile, and Sarah grinned, too, before facing Ben.

"See you later, Dad."

"Have a great practice, sweetie." With that, she left with the pair to enter the stadium as Ben looked on. When they were finally out of sight, he climbed back into the truck and pulled out the first set of papers in the growing light.

*****

Reaching the artificial grass of the infield, the three plopped down their gear. The stadium was empty, save for a lone jogger chugging away in an outside lane. Sarah removed her letterman's jacket, a Scripture prominently embroidered on its back: "Do all for the glory of God" (1 Cor. 10:31).

Amber stood pondering it. "What's that quote on your jacket about?"

"Don't you know a Bible verse when you see one?" chided Kiana.

Sarah, now pulling her hair back into a ponytail, turned and politely answered Amber. "It's just a reminder to do my best with the gifts God has given me and not take all the credit for my accomplishments."

"I can get on board with that!" said Kiana, but Amber's face remained puzzled while squatting down to tightly double tie the laces of her trainers.

"OK, Sarah, Kiana and I are going to start with a four-lap shake-out, what we call our easy warm-up jog, but today you can start with three laps before we stretch. Run at your own pace and don't worry about keeping up with us. We should all finish at pretty much the same time." Sarah nodded. "And just so you know in case you didn't, it's correct etiquette to run outside Lanes One and Two if there are faster runners on the track."

With that, they split up for the next several minutes, but after completing their shake-outs, they reunited on the infield, a light sweat beginning to bead on their brows. "OK. Now we do our dynamic stretches," Amber informed Sarah. "Have you ever done hamstring scoops?"

"No." She shook her head.

"Let's get in a line then. Kiana, you go first, and I'll watch Sarah from behind and help her."

Kiana proceeded to step forward with her right leg and land on her heel, the leg straight, before bending deeply at the waist, sweeping the tips of her fingers across the turf, and then rising back to her full height again in one constant motion. No sooner had she finished with her right leg than she stepped with her left leg and repeated the same motions for each leg several times. From behind, Sarah copied her movements as best she could, until Kiana stopped about thirty meters down field.

"Not bad," said Amber, finishing her own set behind Sarah, "but you need to exaggerate landing on your heel and try to keep your leg straight while sweeping the grass." While speaking, Amber modeled the key points again. "Kiana, let's do another set."

Kiana complied, and they worked their way back to their gear.

"Strike with heel, leg straight, bend deep," called Amber from behind. "Good, Sarah." Sarah allowed herself a slight smile as she got the hang of it.

"Do you feel that in your legs?"

"Oh, yeah."

"OK. Now we'll do what we call 'cross-touches.' This time we'll move sideways." Kiana again took the lead, crossing one foot over the other before pausing, hinging at the hips, and touching the tips of the fingers of both hands to the toes of the back foot. After rising again, she repeated the same process half a dozen times. Keeping an eye on Kiana, Sarah did her best to imitate the movements during the first set, after which Amber once again stepped over and modeled the key details of the stretch.

"Keep your back flat and stick your butt out. Make your hips a hinge, and don't bend." Sarah repeated Amber's movements. "That's it! Good! Now we'll do the other leg on the way back."

Kiana headed the column once more, and when they arrived back at their gear, she looked back at Sarah finishing her last one. "Nice form! You're a quick learner, Sarah." Sarah's smile grew larger.

"Now we do some static stretching," informed Amber. "You'll find this a bit easier, I think."

Sitting in a triangle, they followed Amber's lead as she assumed the butterfly position. Her knees pointed out cross-legged style with the heels of each foot meeting each other and both hands pulling them in towards the groin. She then used her elbows to lightly press down on the inside of the knees.

"I've done this one at school before," noted Sarah, who assumed the position easily.

"Yeah, it's pretty common," Amber acknowledged.

A minute later, Amber repositioned herself by straightening out one leg and reaching for her toes for several seconds while keeping the heel of the other close to the groin. "This one, called the hurdler stretch, is also pretty common."

"I've done this one, too," Sarah commented, imitating Amber. In a second variation, they adjusted the bent leg to have the heel pulled back towards the butt. After switching to stretch the other leg, Amber introduced one last stretch.

"You may not know this one; it's called the pretzel." Keeping her left leg straight, she crossed her right leg over, bent the knee, and placed the foot on the ground just above her left knee. Then she rotated her torso until her right elbow reached the far side of the upright knee. Pressing against the knee with the elbow, she twisted her torso until she was almost looking behind herself. Given Sarah's scrutiny of Amber's positioning, the stretch was clearly new to her. "You should feel that from your butt all the way down the side of your leg, what's called the I-T band, short for iliotibial band."

Sarah's eyebrows raised. "I do."

By the end of the stretching session, the sun, now well above the ridges in the distance, was starting to take the edge off the temperature. Amber and Kiana took off their hoodies, revealing light, long-sleeve jerseys. With only short sleeves beneath, Sarah elected to keep her sweatshirt on. Kiana headed off to the track to begin her workout, while Amber faced Sarah, her hand blocking the glare of the sun.

"Kiana's going to do her own workout today while we do ours. Today we'll be running four hundred-meter repeats. Have you ever done repeats?"

"I doubt it. I'm not even sure what they are."

"We'll do all kinds of different repeat distances over the season, but today we'll be running four-hundreds. I'm going to be running ten of them, but you'll just be running every other repeat to start. Today we'll begin each one together, though we'll have different goal times. I'll be trying to hit sixty-six seconds and you'll be shooting for seventy-two. Make sure you start and stop your watch each time you cross the start-finish line. I'm going to be jogging a lap in between each of my repeats while I recover, but to start I'll let you walk your lap in between, in Lane Three. If I'm not back to start your next repeat, keep loose by walking in a circle until I arrive." Amber clapped her hands. "Ready?"

"Yep!" Sarah gave two thumbs-up, not feeling as brave as she acted. They jogged over to the start line and gathered themselves. Observing how Amber held the wrist wearing the watch across the top of her stomach with her other hand, the thumb over the button, Sarah did likewise.

"Three, two, one!"

On the count of one, Amber punched the button with a beep and darted off, Sarah a step behind. Sarah sprinted to full speed in an effort to stay up with Amber's measured strides around the first curve and found herself still within five meters of her new coach at the one-hundred-meter mark. But mid-way down the back stretch it became clear she would not be able to hold the pace. By the time she reached the two-hundred-meter mark, her lungs screamed, and her legs burned. As she struggled through the second curve and down the home stretch, Amber's lead widened up to forty meters. By the time she gasped across the finish line, groping for the stop button on her watch, her chest was heaving. While walking into the curve, the now-jogging Amber already fifty meters into her recovery lap, Sarah looked at her watch: seventy seconds. She felt an initial wave of relief but how in the world she was going to do it four more times?

A few minutes later, her breathing back under control and the burning subsided, Sarah turned towards the line to start her second repeat as Amber jogged down the homestretch toward her third repeat. Seeing that Amber had stripped down to her racer back top, the steam rising off her body, Sarah suddenly realized how hot she was. Quickly pulling off her sweatshirt, she tossed it on the infield, grateful for the early morning chill. This time, she was determined to set a pace she could sustain. Gauging Amber's speed, Sarah joined her jog about five meters before the line, and a pair of watches beeped as they crossed it.

As on the first repeat, Amber strode steadily ahead along the rail, but this time Sarah did not try to match her tempo, opting instead to set her own rhythm. Halfway down the back stretch, she began to feel the lactic acid seeping back into her muscles, but she passed the two-hundred-meter mark without unduly stressing her breathing. Holding pace around the second curve, she reached the home stretch with a little gas still left in the tank and accelerated, hyperventilating only as she approached the finish line.

The watch beeped. Her chest heaving again, she quickly slowed to a walk and looked once more: seventy-one seconds. The success propelled her throbbing legs forward around the curve. But there were still three more to go . . .

*****

By the time Sarah had finished her five repeats and jogged her half-mile cool down, the time was seven-twenty. Kiana had rejoined them for the post work-out stretch. Since each was pre-occupied with her own fatigue, no one talked until Amber, leading them in a Spider Man pose, piped up. "So, what were your times today, Sarah?"

A little embarrassed at not hitting all her times and unsure of how Amber would react, Sarah listed them with a subdued voice. "Seventy, seventy-one, seventy-three, seventy-five, seventy-three." "That's a fairly typical spread," Amber nodded. "You started out a little too aggressive, had your slowest time near the end, and then rebounded on your final one." Amber repositioned into a pigeon stretch, and the others followed. "As you get used to doing repeats, you'll become more familiar with paces and adjust accordingly. Most important, all your times are within the goal time zip code, so the target time is about right. I'll keep your goal time at seventy-two next time we do this work-out, and hopefully by then you'll be able to run them more consistently and hit them all."

Sarah, taking in a deep breath, suddenly felt better about things. Well enough, in fact, to ask a question. "Kiana, why don't you run the same work-out we do?"

"I'm training for the fifteen-hundred, not the eight-hundred," she explained, glancing over at Sarah, "so I need more endurance and less speed work. But there is some cross-over between the events. I'll join you guys, once in a while."

Amber looked at her watch. "You'd better get going, Sarah. This morning was a good start. We'll pick up at the gym this afternoon. Try to get there as close to three o'clock as you can."

"OK. Thanks." Despite the urgency, Sarah, her muscles revolting, could only slowly gather her things before waving. "Bye!"

"Bye!" the women echoed.

As she began her trek to the parking lot, Sarah overheard Kiana behind her quietly inquire. "So, what do you think?"

Amber's voice replied. "She seems nice. She had a decent first workout. No red flags yet."

Her dad started the truck the moment he saw her coming. After tossing her bag and jug in the bed, she slid in, stared ahead, and exhaled heavily.

Concern knotted his eyebrows as he turned to her. "How did it go?"

Sarah sighed. "This is a whole new level."

CHAPTER 10

The strains of classic seventies' rock pulsed throughout the weight room, muffling the clanking of the machines and the clanging of heavy plates rammed on to the barbells. Stretching along one wall, from the rubber-matted floor to the ceiling, a bank of mirrors doubled its actual size. The first wave of the after-work crowd had started to filter in, utilizing most of the training equipment and stations. Sarah now realized why Amber wanted her to arrive by three o'clock. Four p.m. was an ideal time to wrap up their workout.

"Last set!" Amber, wearing capri-length leggings, picked up the pair of twenty-pound dumbbells resting on the edge of a twelve-inch wooden box and centered herself in front of it while Sarah looked on. Holding one weight in each hand straight down at the side of her thighs, she stepped on to the box with her right leg. Thrusting quickly upward, with her left leg following, she stood upright until the bent left knee peaked above her waist. After she held the position for a split second, the left leg returned to the floor, followed by the right leg, and the next step was reversed, with the left leg leading. Amber repeated the process ten times on each leg, her ponytail bouncing with each repetition, before returning the weights to the box's edge with a sigh and snatching up her small towel.

"Step-ups look easy," she spoke while wiping herself down, "until you do four sets of them at the end of your workout."

Sarah was already getting the idea. Wiping the sweat off her own brow with a shirt sleeve, despite the cranked AC, she began to address the box for her own final set before Amber stopped her.

"Now that you've got the form down without using weights, I want you to do your last set with ten-pound dumbbells to give you an idea what it will be like next time we do these."

"OK." Sarah visited the dumbbell rack and picked up a pair before returning to center herself in front of the box, holding the weights with arms parallel to her thighs. Taking a last deep breath, she began her set, stepping up with one foot, thrusting herself up on the box, bringing the trail knee up above her waist, and pausing slightly in that position before beginning her descent. She quickly discovered just how much more difficult lugging ten additional pounds in each hand made the exercise. Her lungs and legs soon began to complain.

"Half-way there!" encouraged Amber after her fifth repetition. "Stay focused on form!"

By the time she finished the second half, her body was aflame, and sweat beaded profusely once more on her face. As soon as they re-racked the dumbbells, Sarah wasted no time wiping her face yet again on the already-damp collar of her shirt. Amber noticed.

"That's one thing I left off the shopping list. Next time bring a sweat rag. Nobody wants to use sweaty equipment."

While escorting Sarah over to the row of day-use lockers to retrieve her belongings, Amber gave Sarah a last instruction. "I've got a client arriving in a few minutes, so you'll need to do some stretching on your own when you get home. You're going to be tight and sore enough tomorrow morning as it is."

But Sarah didn't get the chance to respond. She recognized a curvy, forty-something woman cutting through the weight room. After spotting them, the woman had immediately changed course. Cathy Sutherland approached wearing slacks, a sweater, and low heels, her exuberant smile framed by a long, layered bob.

"Hi, Sarah! Hi, Amber!" she greeted, still several steps away. All seemed happy for the surprise.

"Hi, Cathy!"

"Hi, Mrs. Sutherland!"

Upon joining them, Cathy reached out with both hands, briefly touching each on the shoulder. "I'm so excited to see the training arrangement has worked out!"

"Me, too," agreed Sarah, returning her smile. "Thanks for helping to make it happen."

"Of course! I'm happy to help out!" Cathy assured her, pulling Sarah into a damp hug. "I can't wait to see how things turn out for you. Your mom would be so proud."

Just then, Sarah's phone vibrated. Separating from Cathy, she checked the text and looked up. "Well, my dad is waiting for me outside," she announced apologetically, "so I better go."

Cathy nodded understandingly before finding her smile again. "OK. I guess I'll be seeing a lot of you around here for a while." She gave Sarah's arm a squeeze.

"See you in the morning, Sarah," added Amber with a brief wave.

"OK. Bye!"

*****

No sooner had Sarah left than Amber observed Cathy lean in a little closer and assume a confidential tone, her smile replaced by a serious expression. "So, how are things going?"

"So far so good, but it's only the first day," Amber answered cautiously, as Cathy started to play with her silver necklace. "I'll know more in a week or two. Sarah and her dad seem nice, and hopefully her mom will, too."

Cathy stared at Amber for a moment, her mouth agape. "Oh, I'm sorry . . . I guess I never mentioned that Sarah is without a mother; she passed away almost four years ago from ovarian cancer."

Amber tilted her head, her eyes narrowed. "Her dad never said anything about that to me either."

"I'm not surprised. Ben plays things pretty close to the vest." As Cathy resumed speaking, a distant look crept into her eyes. "Joy was actually one of my best friends . . . I miss her dearly, as well as the times my husband and I used to share with Ben and Joy at church and school events. Ben has become a bit reclusive since Joy's death and spends most of his time with Sarah now, which is completely understandable."

Amber's tone softened. "How hard did Sarah take it?"

"About as well as one could hope, I guess. But I think it's caused her to grow up a bit more quickly and take her faith more seriously than most teenagers . . . Let me know if there's ever anything I can do to help."

"Thank you. I will."

As soon as Amber replied, Cathy seemed to abruptly remember the task she had abandoned when seeing the two. "Well, I better get back to the books."

"And my client just arrived," agreed Amber, spotting a balding man lingering near the front desk. They both smiled one last time.

"See you around!"

"Bye!"

With that, Cathy whisked back toward the office, leaving Amber still musing over the revelation.

CHAPTER 11

Splash! Splash! Splash! Every time Amber and Kiana raced past, they sprayed Sarah with more rainwater. Not that it mattered; her shoes and leggings had been soaked for over an hour. Still, Sarah wondered if they secretly enjoyed taking advantage of each opportunity.

The rain had started falling long before the Friday practice began. Sarah was glad for both the new rain jacket and the clouds that had raised the early March temperature by several degrees. But pretty much every other part of her body other than her torso and arms was drenched; and the breeze, which asserted itself especially on the back stretch, chased away whatever warmth the clouds had brought. Sarah loathed having to run straight into that breeze three times on each thousand-meter repeat.

As she walked the curve toward the homestretch in Lane Three, Sarah spied her mentors jogging their recovery along the backstretch to join her for their last repeat of the day. Amber had assigned Sarah three one-thousands, half their load, with a goal time of three minutes and thirty seconds, and she had completed the first two in three minutes and thirty seconds and three minutes and thirty-five seconds. Today, she had been allowed an initial one-minute standing rest after each repeat, followed by a one-and-a-half-lap walk. Though her legs still felt drained after a week of challenging workouts, the rest had succeeded in calming her lungs.

Squish! Squish! Squish! Amber and Kiana's footfall soon announced their presence behind her, and Sarah broke into a jog about forty meters from the start line. When they caught up with her ten meters later, she matched their pace.

"Last one!" Amber announced between breaths, fatigue filling her voice. "Think about your race next weekend when you start feeling it."

"Which would be two repeats ago!" joked Kiana with equal exhaustion.

As they neared the start line, all three reached for their wrists, and when they crossed it, they punched their watches in unison. Sarah willed her legs to accelerate. Knowing better than to try to match the swift pace of the women, she settled into her own steady rhythm, focused on her breathing. As she came off the first curve and entered the back stretch, she dueled the dreaded breeze, which buffeted her body, striving to reach the two-hundred-meter mark, where escape awaited on the second curve. Once released from the wind's grip, she leaned in towards the rail and tried to recover a sense of momentum as she rounded the curve.

When she straightened out on the homestretch, the start line loomed distantly ahead. *Splat! Splat! Splat!* The monotony of her footsteps suggested she was making progress, but for several moments the end of the straight seemed to grow no closer despite the backwind. When it finally drew near and passed beneath her feet, she told herself she was almost halfway done, and upon reaching the actual halfway point in the middle of the third turn, Sarah imagined herself sliding down the back side of a mountain after having conquered its peak. The psychological trick helped her attack the wind on the first portion of the backstretch, but fifty meters later the emotional capital had already been spent. Sarah concentrated on thrusting off her protesting legs and driving forward with her increasingly rigid arms. Passing the six-hundred mark at last, she made a mental note: just one lap separated her from the end of practice, from the end of a week of workouts.

With renewed resolve, Sarah began to push the pace and take advantage of the wind at her back. Her measured breathing grew louder as she started to emphasize her exhalation, blowing out the building carbon dioxide. The rhythm hypnotized her as she crossed the start line again and leaned into the rail one last time to attack the final two hundred meters. Sustaining her effort, Sarah followed the curve, and when it unwound on to the back stretch, she saw Amber and Kiana straining to their finish less than one hundred meters away. Slowly, they turned and faced her, their chests clearly heaving and hands on top of their heads. Then they started clapping and shouting words of encouragement she couldn't make out. Desperate to please, Sarah groped for a higher gear despite the burning and found it, battling the wind all the way to a gasping finish.

"Woo!" they cheered as she stumbled forward, trying to suck in air that somehow seemed to lack oxygen. She stopped and bent over with hands on her knees, afraid she was going to pass out.

"Stand up and put your hands behind your head," Kiana advised, shuffling toward her. "You'll get much more air in that way."

Sarah followed the advice before Amber walked over and put her own slippery arm around Sarah's slippery shoulders. "You OK?" A little embarrassed, Sarah nodded firmly before checking her time. What she saw left a stab of disappointment. "What were your times today?"

"Three-thirty . . . three-thirty-five . . . and now . . . a three-thirty-three." She tried to catch her breath.

"Great job!" congratulated Amber, now almost recovered. "That's impressive!" Kiana nodded in agreement.

Sarah looked confused. "But I only made my goal time . . . once."

"I'm surprised you did even that! Goal times assume reasonable conditions . . . and today you're dealing with rain and especially the wind . . . You can take five or more seconds off your times to make up for that! Kiana and I also only made one of our goal times today, and we ran twice as many repeats!"

Sarah's embarrassment flipped to elation in an instant. "Well, I'll be glad to know that from now on!" she said, flashing an enormous smile.

Amber glanced at her watch. "It's getting late, so let's get started on the cool down." But before they took a step, she turned to Kiana. "I'm so beat down right now; what do you say we slow jog it with Sarah?"

"Absolutely! I'm down with that!" Kiana nodded.

The three forced themselves back into slow motion, a now-giddy Sarah in the middle, ready to ask a pressing question. "So, do we always practice in the rain, even if it's pouring?"

"Yep!" confirmed Amber. "Unless there's lightning. You don't mess around with that."

"At school, we didn't practice when it rained, and sometimes even if it rained the day before. The practice field turns to mud."

Amber and Kiana looked at each other with amusement.

"It's kind of hard to train when you're not working out," Amber joked. "And you never know what the conditions will be like on race day. But let's talk about your future now. Tomorrow is your thirty-minute long run, which you'll do on your own. If your dad can't run with you, he can follow you on a bike."

"That will be interesting," commented Sarah with a smirk.

"You should shoot for a seven-thirty pace, roughly about four miles. Just run fifteen minutes out; then turn around and run back. That is, unless you're going uphill or downhill one way; then the return trip won't be exactly as long."

"I think I'll just run from my house over to a park and back."

"Sounds good. By the way, next week you'll still be running every second repetition I run, but you're going to start jogging two laps to recover in between, not walking one. And we're going to keep the pace times the same."

Sarah groaned. "My whole body is already sore, and my legs feel dead."

Smiling, Kiana looked over and caught Amber's eye before asking Sarah a question. "Dead legs? You know what that calls for, don't you, Sarah?"

"No," she answered, innocently.

Amber and Kiana nodded to each other before shouting in harmonic unison: "Ice bath!" Then they laughed.

"What's that?" Sarah stared at them, puzzled over their comment.

Her mentors both smiled from ear to ear, but Amber delivered their response. "You'll find out tomorrow. I'll text your father."

CHAPTER 12

Sarah and her dad drew a few curious gazes as they cruised through the neighborhood. Sarah's long ponytail swished back and forth in a constant cadence as she turned on to their street and logged the last hundred meters, her dad riding shotgun on his mountain bike behind her. The weather had cooperated: though the clouds from Friday had remained, the rain had held off through the morning. Sarah took one last look at her watch and confirmed the time was right before slowing to a stop in the driveway. Her dad pulled up next to her and dismounted next to a second car now parked in the driveway beside his truck. Still-ticking, the Honda four-door sedan belonged to her grandmother.

"How did you do?" he asked.

Still catching her breath, Sarah wiped the glaze of sweat off her face with a sweatshirt sleeve before pushing a button on the watch. "Just over thirty-one minutes and just over four miles," she reported.

"Just what Amber wanted."

"Perfect timing!" announced a familiar voice from the walkway to the front door. They both turned to see her grandmother. She reached up and pushed the bangs of her choppy pixie cut to the side. Today her stout grandma wore a long-sleeve, light blue denim button-down, worn open over a white tee, matched with blue jeans and walking shoes. "I just got here with the ice; it's still in the trunk of my car."

"Thanks! I'll get it!" Before walking the bike into the garage, her dad turned back to Sarah. "As soon as you're ready, take off your shoes and socks and meet us in your bathroom."

"Are we really going to do this?" she whined.

He gave her a smirk. "You're the one complaining about dead legs. I'm just following Amber's orders."

*****

A few minutes later, the three met inside Sarah's bathroom with Grandma, her features tense, leaning on the doorjamb. Sarah, clad in shorts and a tee, stood silently, like a convict facing the gallows. Next to her were two twenty-pound bags of ice stacked by the tub. Meanwhile, Ben pulled out his cell to locate Amber's instructions. Once he found them, he began to read aloud.

"OK. First we fill the tub halfway with Sarah in it." Tentatively, Sarah stepped in and sat while Ben opened the faucet. As the water filled, he continued. "When it gets halfway, we're going to pour all of the ice in up to her hips." His mother held her fingers over her lips as Ben began tearing open the first bag and creating a hole big enough to pour the cubes through. When he turned the faucet off, Sarah's eyes grew wide. Ben checked the time on his watch and then started doing the honors.

As the ice began spilling loudly into the tub, Sarah's voice began to quiver. "This is getting really cold!"

"That's sort of the idea," Ben half-chuckled.

His mother grabbed the front edges of her button down with whitened knuckles and pulled it tighter around her.

"Are you sure this is even safe?" Sarah demanded with an accusing look.

Ben nodded nonchalantly. "At one high school winter camp, some of my buddies and I felt inspired to form the Polar Bear Club. To be initiated, you had to jump into the icy mountain lake." He paused the tale just long enough to grab the second bag and began emptying its contents as well. "While it may not have been the brightest idea, I can assure you there were no fatalities." Ben caught his daughter's eye. "And I wasn't in a house with central heating when I got out, my entire body dripping wet, I'll have you know," he added.

"And I let you go to that camp?" asked his mother, aghast.

Ben smiled. "Let's just say it wasn't an official camp activity."

His personal testimony didn't seem to convince Sarah, who began shivering. "How long do I have to be in here? It's freezing!".

"Ten minutes." Ben casually looked at his watch. "You're almost half-way."

His mother, adjusting her garment again, weighed in. "Ten minutes? Are you sure, Ben?" He re-read Amber's text aloud word for word. Then, the unexpected happened. When Sarah spoke next, her voice had mellowed considerably.

"It's not as bad now . . . I can't really feel anything in my legs. Everything is just numb."

"Makes sense," nodded Ben. "The first shock is the worst part." Then he remembered to check Amber's text. "Mom, will you go start the shower in my room? It says that after ten minutes Sarah should take a warm—not hot—shower for two minutes before getting back into the ice tub for a final two minutes."

Relieved at Sarah's impending reprieve, and the opportunity to do something, his mother left at once without a word and returned a couple of minutes later. "The shower's ready. How long now?"

"Less than a minute. Let's get a big towel so she doesn't drip all over the hallway."

His mother quickly produced one, and at the appointed time Sarah carefully rose out of the tub. Even before she stepped out, they wrapped the towel around her. She then shuffled down the hall to Ben's shower, with Ben and his mother in tow, leaving wet prints on the laminate flooring. Without pausing, Ben watched as she let the towel fall to the floor, lunged over the threshold, and plunged herself under the showerhead.

After basking under its flow for several moments, she exclaimed, "My legs are beginning to tingle!"

"That's from the return of your blood circulation," explained Ben.

"I'm starting to get itchy!" It seemed she could not rid herself of the irritating sensation.

"Time!" announced Ben, and Sarah reluctantly left the comfort of the shower. Following the same procedure, they carefully ushered a wrapped Sarah back to the bathtub without slipping. The initial plunge, accented with a few wails, again proved unpleasant, but Sarah soon announced the numbness had returned. The final minute passed without further drama until Ben started counting down the final seconds.

"Five, four, three, two, one!" Sarah needed no coaxing to exit the tub, and Grandma made sure a fresh pair of towels awaited. While she stood thawing out, her teeth chattering, Ben grinned. "You survived. Welcome to the Polar Bear Club! How do you feel?"

"Like a p-p-popsicle!" Sarah shivered, her expression only slightly less accusatory than before. Even his mother laughed.

CHAPTER 13

Sarah had never seen them laugh that hard, and she didn't mind that it was at her own expense. Amber and Kiana, thoroughly entertained with Sarah's highly editorialized version of her ice bath, switched legs on their hurdler's stretch. Sarah followed suit.

"If they ever make another sequel to *Ice Age,* you've got something to list on your resume," teased Kiana.

"Or *Frozen,*" added Amber.

"Once I thawed out, I felt great," admitted Sarah. "And it was awesome to have my legs back again today."

"Both the ice bath and a day off yesterday probably helped a lot," mused Amber, her fingers pulling back her toes. "Your times certainly suggest they did. Say goodbye to the seventy-two-second goal time on your four hundred repeats; you hit every one of them today, even with the jogging recovery. Next time we'll shoot for seventy-ones."

"Well, that's good news and bad news. I was just starting to feel comfortable at that pace."

"More good than bad, believe me," Kiana chimed in. "Improvement is what it's all about, Baby."

"Yes," agreed Amber. "But let's turn the page." Kiana had already moved on to the pretzel stretch, and the others joined her before Amber continued. "From what I understand, you'll be running with the rest of your team on Saturday in a meet of mostly small schools. Odds are you'll win your race, maybe by a lot. So, the goal this week is not really placement but running a time fast enough to qualify for a higher-level meet, like the Rodeo Invitational, in a couple of weeks. Even though it's your first meet of the season, right now I'd say you should be aiming for your PR, two minutes, seventeen seconds. That should do it and be a good start."

"Starting off where I ended last year? I'd take that!" declared Sarah. "What will you and Kiana be doing?" Before Amber responded, they all changed legs.

"We're leaving Friday for a meet out of state. We're doing pretty much the same thing you are: trying to run season PR's to get in to elite meets later."

That sparked Sarah's curiosity. "What's your time goal?"

Amber paused before replying, as if reluctant to make it public. "Ideally . . . I'd say a two oh five, though I'll take a two oh six," she quickly added.

"Wow," Sarah quietly commented, her eyes widening.

Apparently uncomfortable with the subject, Amber took advantage of the silence to rotate not only to the butterfly stretch but also to another topic. "So, why does your dad always stay in the car?" she inquired, motioning her head in the direction of the parking lot. "What does he do in there during practice?"

Surprised by the questions, Sarah gave it some thought before answering. "I don't mean to be rude, but my dad said you made it very clear during your meeting that you wanted a No Parent Zone at practice." Amber's expression suggested she was guilty as charged. "So, he uses the time to grade papers here instead of at school or at home."

Amber's head teeter-tottered back and forth, like she was weighing both sides of an issue. "Perhaps that rule could use some tweaking." "Honestly, he might stay in there anyway." Sarah sighed at the irony. "Ever since my mom died, he never goes anywhere. He doesn't like it when I call him 'The Hermit', but it's true. Like next week he's going to miss the annual school staff banquet—again—even though he used to go every year."

Amber's features betrayed intrigue until the jingle of Kiana's phone interrupted the conversation. Glancing at the screen, she answered with a bright, big smile after recognizing the caller. "Hi, Momma!" But her smile quickly vanished during a few moments of silence. Then her jaw dropped. "When? Did they take him in an ambulance? What are the doctors saying? . . . Umhmmm . . . OK . . . I'll call you as soon as I know when I can get there . . . OK . . . Yes . . . Love you." After tapping her screen, Kiana stared ahead in blank disbelief. Sensing the worrisome stares of both Amber and Sarah, she explained as if still trying to come to terms with the fact herself. "My dad just went to the hospital. They think it's a stroke."

"Oh, no!" chorused Amber and Sarah, with Amber adding, "That's awful. I'm so sorry."

"My mom had to call 911, and they took him to the hospital in an ambulance," Kiana further informed. "He's alive, but it doesn't sound good." After a few additional moments of stunned silence, her eyes began to well with tears, and her manner grew abruptly urgent. "I need to go right now!"

"Of course!" agreed Amber, already scrambling to her feet. "Let's go!"

Quickly gathering their gear, they all headed to the parking lot.

*****

When Ben saw the trio emerge from the stadium, he could sense something was wrong. Not only were they a few minutes early, but they hurried toward the parking lot at an unusually rapid pace, their bags swinging and faces bearing serious expressions. Returning the set of papers and the clipboard to his satchel, he had everything stowed away by the time Sarah slung her bag into the bed and opened her door. Instead of entering, though, she stood gazing at him, on the verge of tears.

"What's wrong, sweetie?"

Her voice trembled. "Kiana's dad had a stroke! She's really upset, and I don't know what to say to her."

Ben glanced over to see Amber and Kiana hurriedly place their gear in the trunk of Kiana's car and slam it shut before looking back at Sarah. "Will you be praying for her?" Sarah nodded vigorously. "Tell her that."

Hearing the doors of the car behind her already opening, Sarah spun around and called out. "Kiana!" Kiana stopped, turned, and met Sarah's teary eyes. "I'm so sorry! I'll be praying for you and your family!"

Kiana managed to form her lips into a mournful smile. "Thank you, Sarah. Thank you!" With that, she closed the door and cranked the engine.

CHAPTER 14

"We're running late!" Ben yelled down the hallway. He stood by the front door with a granola bar in his hand, his satchel and thermos already stashed in the car. A still-groggy Sarah trudged out of her bathroom into the kitchen, where she grabbed her water jug on the counter and then picked up her gear bag laying near the door. "Please don't make me play hardball with you," he pleaded, stuffing the granola bar in the front pocket of her hoodie before doing a double-take. "You've got some toothpaste on your lip."

Wiping it off with a sleeve, Sarah plodded out the door straight to the truck without a word, while Ben paused to lock the door behind him. When he turned, he noted the lightening sky. The sun, rising a minute earlier each day, was already on the brink of piercing the horizon. Next week, when daylight saving time kicked in, they would leave for practice in the dark. He wasn't looking forward to that. Getting Sarah out the door was already hard enough.

The pulsing of his cell cut short his thoughts, and he paused his brisk stroll to the truck to pull it out. His eyebrows rose when he saw the identity of the caller. Swiping the screen, he held the phone up to his ear, his tone cheerful. "Hi, Amber. What's up? OK . . . Sure, no problem. What's your address?" He repeated it back to her. "OK, see you in a few. Bye."

Sarah cracked open the passenger side door. "What's going on?" "Amber's having some car trouble," explained Ben, punching the address into a maps app. Then he looked up with a shrug. "So, we're taking her to and from practice today."

*****

The sun shone down brightly as Ben weaved the aging Ford purposefully through the neighborhood. With all three sitting in the cab, Sarah squished in the middle, space was a little tight. Still fresh from practice, both runners found it hard to stop perspiring, a fact that didn't enhance the smell. Ben had actually considered cranking the AC at seven-thirty on an early March morning. When they turned on to their street, Amber was updating them on Kiana, her eyes taking in the varied landscaping of the closely-spaced homes passing by.

"Yeah, Kiana's dad has stabilized. But there appears to be some permanent damage. It looks like she's going to be gone for at least a couple of weeks. I feel terrible for her. Of course, my car has to pick the moment she's left to break down."

"That's sad," lamented Sarah, her arms wrapped around her knees. "I'm going to keep praying for her and her family."

"Positive thoughts can't hurt," Amber noted.

Ben pulled into his driveway and kept the engine idling as first Amber and then Sarah exited the cab. Before Amber climbed back in, Ben delivered some instructions to his daughter. "You've got your key, right? Be sure to lock the door behind you. I'll be back in twenty minutes, so I can still make your shake and get the rest of your stuff in the car. But don't dawdle; get ready for school."

"OK. Bye, Amber." She waved.

"See you this afternoon," replied Amber, returning the gesture. While Sarah retrieved her gear from the bed of the truck, Amber climbed back in and pulled the door shut. She promptly leaned into it, wedging an elbow into the windowsill while the other arm hugged the gear bag sitting on her lap. When Sarah was clear, Ben backed out, and once he saw her step inside, they rumbled on to Amber's apartment. For a few moments, Amber played with the zipper on her bag while staring out her window, and Ben wondered whether he should turn on the news. Instead, he elected to break the silence before it became too awkward.

"So, how is Sarah doing?" He glanced in Amber's direction.

"She's had a good first week and a half," she replied in a business-like manner, still gazing out her window at the neighborhood. "She's playing a bit of catch-up with the late start on serious training, but hopefully we can make up that ground and she'll reach May with fresher legs. I'll know more after she races on Saturday." Ben merely nodded in reply, leaving them to listen to the throes of the engine until Amber spoke again. "Is she enjoying it?"

"Once she gets there. Getting her out of bed can be a chore, and next week is the start of daylight savings. If you could put in a word, it might carry more weight than mine."

"Sure . . . I'll do that," she nodded to the houses outside. With the common ground of Sarah covered, another, longer silence set in until Amber severed it. "Sarah gave quite an account of her ice bath the other day," she announced, sarcasm subtly creeping into her voice. "She claims you enjoyed playing the role of gleeful executioner."

Ben grinned a grin he guessed Amber didn't see before replying in a more light-hearted tone. "Sarah can be quite entertaining at times, part drama queen and part stand-up comic. She may have a career ahead of herself in Hollywood." Ben sneaked another look over at Amber, this time to see her grinning, too. "I don't think she would have gone through with it if the idea hadn't come from you." Amber's eyes migrated from the window to the windshield. "Did you really jump into a frozen lake?" she asked with a hint of disbelief, her free hand leaving the zipper to toy with a stray strand of blonde hair that had escaped her ponytail.

"Well, it was only half-frozen . . . " As Ben made a turn off the main thoroughfare towards Sarah's apartment complex, in the corner of his eye he saw Amber's grin spread into a smile. This time the silence was short-lived.

"Hey, I feel like I owe you an apology," she blurted with a nervous laugh.

"Don't worry about it at all," Ben assured her, waving away her statement. "Giving you a lift is absolutely no problem."

"No, it's not about the ride—thanks again, by the way," she added, darting her eyes in his direction. "It's about our meeting at the coffee shop." Ben shot her a confused expression. He wasn't sure she saw it, as she had resumed her study of the traffic ahead. "Looking back, I may have come off a bit too defensive about a few things, including my concern about 'parental hovering.'"

"Oh, that." Amber glanced again in Ben's direction.

She removed her elbow from the windowsill and half-turned towards him, her features sincere. "Look, training a teen with a parent is a new experience for me, and I didn't know what to expect." She started to shake her head. "I certainly didn't intend to banish you to your car or deny you the chance to be involved in Sarah's training."

"Be careful!" Ben advised sarcastically, his smile growing wider. "If you give me an inch, I may take a mile. Soon you'll find me demanding to plan your workouts!" He gazed at Amber as her smile acknowledged the irony. After a short pause, Ben continued, catching her eyes. "Perhaps I'll creep out from under my rock once in a while." Blushing, Amber pulled in her lips and nodded before turning to ponder the townscape out her window anew.

As Amber's apartment complex came into view, Ben turned serious again. "Do you need any help getting a tow or a ride anywhere? We can pick you up again tomorrow."

"Thanks, but I'll be fine," she pleasantly declined. "I may have to cancel on my first client of the day to make a couple of calls, but insurance will handle the tow and the dealership should offer me a courtesy car until it's fixed." A couple of speed bumps later, they rolled to a stop in front of Amber's apartment.

"OK. Just call if you need anything."

Amber opened the door and placed one foot on the curb before pausing and facing Ben once more. "I really appreciate your help today, Ben." Then she lowered her head and began to laugh before looking up again. "It's quite the twist, you know; I'm also the one that broke the 'no providing transportation' rule."

"Some things can't be helped. It happens to all of us," Ben assured her.

She flashed a parting smile. "See you tomorrow."

"Bye," Ben said quietly, holding up a hand in farewell.

Amber stepped out, shouldered her bag, and closed the door. Ben waited until she reached her apartment and disappeared inside with a wave. Then, after a squeeze of the steering wheel, he shifted the truck into gear and hastened home.

CHAPTER 15

Sweat dripping from her nose bugged Sarah to no end, but that was actually the least of her worries. Her entire body trembled from the struggle to maintain proper plank form. With her elbows tucked in against her ribs and the toes of her shoes digging deeply into the yoga mat, she blew out yet another batch of air and willed herself to not let her butt pop up or slouch down despite the ever-mounting burning in her abdomen and shoulders. Sarah looked up at Amber, who faced her in the same ramrod-straight position, for a sign that the end was near. Instead, she found her coach almost casually looking around the otherwise vacant dance room as if considering how she might redecorate it. Just when Sarah thought she had no choice but to surrender to the pain, Amber calmly spoke the words she had been waiting to hear.

"Five, four, three, two, one." Both sank their knees to the mats, Sarah more quickly than Amber, and caught their breath before wiping themselves down with their towels. Taking swigs from their water bottles, they rotated to sit, Amber leaning back on her arms with her knees up and Sarah hunched forward cross-legged. They somewhat matched, both layered in now-damp tank tops.

"OK, I'm going to cut the gym portion a little short today since we're both racing in two days," Amber announced, rolling her head in a circle to loosen her neck and shoulders. "There won't be a weight work out tomorrow either. In fact, I'm leaving early in the morning to travel to my meet, so you will be on your own for an easy thirty-minute recovery run—say an eight-minute pace—and a few practice starts."

"Where are you going?"

"I'm flying to Tennessee."

Sarah was impressed.

Amber continued. "Remember, since you're running in a pretty small-time meet, your goal is time, not placement. You will need to sprint hard at the start to avoid getting caught in traffic. Shoot for a thirty-three-second first two hundred and a sixty-seven first lap. If you can hold on to run a seventy-second final lap, you'll be right on your PR."

"OK, but how will I know if I'm on pace?" Sarah asked, the question muffled as she pressed her face into her towel again. When she pulled it away, she found Amber looking at her with surprise.

"How will you know? . . . Right." Leaning forward, Amber used her hands to diagram an imaginary track. "Most every high school invitational, even the small ones I would think, will have a clock at the start-finish line, but not always one at the two-hundred-meter mark. So, I would suggest having your dad positioned on the backstretch to call out your two hundred and six hundred-meter splits."

"I think he'd actually like doing that." Sarah grinned.

"Good. You may not be pushed Saturday, so you must push yourself with your split times." Sarah nodded.

A few early birds from the boot camp crew entered the room and began staking out their spots for the class scheduled to start in ten minutes. Taking that as their signal, Amber and Sarah rose and walked over to a dispenser mounted on the wall to tear off some antiseptic wipes and sanitize their mats. After rolling them up and returning them to the storage bin, they made their way out of the dance room to the water station in the weight room to refill their bottles.

On their way, Sarah checked the notifications on her phone. While doing so, she noticed Amber look with interest at the photo of Sarah as a child with a woman's arms wrapped around her on the lock screen. After Sarah filled her bottle, Amber then caught Sarah's dark brown eyes as she started filling her own.

"Who's with you in that picture?" she asked, nodding toward the phone.

"My mom."

"I thought it might be. Mrs. Sutherland told me about what happened . . . You know, I lost my mom a few years ago, too, and that was hard to deal with even as an adult." Amber paused just long enough to screw the lid back on her bottle. "Do you feel comfortable talking about that?"

Sarah lowered her gaze and shrugged. "Sure. It's not as bad as it used to be." She met Amber's gaze again. "The months she was sick and just after she died were the worst. Everyone was really nice, but it felt like putting a band-aid over a huge hole. My mom was hurting. I was hurting. My dad and grandparents were hurting. I felt so helpless." Sarah saw Amber's eyes begin to well. "It doesn't sting so much now, just kind of an ache that comes and goes."

"I'm so sorry to hear that, but it makes total sense," Amber commented, drifting a couple of steps away from the water station, with Sarah following her. "I can only imagine how difficult these past few years must have been for you."

"Yeah. I can't imagine getting through it without my dad and grandma, who are always there for me. We've all grown really close."

"That's great to hear." Amber took a half step towards the day-use lockers before stopping when Sarah continued.

"But another thing that got me through was a promise from God," she revealed, her voice hitting a more hopeful note. "My dad pointed out a verse that reads, 'My grace is sufficient for you, for my power is made perfect in weakness.'" Sarah paused. "I clung to that promise, like nothing else . . . and I still do."

Amber swallowed hard before speaking. "Thanks for sharing your story with me. I'm glad you felt you could." She reached out and placed a hand on Sarah's shoulder. "You're a courageous young woman, and I know your mom would be so proud of you."

"Thanks," said Sarah, smiling faintly.

They crossed over to the day-use lockers, and Amber assumed an upbeat tone while taking off her hair tie and redoing her ponytail. "I'm also glad to see your dad has joined us in the stadium at practice."

"Yeah, me, too." Sarah giggled. "He told me you gave him permission to leave the dungeon and grade his papers in the stands. Did you see the little folding stadium seat he brought?" Amber nodded as they laughed. "Honestly, I was amazed when he actually came down to the field and talked with us during stretching at the end of practice yesterday . . . Maybe there's hope for 'The Hermit' after all."

Still grinning, Amber looked at her watch. "Well, I need to pack for my trip, so I better get going." She turned to open one of the locker doors, and Sarah began collecting her personal items from another as well. "I can't wait to hear all about your race next week at practice," Amber added. Closing the locker, she held up a finger, as if suddenly remembering. "Oh, and one last thing."

Sarah looked up with curiosity. "What's that?"

Amber smiled. "Make sure you load up on the carbs. Plan a family pasta party Friday night!"

Sarah relaxed. "As Kiana might say, I think my dad just may be down with that!"

CHAPTER 16

"Coach Sutherland said there will be only one JV and one Varsity heat for all distance events," Ben informed Sarah. Draining the last of the coffee from his thermos, he placed it in the holder below the cab's dash. "So, I don't know how big your race will be; it could be small or could be huge."

Sarah merely nodded beside him, and Ben realized her nerves were already setting in.

The truck slowed when the kiosk for St. Timothy's Episcopal High School appeared. They were arriving a full hour before the scheduled start of the girls Varsity 800, as Coach Sutherland had advised. Less than half an hour away on the other side of the valley, St. Timothy's made for a convenient venue. Ben entered the mid-sized parking lot and found a few spaces to choose from before backing into one less than fifty yards from the stadium entrance. Emerging into the cool and cloudy morning, they walked parallel to a chain link fence until greeted by a cheerful woman wearing a St. Timothy's booster tee and a wide-brimmed hat. Seated in a lawn chair, she had a cash box in her lap.

"Hello!" Spotting the racing jersey beneath Sarah's half-zipped sweat top and open letterman's jacket, she explained, "Athletes get in free; adults are five dollars." Ben decided against insisting he was a coach and forked over the money. With a wide smile, she pressed his hand with a rubber stamp as a reward. "Thank you and enjoy the meet!"

They made their way through the gate to the edge of the track, where they joined a line of onlookers. To the right lay the start-finish line, where a pair of pop-up tents stood on the infield. Sheltered underneath, three men huddled behind tables cluttered with electronic equipment, absorbed in their digital timing duties. Nearby, a digital clock sat atop a tripod, paired with a portable electronic results sign board propped up on the ground below it.

"At least they've got automatic timing," noted Ben with relief. Sarah remained tight-lipped.

Hearing the crack of a gun, they turned to see a boys one hundred ten meter high hurdle race just beginning. Not all the lanes were filled. The hurdlers charged toward them, most hopping over the obstacles rather than striding over them, and a few knocking hurdles over as they ran. Near the finish, one boy took a nasty fall that drew several groans from the spectators.

"Ouch!" commented Ben, quietly under his breath. "That had to hurt." But the boy immediately sprang back up, likely from sheer embarrassment, and completed the race to a smattering of sympathetic applause.

To Ben and Sarah's left, the permanent home stands offered wooden benches that stretched between the twenty-yard lines six rows deep. On the visitor side, three portable bleachers, almost empty, straddled midfield, spacing themselves at ten-yard intervals. No barrier separated athletes and parents from the synthetic track on either side.

Before they could begin locating the team hub, Ben and Sarah had to bend around a makeshift snack bar consisting of a couple of long tables, the prices scrawled with markers on poster board taped to the edges.

Reviewing the stale donuts, cooling Costco Pizza slices, and boiled hot dogs stacked in a cooler, Ben couldn't help himself. "Maybe we can eat lunch here after your race instead of Burger Shack."

That finally got a response out of Sarah, who scrunched her nose and frowned. "Gross."

Ben observed half a dozen team pop-up tents from the relatively larger schools spread out along the higher rows of the stands. Since Montevallo Christian Academy did not possess a team tent, it took a few more seconds to locate Coach Sutherland and the team base near the far end. As they walked up the steps, one family was just leaving while a couple of others still awaited races.

"Hi, Ben! Hi, Sarah!" greeted Coach Sutherland. Lounging back on the bench behind him, his arms spread out, he wore a team hat and wind breaker embroidered with his name and title on the chest. He had no hurdlers or field athletes to coach.

"Good morning one and all!" Ben replied to the group. He proceeded to exchange pleasantries with the parents, while Sarah chose from a few options to set her bag on the splintered and paint-chipped bench. She began saying hello to a couple of teammates when Coach Sutherland interrupted both Ben and Sarah with an update.

"The meet is running a little ahead of schedule, so let me get Sarah her number bib right away." His hand was already rifling through a large manila envelope. "Sarah may be racing in as little as half an hour," he added. No sooner had he finished speaking then a man holding a megaphone walked over to the edge of the track near the fifty-yard line and made an announcement in a gravelly voice. "First call, boys and girls eight hundred meters! Second call, boy and girls one hundred meters! Last call, boys and girls four hundred meters!" Finding the bib, Coach Sutherland handed it over to Ben, along with four safety pins. After Sarah stashed her letterman's jacket in her bag and unzipped her sweat jacket, Ben quickly got to work on attaching the bib to Sarah's slightly baggy jersey, a dark blue tank top emblazoned with the gold, interlocking letters "MCA" across the front. The job complete, Sarah tucked the jersey into her spandex shorts beneath her sweatpants, zipped her sweat jacket back up, and grabbed both her bottle and spike bag.

Facing the track, she surveyed the infield. The check-in tent was located in the end zone near the timing tent. Small clumps of athletes, either warming up or cooling down, scattered themselves over the balance of the infield, while long jumpers and high jumpers competed along the fringes. Before Sarah left to check in with a JV teammate, Ben called her over to have a last word.

"Remember, today is about time, not placement; so don't worry about anyone else," he urged. "Give yourself a chance to run at the Rodeo."

"OK," she replied quietly with a nod.

As they left, a chorus of well wishes following them, Ben decided it was a good time to start his own pilgrimage to the backstretch as well. "Hey, Jack. I think I'm going to go get set up at the two hundred mark to give Sarah her splits," he informed his friend.

"Sounds good!" Jack nodded while smoothing his mustache. "But don't start your time on the sound of the gun if you're timing from across the field. The sound will take almost a second to reach you from that distance, so be sure to look for the smoke at the end of the barrel instead."

Ben cocked his head as he thought over the advice. "I wouldn't have thought of that. Thanks for the tip, Jack. I'll do my best!"

*****

The girls JV eight-hundred-meter heat seemed like it would never end. Though most runners finished long before, a pair of turtles reached the second lap at a jog and barely sustained it to the finish line. Once they finally crawled across, the starter, an elderly man in the customary red hat and sports coat, brought the waiting Varsity heat on the track without further delay.

Unlike most meets, starting position was not assigned by ranking, so the girls milled about before choosing a spot to their liking along the arced start line. Despite wearing the "number one" stickers on her right hip and chest as the runner with the fastest entry time, or first seed, Sarah, bouncing lightly on her feet, found herself somewhere in the middle of ten or so girls. Left and right, she glanced at her opponents, trying not to get psyched out by the older and more developed girls or overconfident about some who looked like they still belonged in junior high. She thought she recognized one or two of them from last year's small schools regional meet. Seeing the starter return to the infield, Sarah made sure her jersey was tucked into her shorts and tightened her ponytail. Then she remembered Amber's admonition to get out fast.

Receiving a thumbs-up from someone in the timing tent, the starter slowly raised the gun with one hand and issued a command to the runners with a megaphone in the other.

"On your marks!"

The girls bent forward and cocked their arms. With a pull of the trigger, Sarah lurched off into the mad rush of the first fifty meters. Try as she might, she couldn't outsprint the girls on each side; in fact, one girl starting almost the furthest outside, sprinted a step ahead of everyone and cut in towards the railing at a severe angle, wreaking havoc within the pack. Forced to break stride, Sarah instinctively circled around all but the slowest runners and took up a position on the outside of the pack, where she had a clear path forward. Though necessary, the maneuver cost her a precious second or two.

By the time they rounded the opening curve, Sarah, finally attaining her race speed, rejoined the leaders of the trail pack. However, she was concerned to see the girl who had cut them off already almost ten meters ahead of everyone and extending her lead. Thinking back to her repeats with Amber, Sarah resisted the temptation to give chase at a full sprint and instead settled into a vigorous but sustainable pace and breathing pattern all the way down the backstretch that edged her towards the head of the trail pack. Soon, she began to hear her father's bellowing voice.

"Thirty-two, thirty-three, thirty-four, thirty-five, thirty-six!"

Just before they entered the second curve, Sarah ducked into Lane One ahead of the rest of the trail pack. Still, she thought she crossed the two hundred mark at thirty-four seconds, a second too slow.

Leaning into the rail, Sarah gauged the leader almost fifteen meters ahead and heard the footsteps of her closest competition behind right on her heels. She responded by extending her stride and pumping her arms until she straightened out on the home stretch. The effort did not succeed in closing the gap with the leader, but at least it had stopped widening. When passing the cheers of the

Montevallo faithful, the gap remained stable, and Sarah began to worry whether the lead was surmountable.

Before her fears spiraled too far, though, the frontrunner's arms began to flounder, and her legs started to lock up as she neared the start line. By simply maintaining her pace, Sarah shaved five meters off the lead by the time they crossed the line. When she whisked by, the clock read 1:08. She still had a second to make up, she told herself, whatever her placement.

The narrowing gap powered Sarah into the third curve. Sensing the opportunity, she bit off another five meters of the lead by the mid-point, and with a surge of energy she swept past the faltering frontrunner by the end of the curve, continuing her momentum on to the back stretch. The former leader had faded so quickly, Sarah wondered if she realized from the outset that it was a two-lap race. Midway down the backstretch, Sarah could still faintly hear one competitor giving chase from behind, but not as close as before. The bigger issue was the time.

"One-forty, one forty-one, one forty-two, one forty-three, one forty-four!" As best Sarah could tell, her surge had put her back on pace at the six-hundred mark. But the brief flood of relief she felt was soon dispelled when the burning of her legs and lungs began to assert itself in earnest as she rounded the final curve. While expelling air from her lungs, she also expelled all thoughts other than running at the Rodeo. Trying to cover as much ground with each step as her increasingly heavy legs could manage, she straightened out on the homestretch, the faint but reinvigorated cheers of the Montevallo fans fueling her. Picking out the clock almost one hundred meters away, she focused on the digits with the goal of reaching the finish line before the seconds numeral reached eighteen. Feeling like she carried a piano on her back, the numbers seemed to change in slow motion. Sarah no longer heard anyone behind her; in fact, her focus proved so intense that she didn't hear anything at all but her labored breathing.

Two fourteen, two fifteen, two sixteen. As the finish line flickered by, Sarah thought she glimpsed the clock lingering at 2:16, a hope that helped her ignore the pain as she stumbled forward and attempted to calm her heaving lungs. Circling as she shuffled back, she saw her nearest competitor had just crossed the line with others now following. The early leader, clearly new to the event, limped across almost last.

Sarah approached the second-place finisher, bent over while still trying to catch her own breath, and placed a hand on her sweaty back.

"Great race," she gasped.

The girl, standing up, replied as best she could. "You, too."

Coach Sutherland yelled her name from the edge of the track, and she turned. He was pointing to the electronic results board. "Two seventeen point one nine! That's more than a half-second PR from last year! New school record!"

Her initial frustration over just missing the two sixteen quickly turned to joy as she realized her achievement. Saying a silent prayer of thanksgiving, Sarah suddenly found herself infused with three times the energy of a moment before as she stepped back into the infield.

"Rodeo Invitational, here I come!" she quietly celebrated.

Ambling to midfield, Sarah spied the lone figure in the bleachers at the two hundred-six hundred mark and waved. He clapped his hands above his head and gave two thumbs-up. She returned both gestures with a smile so broad she was certain even her dad could see it.

CHAPTER 17

Ben studied the sparkling red vinyl upholstery of their booth, which matched those on the soda fountain stools, and wondered where one got their hands on that type of material in the twenty-first century. Not to mention the linoleum table tops and the retro juke box, playing Charlie Gracie's 1957 hit "Butterfly." The former Billboard number one rockabilly ballad perfectly complemented the charm of the throw-back diner. Burger Shack had been a Turner family favorite before Joy's death, and it remained so after.

A college-age waitress in a red-and-white-striped dress with puffy sleeves, accented by a small white apron, finished refilling their waters, a paper hat tilted to the side of her bobbed hairdo. "Can I get you anything else right now?" Eyeing their partially devoured burgers, fries, and milk shakes, Ben and Sarah, still dressed in her track gear with a medal hanging around her neck, shook their heads.

"I think we're good, thanks," Ben replied.

"OK. Enjoy!"

Ben picked up another French fry and held it up to the light. "I love the fries here: soft on the inside, just a hint of crispiness on the outside, and ever-so-lightly salted." He took a slow bite, his eyes closed to relish the experience.

Sarah did not share his culinary ecstasy. "Dad, that's not just a little weird; it's actually creepy. People are probably staring at us."

Ben deferred to her sensibilities but also used the opening to introduce another line of conversation between bites. "What's weird is your choosing a starting position for your race in the middle of the pack. That cost you an even more impressive PR. Can you learn anything from that?"

Sarah shrugged her shoulders. "Yeah," she admitted. "I need to get out faster. Take my start drills more seriously in practice."

"That's true. But there's also another lesson: don't get caught in the inside traffic. There's a reason why they start the highest seeds at the post-season meets on the outside in a staggered waterfall start. Remember that?" Ben stopped just long enough to squeeze a puddle of ketchup from the bottle on to his plate. "That way, if they don't take the early lead, they have the option of taking up a position on the outside of the pack as it rounds the curve. Either way, not only do they have a clear path that helps them avoid breaking stride, but they also avoid all the pushing, shoving, and elbowing, not to mention spikes. Think about that next time you have a choice in where you start. Today you had to take a serious detour because of a girl that turned out to be a non-factor in the race, which was the ultimate irony."

Sipping on her shake, she simply nodded. Ben paused long enough from his lecture to take another bite from his burger before continuing.

"The good news is that from here on out, you likely won't have rookies like that in your races. At the invitationals, you'll be competing against experienced runners who have qualified based on time. Who knows? It may even play to your advantage. You may miss most of the opening chaos regardless of where you're lined up because they may be faster than you off the line. Your strength is maintaining speed and endurance after the start, not raw speed off the line. You showed that again today."

Sarah, reaching the bottom of her shake, began to make obnoxious noises while sucking on the straw, drawing the attention of a couple of nearby tables. Ben couldn't resist. "OK, who's weird and making people stare now?"

Blushing, Sarah halted the slurping and put the glass down before pouring in the leftovers from the tin. "Now that I've got a new medal for my collection, I'm thinking about rearranging them on my wall." She took a moment to slide her fingers down the ribbon and then test the solidity of the medal.

"Sure. As long as you patch up the old holes and touch them up with paint."

One thought led Sarah to another. "I wonder how Amber did today. She said the results would be posted online soon after her race, but I forget what the site was called."

"Hmmm. I'll be interested to hear," Ben admitted. "But it's clear that this 'whole new level' thing she's doing with you is working. You could have run at least a two sixteen today in your first race of the season with a better start."

As Ben finished speaking, Sarah's phone vibrated on the table. Sliding it over, she peeked at the caller. Then her eyes darted toward her father, her eyebrows raised. "It's Amber!"

"Go ahead and take it," Ben said with a nod, glad for the chance to catch up on his meal.

Sarah quickly swiped the screen. "Hi, Amber! . . . Having lunch with my dad . . . Yep! A low two seventeen! Beat my PR by over half of a second! . . . By about two to three seconds; the second-place girl was like 10 or more meters behind me . . . I ran almost exactly the way you told me! Just a little slower on the first lap and a little faster on the second." Sarah shot a glance at Ben across the table. "I did have a little trouble getting out at the start. I'll tell you about it later. But how did you do? . . . Awesome! . . . Congratulations! . . . "

While Sarah finished speaking with Amber, Ben's attention drifted as he tried to place the song currently playing on the juke box. When he finally identified it as Jackson Browne's seventies' anthem "Running on Empty," he thought it odd; as much as he liked the song, it didn't really fit the era.

"OK, I will . . . Bye!" Sarah cheerfully placed her phone back down on the table. "Amber said to be sure to say 'Hi' to you and sorry for interrupting our lunch."

Ben nodded before dipping another fry. "That was nice of her to call. I think she's becoming genuinely interested in her little prodigy. How did she do today?"

"She's happy. She ran a high two oh five, good enough to get her into the fast heat of the next invitational she wants to run in. She said it's also probably good enough to get her into the Western Relays next month."

"Great!" Ben smiled. "I'm glad for her."

"By the way, she repeated that she thinks my time today almost guarantees I'll be accepted into the Rodeo Invitational in a couple of weeks."

"How exciting! What a start to the season!" On a more sarcastic note, Ben added, "Maybe meeting that challenge will also help you get out of bed in the morning."

Sarah frowned. "Don't expect any miracles." Then she appeared as if she had just realized something. "Amber would probably kill me if she knew I was eating a burger, fries, and a shake."

"With whipped cream, a cherry, and the extra in a tin, I might add." Ben grinned before reaching a hand across the table. Placing his hand over Sarah's, he assumed a confidential tone. "Well, as they say, 'What happens in The Burger Shack stays in The Burger Shack.'"

CHAPTER 18

"Switch." Following Amber's lead, Sarah changed legs as they progressed through the pre-workout stretching routine. Practice on this particular Monday, however, would prove anything but routine.

The arrival of daylight-saving time had sprung the early morning forward into darkness. Several lingering stars had dotted the sky on the drive over, and they had already completed their shakeouts and dynamic stretches in the pre-dawn gloom. Only as they neared the conclusion of their static stretching did the sun flirt with the notion of breaching the horizon. Amber gazed in the direction of the increasingly-visible Ben, set up in the stands near the start of the home stretch with his folding stadium chair, trusty thermos, and seemingly ever-present papers.

"Did you see how your dad was grading during your shakeout?" Amber asked, a trace of incredulity in her voice.

"Yeah." Sarah chuckled. "He was using the flashlight on his phone. I didn't know he knew how to use that." After more thought, her tone grew affectionate. "That's dedication for you."

"I'll say," agreed Amber, transitioning to a new stretch. A comfortable silence fell between them. Though cool, the bite of the early morning had relented as the calendar advanced past mid-March. Only the last vestiges of snow remained visible on the high ridges in the distance. Today they would start their 1000-meter repeats without sweat jackets, preferring only long-sleeve jerseys.

Sarah's voice interrupted the stillness. "I miss Kiana."

Taking her eyes off Ben, Amber refocused on Sarah with a sympathetic expression. "That makes two of us. Her dad was released from the hospital to a rehab center where he's getting therapy. But it doesn't seem like he'll be going home any time soon, and I doubt Kiana will return until he does. It's going to be a real adjustment," she concluded, seeming to comment about herself as much as anyone.

Amber shifted the topic to the matters at hand. "As I said on the phone, your time Saturday should get you into the Rodeo Invitational, and a good showing there can then qualify you for the biggest meet of the regular season, the Western Relays. Western Relays has both a high school division, with the best talent in and out of state, and a college/open division that draws some of the best runners in the country. I've already qualified to run there, but I'm hoping to shave off more time in my next race to make it into the fastest heat."

Sarah's voice instantly rose an octave or two. "You and I will be running at the same meet?"

"Don't get ahead of yourself," Amber cautioned. "It's possible, but first things first: you still need to qualify at the Rodeo. I'm not certain if even a low two seventeen will be good enough to do the trick." Amber caught Sarah's eye. "Keep that in mind as you're dragging yourself out of bed and working out in the dark each day for the next two weeks."

"Got it." Sarah's tone signaled a renewed resolve.

Amber matched it as she rose to her feet. "Then let's get to work."

Ten minutes later, Sarah jogged her recovery in Lane Three, glad to be halfway done with the workout. With two repeats in the bank and under the goal time, only two remained. She thought of Amber and felt a mixture of pity and amazement; completing eight one thousands sounded awful. The sound of Amber's breath drew closer behind her, and within seconds her mentor whisked past with her head up, shoulders back, arms pumping 'ear to rear', and knees high. Sarah wondered how she could keep such perfect form even when tired.

Then the workout abruptly went off script. About fifty meters ahead, nearing the finish line, Amber strangely began to slow down for several steps before clutching the back of her right leg. Suddenly unable to place any pressure on it, she hopped awkwardly on her left foot for a few more steps before finally collapsing to a knee. Doubling her speed, Sarah ran up from behind and stopped short to find Amber's eyes shut hard, her teeth barred, and her breathing rough.

"Oh my gosh! Amber, are you OK?" Sarah, her eyes wide, knew she wasn't but didn't know what else to say. Amber merely shook her head and wiped her red-rimmed eyes. Desperate, Sarah spun around and called down the track to her father.

"Dad! Dad! Amber's hurt! Come help!"

*****

Quickly setting aside his papers, Ben hustled down and over to find Amber, now sitting, pulling her knee to her chest and attempting to massage the hamstring through her leggings. The grimace on her face removed any doubt the pain remained severe. He crouched down and gently placed a hand on her shoulder.

"How bad is it?" he asked quietly.

When Amber finally found the words, they came in batches. And Ben noted her tone couldn't fully conceal the fear. "It's either a pull . . . or a bad cramp. Can you guys . . . help me over to the infield?" Each hooked an arm under an armpit, and they managed to lightly drag her a couple of yards on to the artificial grass, where Amber proceeded to lie on her back, keeping the hurt leg bent. Taking a moment to think, Amber beckoned to Sarah. "Can you bring me my water jug? Then go ahead and finish your workout while I try to hydrate and stretch this out."

"OK." Sarah quickly retrieved the jug and then hesitantly returned to the track, looking back over her shoulder with concern written on her face.

After taking a couple of long swigs, Amber turned back to Ben, who now kneeled beside her. "Ben, would you please, very gently, help me try to extend my leg."

"Of course." Ben stood and repositioned himself to face Amber. Stooping over, he placed both his hands under the calf of her bent leg, while she, sitting up again, interlocked her fingers under her hamstring. "Tell me if I need to stop," he instructed. With extreme care, he slowly pulled the calf toward himself until the leg was almost straight. Meanwhile, Amber winced audibly until the tension grew unbearable.

"OK, stop! Now ease it back, please." When her foot rested back on firm ground, Amber took another couple of long drinks from her jug as a huffing Sarah ran by.

Ben took a knee again. "What do you think?" he asked, his earnest features illuminated by the rising sun.

Amber's words, now tinged with hope, began to flow more freely. "I'm starting to think it's just a really nasty cramp from dehydration and lack of electrolytes. I'm racking my brain to think of how much I drank yesterday . . . I know I forgot to drink hardly anything this morning." She shook her head with a look of disbelief. "On the other hand, if I pulled it—well, that may be the season. But I could feel it coming on for several steps before it really seized up, so I think it's a cramp. A pull is usually more sudden. And a pull wouldn't start responding to stretching and hydration like this."

"So, it's feeling better?"

Amber looked up to the brightening sky as she considered. "It's definitely relaxing some, and the pain isn't as intense," she determined at length, quickly adding, "But there's no way I can run on it right now. Even walking will be a challenge until it goes away. I'm definitely done for today."

"OK, well, there's no way you should be driving right now. We'll take you home as soon as Sarah finishes this repeat," he said, peering into her green eyes. He decided they were more precisely the shade of jade.

Amber held his glance for a moment, before peeling her eyes away and studying the grass. "You don't have to do that; I can manage," she mouthed without conviction.

"I really don't think you should," Ben insisted. Seeing Amber's expression melt into resignation, Ben yelled to Sarah, nearing the end of her repeat, as she passed by again. "Finish this one; then come back and help pack up! We're taking Amber home."

Cautiously, Ben helped Amber to her feet, surprised by how light she felt. While she wrapped a damp arm around his neck and broad shoulders, his arm steadied her slim waist. As they began hobbling together towards the parking lot, he mused there were worse ways to spend a Monday morning than coming to the aid of a beautiful damsel in distress. It certainly beat grading papers.

By the time Ben had Amber securely situated in the truck, Sarah had caught up. Shouldering both Amber's gear and her own while clutching Ben's satchel, chair, and thermos, she looked every bit the part of the loyal pack mule.

*****

"All I could think about on the way home was 'déjà vu'!" Amber almost shouted to Ben in the kitchen. After making her comfortable on the couch, with pillows behind her back and under her leg, he had gone to forage for Gatorade and ice.

"Yeah, I was thinking the same thing," he said, returning with a jumbo-size bottle and a bag of frozen veggies, which he handed to her. As Ben looked on, Amber gulped down a few mouthfuls of electrolytes and wedged the bag between the pillow and her hamstring. "You haven't caught many breaks since Kiana left town."

"It seems to have become the pattern of my life," she sighed. Catching herself, Amber shot a glance over at Ben, now retrieving a blanket from the loveseat on the other side of the living room. "Listen to me, throwing a pity party for myself. I'm sorry." He returned to the couch, unfolding the blanket.

"It's perfectly natural to vent a little frustration, especially when you're still hurting," he assured her. Bending over to lay the blanket across her, Ben pulled it down over her sock-covered feet. "You've had a challenging morning to say the least."

"I still feel a bit foolish," she admitted. "After all, I'm complaining to someone who's endured far worse."

Ben hesitated before releasing his grip on the blanket. Standing up, he faced Amber to find her eyes locked on him. His manner became subdued as he set his hands on his hips. "So, you know about Joy." The ensuing silence served as confirmation.

"You've done a wonderful job with Sarah and should be very proud," she replied with utmost sincerity.

Ben's face flushed almost imperceptibly. Shifting his feet, he folded his arms across his chest. "Thank you. I appreciate the compliment. But believe me it's by God's grace and a huge assist from my mom."

"You're humble, too." Amber's pursed lips soon twisted themselves into a smile. "Speaking of your mom, as Sarah tells it, she wasn't a fan of the ice bath either."

That made Ben grin. "I guess you could say she warmed up to the idea . . . once it was over, that is." Seeming to remember the time, he scanned the room and asked, "Are you going to be OK? Anything else I can get you before I go?"

Amber tested her leg. "It's starting to loosen up a lot, so I think I'm good." On second thought, she pointed to the edge of the coffee table. "Can you please hand me my phone?" He leaned over and handed it over. "Thank you, Ben, for all you've done. I really mean it."

"Happy to help! I'm just glad you're feeling better. And let me know if you change your mind about calling an Uber to go get your car."

"I will, but I think I'll be fine," she insisted with a dismissive wave.

"OK, then. Hopefully, I'll see you back up on your feet tomorrow morning."

As soon as Ben turned to leave, a frown of indecision replaced Amber's smile. Sensing a unique window of opportunity fast closing, she found her tongue just a step before he reached the door. "Ben!"

Halting, he turned back toward her, a look of curiosity on his face. Having just regained his attention, Amber suddenly wasn't certain she was actually ready for it. She plunged ahead. "Before you leave, can I ask you a personal question?"

"Sure . . ." he replied, a little hesitant.

Gazing down and fiddling with the blanket, Amber steeled herself before continuing. "Both Cathy and Sarah have mentioned that you avoid social situations. Sarah even says she calls you 'The Hermit.'"

"Is there a question in there somewhere?" he asked evenly, his eyebrows arched.

She looked back up and met his steel blue eyes. "Is it true? Why don't you go to events like your staff banquet any more, especially when you have such good friends like Cathy and her husband?"

A wry smile spread across Ben's face. "That *is* a personal question." He nodded.

Both of Amber's hands flew to her reddening face, the fingers covering her mouth. "I'm so sorry; I shouldn't have pried. I promise I won't—"

Alarmed at her anguish, Ben took a few swift steps back toward her while cutting her short, his voice suddenly soothing. "It's OK, it's OK. No worries, Amber." Her still-widened eyes implied additional reassurance was necessary. Stepping even closer, his brow furrowed, he persisted. "Really. I shouldn't have put it like that . . . I said you could ask, and I should have the courage to answer."

Relieved, Amber let her hands fall back to her lap. Meanwhile, Ben blew out a deep breath and took a seat near her on the edge of the coffee table. Leaning forward, elbows on his knees, he rubbed his eyes before continuing. "It is true. Part of it involves avoiding memories. Many events remind me of Joy's absence, though, honestly, the feelings surface whether I go or not." She nodded sympathetically but remained silent. "But the school dynamic is also awkward; not only is it small enough to be a fishbowl, but the banquet is a couples-oriented event. I'd feel like a third wheel."

Amber nodded again, pondering his words before speaking. "I get it . . . That makes total sense. I'd probably feel the same way in your shoes." She paused. "But I still hate to see someone like you miss out on the simple pleasures in life, like enjoying time with old friends and colleagues." She then took up a more buoyant, even defiant tone accented by a tilt of her head. "For what it's worth, I'm an outsider who couldn't care less about what your colleagues may say about me. And I also just happen to know the track coach's wife." She set her jaw as she smiled. "If you change your mind, I'd be happy to serve as your plus one for the evening."

He hadn't seen that coming. But rather than give any indication of his surprise, Ben calmly sat up, placed his hands on his knees, and remained quiet for a few moments as he considered the offer. When he finally spoke, he did so with exaggerated solemnity, looking directly into Amber's eyes. "In that case, I have one serious concern."

"What?" Taken aback, Amber asked the question almost in a whisper.

"Do you even own a dress?"

Spying Ben's smirk, Amber quickly recovered and matched it. "Hmmm . . . I think I might have seen one in my closet the other day." Then she laughed.

CHAPTER 19

Ben scanned the restaurant bathroom to make sure he was alone. Satisfied, he stepped up to the long mirror that ran along the wall above three marbled wash basins. Running his fingers through his hair, combed back in the front and on the sides, he smoothed a couple of rebellious locks before pulling up on the open collar of his ironed button-down to raise it crisply above the lapel of his sports jacket. Finally, he dusted off each shoulder with a flick of his hands. The grooming review complete, he stepped back out into the lobby in slacks and leather Oxfords to check his phone for the third time and await Amber's arrival.

The next five minutes passed slowly with Ben half-admiring the vibrant array of Italian blown glass stretching across one wall. The variety of sizes, shapes and color schemes rendered each piece unique. The wall facing it added a more subdued but incredibly quaint ambiance: a collection of majolica earthenware, each piece presenting its own intricate design. Together, the decorations helped make Alfredo's a local icon.

Ben's eyes kept returning to the inlaid oaken doors each time they parted, only to glimpse strangers on a Saturday night date or colleagues with their spouses following the sign pointing to the banquet room. One or two seemed surprised to see him as they waved across the lobby. Ben looked at his phone for a fourth time. Amber was technically two minutes late.

Moments later, the door swung open again, and this time Ben caught his breath. A woman resembling a Hollywood starlet tiptoed in wearing strappy heels and a flowy halter dress, a clutch pinned beneath her toned arm. As she stowed her aviator sunglasses, her eyes searched in the opposite direction for a familiar face. Her hair, a riot of loose blonde curls, cascaded over her bare, defined shoulders, framing a face that glowed from countless mornings in the sun. With her eyes shadowed and lined, and her lips tinted, she appeared remarkably sophisticated. Ben had to convince himself that he was the one she was looking for. As he stepped forward, Amber finally spotted him and brandished a brilliant smile.

"Wow, look at you!" gushed Ben, both hands extended. "So, I guess you found your dress, and I might add you look great."

"Thank you! And you seem to have won the battle with a button-down. Who knew you had Oxfords and a sports jacket in your closet!" They laughed.

"Thanks for coming. Are you ready to enter the rumor mill?"

Amber nodded confidently while flashing another smile. "Bring it on!"

Ben couldn't help but grin at her audacity. "Well, Jack and Cathy are waiting for us inside at a table for four," he informed, making a gesture towards the banquet room for Amber to precede him.

"Perfect!" she replied and followed his lead.

*****

Almost the moment the master of ceremony stepped away from the microphone, the program ended, a bow-tied waiter placed two slices of New York-style cheesecake in front of Ben and Amber. Circling the table, he did the same for Jack and Cathy.

Amber looked at her piece with longing eyes. "So, does this qualify as carbs in your training diet plan?" he asked.

"That's a bit of a stretch," she conceded, picking up a dessert fork, "but I'm not going to deny myself at least a couple bites. You can have the rest."

"Now that's what I call a win-win situation," Ben grinned.

Jack, who for one night had traded in his team gear for a tie and blazer, interrupted Amber's giggling. "Congratulations on your award tonight, Ben," he mocked. "Frankly, I'm a bit jealous of you."

"Oh, I bet you are! If only you could have won 'Most Likely to be Off-Campus at Lunch.' A highly coveted prize!" Ben slid his certificate, lying on the table, a few inches further away from Jack. "Keep your hands off!"

Amber, with feigned admiration, touched Ben's shoulder and looked up at him through her eyelashes. "I'm so proud of you, Ben! The work you must have put in!" All four burst out laughing.

"I don't know, Honey," countered Cathy, elegant in her black Ann Taylor dinner dress, featuring a squared neckline and capped sleeves. "'Most Likely to Need a Substitute' is pretty special, too!" The table erupted again, enough to draw the attention of a neighboring table or two.

"Hey, we should really be toasting Sarah and Amber!" insisted Jack, picking up his glass. "Not only did our track star run a PR in her first meet of the year, but now she's been accepted into the Rodeo Invitational. Congratulations!"

"Hear, Hear!" Cathy agreed. They clinked glasses with one another.

"I'm flattered to be included," said Amber, "but Sarah is the one doing the work, and I think she's just getting started. Hopefully she can meet the occasion next week."

Cathy subsequently redirected the conversation. "So, Amber, I know you're training for some big meets yourself. How are things going?"

Putting down her fork, Amber began playing with the stem of her glass. She looked a little uncomfortable having the spotlight shine on her. "Well, as Ben knows only too well, I had a bit of a scare with a bad cramp earlier this week. But overall, I'm encouraged by the early results. For this point in the season, I've been running my best times since college."

"Well, that's great news!" said Cathy.

"Yeah," Amber continued. "I've already run a time that will qualify me for the open division of the same meet we're hoping Sarah will get into in April. I would still like to improve in my next race, though, to qualify for the fastest heat."

"Is that the Western Relays?" inquired Jack. Amber nodded while taking a sip of her iced tea. Jack turned to Cathy. "That's the biggest meet in this part of the country, with both high school and open divisions. Some of the biggest names in track and field compete there." Turning back to Amber, he asked, "So what is your ultimate goal?"

"Well, for starters," she began, now using her fingers to rotate the glass back and forth, "breaking my career PR, set several years ago back when I was in college."

"Do you mind my asking what that is?"

Blushing, Amber, hesitated before answering. "A two oh three."

Her tablemates, including Ben, stared at her. "Wow! If you succeed in breaking that, how far could you go?"

Amber looked first at Ben and then down at her nails, French-manicured for the evening, which now tapped the base of her glass. "My ultimate dream would be to earn a spot on the Olympic team at the U.S. Trials. But I've got to qualify to run at the Trials first," she quickly added. The raised eyebrows around the table suggested a reappraisal of Amber.

Intrigued, Jack brought Amber's inquisition to a close with one last question. "So, what does it take to qualify?"

Amber's swift reply made clear she had memorized the time long ago. "Running a two oh two point five or lower at a sanctioned meet this season."

"Wow! That's really something!" Jack said, his eyes wide. "Well, best of luck, and keep us posted!"

Wanting to spare Amber further unease, Ben made a show of checking the time on his phone. "OK, you empty-nesters. Seeing that I have a child at home, I need to get going. I told my mom I'd be back around ten."

"Oh, the days," sighed Jack, only half-sarcastic.

Ben stood up, followed by the others. "Thank you, Guys, for a wonderful evening," he said sincerely. "I'm glad we did this; it's been too long."

"Believe me, the feeling is mutual," agreed Jack. "And it was great to finally meet you in person and get to know you, Amber."

"Yes!" concurred Cathy. "We loved spending the evening with you both."

The four exchanged handshakes and hugs before Ben, feeling as if a dozen sets of eyes followed him, escorted Amber out to the lobby, where she held up a finger. "Do you mind if I visit the restroom on our way out?"

"No, not at all!" replied Ben. "I'll meet you right back here."

No sooner had Amber entered the last open stall than she heard a pair of women enter the bathroom. While they waited, they continued their conversation. Amber couldn't help but listen in from behind the door.

"Did you see that young thing Ben Turner brought with him tonight?"

"How could you miss her with that hair? She must be half his age. His wife would probably roll over in her grave if she could see it. The disrespect. And what about the daughter? I wonder if she's met her. Poor girl. They could be sisters!"

"I heard he met her at the gym Cathy Sutherland works at. I was surprised to see them sitting at the same table together. Cathy and Joy Turner were good friends."

"Well, they say gyms are the new bars these days."

The flush of the toilet preceded Amber's emergence from the stall. Upon seeing her, the middle-aged women turned ashen and looked away. But Amber stared at each, indignity in her eyes before stepping to the nearest sink. One of the women took an awkward step toward the now-open stall, but she stopped when Amber spoke into the mirror.

"Ben warned me the school was a gossip mill, so I can't say I'm surprised. But I must say I am shocked at just how ill-informed you are." She turned to pull out a towel, and while drying her hands gave one more parting shot. "I'm so glad to know he's surrounded by such a loving Christian community at school." Without looking back, Amber strode out the door, her face still burning when she rejoined Ben by the blown glass display.

Ben glanced at her with concern. "Are you OK?"

"Absolutely!"

"What happened?"

"I just kicked a little butt."

Ben's eyebrows raised. "Wow. I need to visit the women's bathroom more often. Should I call an ambulance?"

"Not this time," grinned Amber. "But I see why it took some courage for you to come tonight. Come on, let's get you home to Sarah."

Ben walked Amber out to her car, located at the far end of the lot, where they stepped into a pool of light below a lamppost and faced each other. "Thanks for making tonight possible," Ben said. "It wouldn't have happened without your encouragement. Seriously, I had a great time."

"So did I! It was really fun." Amber pushed a wind-blown lock of hair from her mouth to behind her ear, exposing her multiple piercings and a large golden hoop earring. "I'd be glad to do this again some time." She turned to unlock her door, and Ben held it open while she slid in.

"I don't know if I'll recognize you at practice next week!"

"Right back at you!" Amber smiled. "Good night!"

Ben shut her door, and the engine roared to life. Stepping back and waving, he shouted, "Good night!" as she reversed out of the space and drove off into the night. Slipping his hands into his pockets, he then turned and stepped into the darkness in search of his own car.

CHAPTER 20

Sarah and her grandmother, swathed with blankets, proved so entranced by *The Wizard of Oz* that neither seemed to take notice of Ben's presence until his keys clattered on the couch's side table. Pausing the movie, they turned in tandem, redirecting their attention from the screen to him with expectant expressions. Sarah, resting her arm across the back of the furniture, asked what they both were wondering.

"How was the banquet?"

Ben smiled. "Fun, thank you. I had a great time with friends." He shifted to a mischievous look before continuing. "I won a very special award," he said, holding out his certificate, "and I love you so much I'm going to give it to you." Reaching out to receive it, Sarah began to read with interest but soon lost interest.

"'Most likely to be Off-Campus at Lunch?' Gee, Dad, thanks; I'll cherish this." Putting it aside, she refocused the conversation on more critical matters. "Do you have any pictures? What did Amber wear?"

"No pictures, and she wore a very chic sweats ensemble with a head band."

Sarah's face betrayed her disappointment. "Really?"

"No!" Ben laughed. "She wore a beautiful dress; I hardly recognized her, and she said the same about me!"

Removing his sports jacket and starting to loosen his tie, Ben moved away from the living room, walking slowly down the hallway towards his own room. His mother rose and followed him, reaching Ben at his door. Seeing her solemn countenance, he stopped and laid his coat over his arm while the movie resumed in the background.

"So," he asked in a suddenly tired voice, "how do you feel about my going?"

Angling her head in an effort to catch his eyes, she faintly smiled with pursed lips. Her voice was soft. "Happy . . . You?"

Looking back towards the living room, Ben paused before answering quietly. "Can you feel happy and guilty at the same time?"

Nodding, her response took the form of a hypothetical question. "If the situation was reversed, Joy was in her thirties living with Sarah and you were gone, would you want her to live out her life alone and looking backward? To deny herself companionship and a future?"

After pondering, Ben slowly shook his head and met her eyes again. "No. I'd love them both too much to want them stuck in the past while life moved forward all around them. But then again, I wouldn't want them to forget me, either. I'd always want to keep a special place in their hearts."

"Exactly!" replied his mother with a decisive nod of the head. Then she unfolded her arms and allowed her hands to accent her heartfelt appeal. "So why don't you follow the Golden Rule and 'do unto others as you would have others do unto you?' Because Joy loved you, she would want the same for you as you would want for Joy: a fulfilling life. And believe me, there's exactly zero chance you'll ever stop cherishing Joy with my darling granddaughter reminding you of her every hour of every day." Though remaining silent, Ben nodded, and his mother pressed the point home. "If the time ever comes that you fall in love again, you'd never tolerate a woman who wants you to forget Joy. And any woman who truly cares for you will never ask you to. She'll honor her memory, not be jealous of it; she'll share your grief, not push it away." Shaking her head, her tone turned abruptly firm. "You wouldn't settle for anything less!"

While he absorbed the words, Ben exhaled, as if releasing a burden. Then he stepped forward and embraced her. "Thanks."

"You're more than welcome!"

His mother rubbed his back for a moment before they separated. When they did, Ben's demeanor grew decidedly more upbeat. "And thanks for coming over to stay with Sarah tonight."

"Oh, yeah. That's always a real hard sell!" she replied, her face suggesting he should know better.

Ben ducked into his room to hang up his coat, and they returned to collect her things from the living room, only to find Sarah asleep on the couch. After exchanging grins, Ben walked his mother to the door and bid her good night. Then, after sliding the controller out of Sarah's limp hand and punching off the movie's rolling credits, he pulled a blanket over her and retired to the study.

Groping through the dimness, he found the desk lamp beside the desk top screen and switched it on. With a roll and a click of the mouse, he roused the screen, selected a browser and began typing key terms into the search bar. After adding and subtracting a couple of words to refine the search, a dozen promising results appeared on the screen. He decided to attack them chronologically.

The first article, from a local newspaper, presented a photo of the teenage version of Amber, modeling longer and darker brown hair, in a high school uniform near the top of a medal podium. Ben was struck by the relative lack of muscle definition in her shoulders and arms. Reading a couple of paragraphs, he discovered she had placed second in the Texas State Championships her senior year. Clicking on another link, Ben observed a smiling Amber, clad in an Arkansas tee, seated at a table decorated in red and white while signing a college letter of intent, flanked by her parents and coach.

Additional clicks, mostly from the University of Arkansas athletics website, followed Amber through her college career. By her sophomore year she had gone blonde and made the medal podium at the Southeastern Conference Championships; by her junior year she was the 2009 SEC 800-meter champion and an NCAA National Championships medalist.

Then information became harder to find. Ben located one article from her senior year that mentioned the end of Amber's quest for an NCAA championship due to a stress fracture in her foot. A little more research produced a roster picture from the following year, 2011; beneath Amber's name it noted *Redshirt Senior*. "So, she got a fifth year," Ben murmured to himself, but he found no additional collegiate accomplishments for Amber, only a roster photo of a younger-looking Kiana the same year listed as a junior. Over the last five years, all Ben could find were a few times listed in random track meet results pages, one from just a month ago, each labeling her as "unattached."

Ben closed the browser. Leaning back in his chair, he rested his elbows on the arm rests, making a steeple with his hands, and sat staring at the desktop screen for a couple of minutes.

"Whatcha doing, Dad?"

Ben was too lost in his thoughts to be startled. Swiveling around, he smiled at Sarah when he saw she still had the blanket draped around her shoulders like a cape. She looked like a bedraggled superhero.

"Just thinking about the past . . . and the future." Thankfully, Sarah didn't find the answer too strange or ask what he meant. She was too sleepy. "Come on, let's get to bed."

Standing up, Ben walked Sarah to her room on the way to his own without turning off the desk light.

CHAPTER 21

It was an unseasonably temperate Monday morning. Though still the last week of March, their phones claimed an early morning temperature of sixty-seven degrees. Four four-hundred-meter repeats and jogging recoveries later, it felt like half that again to Sarah. Copying Amber, she had shed down to her cropped racerback top for the first time this season. Even Ben, grading in the stands, had opted to remove his jacket.

Sarah focused on her fifth and last repeat of the day. She had made a deal with Amber during the pre-workout stretching, and only seventy seconds separated her from taking care of her end of the bargain. Looking over her shoulder, Sarah saw Amber had two hundred meters to go before meeting her at the start line, so she looped back to synchronize with her arrival, matching Amber's jog pace twenty meters from the line.

"Last one!" Amber gasped between breaths. "Don't give in to the pain!" Sarah let her silence speak for her resolve. Nearing the line, their arms swung across their waists to reach their watches, and upon crossing it a pair of beeps sent them accelerating into the first curve.

Again, Sarah did not try to match Amber step for step, but she did attack the first one hundred meters with an increased determination, keeping her mentor a step closer than usual by the end of the curve.

Energized by her start, Sarah lengthened her stride and tried to keep her breathing rhythmic, her arm motions full range. As the two-hundred-meter mark approached and then flicked by beneath their feet, Sarah sensed Amber's lead had increased less than normal and wondered just how close she could stay for the balance of the lap.

Pulling hard on the second curve, she tried to forget the fire stoking in her legs and lungs and concentrated on the challenge of sustaining her rhythm over the last one hundred-and-fifty meters unwinding before her. Straightening out on the home stretch, she blew her breaths out like a forceful mantra, causing her father to look up from his papers. Intent on the charging figure of Amber ahead, her legs driving, knees high, and carriage erect, Sarah emulated the movements until, with fifty meters left, she despaired over keeping the pace. Forty, thirty, twenty, ten: Sarah counted down the final meters and finally pressed the button on the side of her watch in a state of anaerobic numbness. Still, she wasn't too incapacitated to detect the surprise in Amber's face when she turned to observe her sooner-than-expected finish.

"What did you just run?" Amber demanded, though still trying to regain her own breath.

Sarah shuffled along a few more steps before even making an attempt to read her watch. When she did, the pain fell away. "A high sixty seven."

Amber just stared at her before letting her quiet words do the talking. "You're for real, girl. And don't you forget that."

If Sarah hadn't already been flushed from the effort, Amber would have seen her blushing. Uncertain of how to react to such a supreme compliment, especially coming from Amber, she simply mumbled, "Thanks." Then she remembered.

"OK," she said, still gasping, "I held up my end of the bargain . . . I focused on the workout first . . . and made all my times. Now it's time for you . . . to keep your end of the deal . . . on our cool down. Start dishing!"

Amber's look of astonishment melted into a grin. "Well, now I know what motivates you!" As they began to jog, Amber's voice signaled her unconditional surrender. "OK, so what do you want to know?"

"Let's see," began Sarah, a smile stretching from ear to ear. "Let's start with what you wore. My dad said your dress was beautiful."

"A flowy halter dress," said Amber while nodding. "One of my favorites."

"What color?"

"Burnt orange . . . I'm an autumn."

"Cool. What shoes did you match with it? And jewelry?"

"Pretty simple. A pair of strappy heels and a pendant necklace. I also wore a pair of big hoop earrings along with my studs."

"Nice! And how did you do your hair?"

"Down with some loose, messy curls . . . I don't think I look good with my hair up, especially in a formal bun."

"Cute. You know, the spring dance at school is coming up in a couple of weeks. Would you come over and help me get ready and take pictures?" Sarah smirked when noting, "My dad isn't very talented in those areas."

"Sure, if I'm in town. That sounds like fun. When is it?"

"Not this Saturday but next, starting in the late afternoon."

Amber's eyes sought the horizon as she checked her mental calendar. "I don't have a meet that weekend, so I think that works. I'll double check and get back to you. Are you going with anyone?"

"My two best friends, Marcie and Tiffany."

"That's good," said Amber, shooting Sarah a knowing look. "You'll probably have more fun that way."

As they neared the end of the second curve, Sarah stopped talking long enough for them to pass her father before continuing. When she did speak, she struck a hushed, secretive tone. "So, do you like my dad?"

Amber rolled her eyes over to Sarah and paused before replying. "What kind of a question is that? Of course I like your dad! He's a great guy, and we're becoming good friends. You're lucky to have him for a father." Before Sarah could pursue the topic further, Amber changed it.

"I'm going to ease things off for both you and me Thursday and Friday with the invitationals coming this weekend, so tomorrow and Wednesday we need to hit it hard again. I thought about easing you off Wednesday as well, but since the Rodeo isn't the main goal, I want to train you through it as much as possible. I'll wait to taper us more, hopefully, for the Western Relays and your big post-season meets still ahead."

A dreamy smile filled Sarah's face. "Wouldn't it be crazy if we ran together at Western Relays?"

"Not really," replied Amber. "After today's workout, I'd bank on it."

CHAPTER 22

Thunk! Sarah dropped her bag and turned to join Ben as he scanned the Arroyo Hills High School stadium. The sight confirmed what they already suspected from the parking chaos surrounding the school and the length of the lines they passed at the ticket booth on their way to the team entrance. They were not at St. Timothy's anymore.

Rising twenty rows skyward, concrete bleachers boasting aluminum benches mirrored each other on both sides of the track, stretching from one end zone to the other. A rainbow of team pop-ups, representing every large school in the greater valley region, lined the top row beneath the press box on the congested home side, while several more dotted the half-full visitors' side, where Ben and Sarah had sought refuge. At one end of the stadium, adjacent to the first curve, a large digital scoreboard towered over the snack bar and restroom complex, constantly updating race entrants and results. The track itself was cordoned off from spectators with a chain link fence, and in the heart of the infield, a rectangular area had been further enclosed with a string of triangular flags. Within it, runners on deck completed their final warm-ups when allowed to enter the infield one heat at a time. Around each edge of the rectangle, four field events progressed at once: long jump, triple jump, high jump, and pole vault.

Sarah sighed. "It's weird being here without the team. And there's way more people than usual!"

"No doubt about that," Ben agreed, arms folded across his chest. "I'm glad Coach told us to get here more than an hour before your event. Who knew we'd have to hunt for a parking spot half a mile away?" He was glad to spy a time clock at the two-hundred-meter mark. That simplified providing Sarah her splits. Facing her, he added, "By the way, he wanted you to know that he would be here if the team didn't have a meet today."

If she found the message meaningful, Sarah, in the throes of pre-race nerves, made no show of it. Instead, she changed the topic. "I'm going to see if Amber has run yet." Taking a seat, she started scrolling through an online meet results site on her phone.

Ben sat down beside her and opened the team packet he'd picked up from the Team Welcome table. "Coach said there would be two varsity and two frosh/soph heats for each running event and gender," he informed Sarah. He pulled out the stapled heat sheets from the large manila envelope and flipped through them. "It looks like you're in the fast Varsity heat, sixth seed. Both heats have twelve runners."

But Sarah was not listening. "Oh my gosh! They posted the results from Amber's race. She ran a high two oh three! That's crazy!"

For a moment, Ben forgot about Sarah's bib, a look of interest spreading over his face. "Is that a new PR for her?"

"For the season. I think it's just a few tenths off her best ever!" When Sarah looked up, her eyes were shining.

"Wow!" said Ben, clearly impressed. He took a moment to ponder the magnitude of the feat. "She's got to be higher than the moon!"

"I'll say."

"Well, good for her!" Rousing himself from his thoughts, Ben proceeded to remove the bib and safety pins from the packet and handed them to Sarah.

"Can you pin this on for me?" she pleaded, frowning.

Ben raised his brow. "Shouldn't someone who's begging to get a driver's permit be old enough to start doing that?" Shaking his head, Ben complied anyway after Sarah unzipped her sweat jacket. "What does Amber want you to do in your race?"

The excitement over Amber's race results succeeded in further loosening Sarah's tongue. "She kept it pretty simple: run at least a two sixteen to make sure I qualify for Western Relays. That means taking a second off my first lap from last race while still running the same time on my second lap. Anything more than that is, as Amber put it, 'icing on the cake.' She thinks it's doable with faster runners around me."

The booming public address system abruptly echoed throughout the stadium. "Final call, girls and boys four hundred meters! Second call, girls and boys one hundred meters! First call, girls and boys eight hundred meters!" Ben picked up the pace with the safety pins.

"Well, we'll soon find out," he said. "Did you see the athlete check-in area on the way in?" His hands occupied, Ben tilted his head in the direction of a spacious practice field situated behind the scoreboard, accessed through a gate in another chain link fence. Beyond the meet clerk's tent at the entrance, dozens of athletes could be seen shaking out and stretching. Sarah merely nodded tensely as Ben snapped closed the last pin.

"You better get going. Be sure to take your spikes and water bottle." Rethinking matters, Ben put out a hand to stop her. "Let's pray first."

Sarah's expression showed full agreement, but she deferred. "You do it."

Ben put his hand on Sarah's shoulder, and they closed their eyes. "Lord, we ask that You enable Sarah to run to the best of the ability You have gifted her with today, without fear, for Your glory. Amen."

"Amen."

Ben gave Sarah the most confident smile he could muster. "I'll be at the two-hundred-meter mark. God's speed!"

Without another word, Sarah turned and started her solitary journey, her ponytail bouncing with each step down the stairs.

*****

As soon as the last heat of the girls frosh/soph eight hundred thundered by, the official at the gate gave the signal for the girls in Sarah's heat to cross the track to the infield re-warming area. Wearing a pair of sticker sixes on her thumping chest and the right hip of her shorts, Sarah jogged with them past the first heat of Varsity girls, tentatively making their way to wait by the start line. When the coast was clear, she accelerated into a full sprint for thirty meters to get out the kinks and anxious energy. While doubling back along the line of flags, she surveyed the bustling venue and wondered if she really belonged there.

Sarah switched her gaze to the competitors milling around her and recognized most of the school names scripted on their jerseys. One girl, wearing the number three, was from Saddleback Canyon, the school she passed every day on the way to her own school. Studying her face and development, Sarah mused the girl had to be at least a couple of years older than herself. Nearby stood a pair of uber-defined runners, the second and fifth seeds, sporting the distinct silver and royal blue uniforms of the vaunted host school. To Sarah's shock, the higher of the two seeds, a powerfully built Latina, a few inches shorter than Sarah with long, thick brown hair, spoke to her while staring at the interlocking letters on her racing jersey.

"What school are you from?" she asked while bouncing up and down on her toes, genuinely curious. "I've never seen that jersey."

"Montevallo Christian Academy," replied Sarah, a tremor in her voice.

"Where's that?" Given the girl's expression, the name was clearly new to her.

"About fifteen minutes from here."

Sarah's answer seemed to surprise her. "Oh . . . Well, good luck!"

"Same to you!"

The crack of the gun announced the start of the first Varsity girls heat, and Sarah decided to cram in a couple of more practice starts to finish getting loose and slow her pulse before reporting to the start line. When she rejoined the girls in her heat, they had clumped together by the timing tent to watch the finish of the first heat. Sarah, quickly counting only eleven, including herself, figured someone had scratched from her heat. As the exhausted winner of the first heat stepped off the track, Sarah checked the scoreboard: a low two eighteen. At least she belonged in the fast heat, Sarah told herself. Then she recalled Amber's supreme compliment from earlier in the week. Repeating the words in her mind took the worst edge off her nerves, and she took a deep breath.

Moments after the last runner finished, the assisting red coat beckoned Sarah's heat on to the track, allowing them one more practice start down the straight before calling them back to the start line. Results from the just-completed heat echoed from the PA system as Sarah circled back, her knees weak again. When she arrived, girls were already lining up along the arc, the top seed against the rail and Sarah once again wedged in the middle. This time she had no choice in the matter.

"Next up is the championship heat of the Girls Varsity eight hundred meters!" The announcement caused her heart to pound again, as did spying her name listed on the scoreboard. Constantly shaking out her arms and legs, she felt like a specimen under a microscope, scrutinized by a couple of thousand unseen eyes.

"Spread out, Ladies!" directed the red coat, motioning with his hands, and the line of runners expanded along the arc as the lower seeds stepped further out. The rest spaced themselves accordingly. "Now take a step back from the line!" he ordered. When satisfied with their effort, he retreated to the infield and handed the heat over to the lead red coat, who stood on top of a small ladder with a microphone in one hand and a pistol in the other. Once he raised the gun above his head, the spectators in the area hushed. Then he spoke, his firm monotone projected to the runners by a portable speaker.

"On your marks!" Eleven girls stutter-stepped up to the line, leaned forward, and froze with one arm cocked. "Crack!"

Sarah thrust off the line, jump starting the turn-over of her lanky legs, but try as she might, the shorter-legged runners around her achieved the feat more quickly and pulled a step or two ahead in the first twenty meters. The collective speed of the elite group turned out to be a blessing in disguise, though; as the outside runners cut towards the rail in a flurry of elbows, Sarah avoided the skirmish without breaking stride by angling on a direct line behind them to take up a position in Lane Three on the outside shoulder of the pack. Her acceleration continued unimpeded until she reached race pace and passed a pair of girls in the rear as they came off the curve. Then, while the rest of the pack relaxed its initial sprint, Sarah sustained her speed and glided forward down the stretch along the edge. Within fifty more meters, the pack began to thin, and she joined the front runners, just a step behind. Content with her position, Sarah focused on settling into a steady breathing pattern as the ever-shifting digits on the two-hundred-meter clock loomed ahead. Checking it as they passed, she glimpsed a thirty-three.

"Right on time!" The voice bellowing above the stampede of spikes sounded like her father's.

Entering the second curve, Sarah slightly eased off the pedal and drifted towards the rail into the outside edge of Lane One, tucking in behind a pair of leaders and matching strides with another girl beside her on the rail. The breath of at least one additional runner stalked close behind. Approaching the end of the curve, Sarah pushed on the accelerator again, timing her surge to coincide with her arrival on the home straight. She edged into Lane Two with notions of challenging for the lead, but her competitors promptly responded, and she succeeded only in mirroring their strides all the way to the start line, the trailing runner still literally breathing loudly behind her. The frantically-changing numerals on the clock read one oh seven something as the frontrunners crossed the line, and Sarah, realizing she was right where she was supposed to be, sensed her confidence rise.

Entering the third curve, Sarah inched back over the border line into Lane 1 to pace once again next to the girl on the rail, and just in time, too, to prevent the insurgent trailer from pulling even and forcing her into staying in Lane Two. Then the burning began to set in. It started in the hamstrings and soon spread into the quads and calves. Next, her chest and arms caught fire. Sarah responded by redoubling the effort to pump her arms and concentrate on her exhalation. Blowing the air out of her lungs in a forceful cadence, she straightened out on the back stretch and assured herself it would all be over in roughly forty seconds.

Just when Sarah thought it was still anyone's race, the number one seed began to separate from the front group, and the breathing behind Sarah started to fade. Nearing the six-hundred-meter mark, she found herself in a trail group of three, and the form of the girl on the rail beside her was beginning to fall apart, her breathing even more labored than her own.

The ever-spinning clock fell away one last time, with Sarah right on a one forty-one, when a voice again penetrated her focus. "You're on PR pace!"

The news injected Sarah with a vital shot of energy. Briefly stepping on the gas, Sarah passed the girl on the rail and ducked inside to the rail herself, a step or two behind the second-place girl sheathed in silver and royal blue. For the first time, it dawned on Sarah exactly who she was chasing. Rounding the curve, Sarah's body screamed for mercy, but the thought of running with Amber at Western Relays gripped her mind and blunted the pain.

Timing a last slingshot off the final turn, Sarah reached out with her feet on each stride, forced her arms from 'ear to rear', and strove to breathe while keeping an erect carriage. Fifty meters from the finish, she had cut the lead of the Arroyo Hills girl in half, and twenty meters later pulled even with her. Even in the fog of competition, Sarah could hear the stadium come alive at their duel. She strained to sustain her push but, starting to lock up, couldn't make her increasingly frozen limbs respond to her opponent's last-second spurt. She crossed the line in third place, a step behind, with the fourth-place girl from Saddleback Canyon a couple of steps further behind her.

Staggering to an awkward stop, Sarah worried whether the human heart could actually jump out of the rib cage. With her lungs still groping for oxygen, her hands behind her head, a red coat immediately approached to herd the finishers off the track. Zombie-like, she stepped to the infield, oblivious to the tense clump of frosh/soph boys she passed, poised to step on the track. Then she heard her name echo throughout the stadium. Searching out the scoreboard, Sarah felt her body shiver at what she saw: 3rd / Sarah Turner / Montevallo C. A. / 2:15.57.

Tears had already begun welling in her eyes when she felt a damp hand pat her sweaty back. Startled, Sarah looked over to see the fatigued smile of her Arroyo Hills opponent. "Great race . . . You really pushed me," her friendly rival haltingly complimented, still trying to catch her own breath, before giving Sarah an affirming look and adding, " . . . I know your school now!"

Touched, Sarah returned the gesture. "Congrats on second! . . . And thanks for pulling me to a PR!"

With a pair of nods, they drifted apart, and Sarah, still collecting the remainder of her breath, meandered toward the visitor side of the infield, searching for her dad in the stands. Moments later, she heard the familiar voice calling her name. She finally placed it when she saw him near midfield, leaning forward against the railing at the bottom of the bleachers and waving his arms. After waving back in recognition, Sarah punched both her fists above her head. Somehow her wide smile broadened when she heard her father say it.

"Woo-hoo!! Like that icing!!"

CHAPTER 23

Ben did not need to knock; the door was already open. Tiptoeing carefully through the maze of clothing strewn on the floor, he succeeded in reaching Sarah's bed unscathed. Sarah, propped up by pillows piled against the wall, sat swathed in the sheets and comforter pulled up to her waist, like a butterfly in the midst of shedding its cocoon. Above her head, her expanding collection of medals had been rearranged to include two recent additions.

"Here you go," said Ben, handing her a box of lozenges. "This should help with the burning in your throat. I hope you like wild cherry." Sarah, breaking in her new Rodeo Invite sweatshirt, set a textbook down in her lap and gratefully accepted the box before grabbing another tissue and blowing her swollen, red-rimmed nose. The small waste basket beside her bed already brimmed with crumpled used tissues.

"Arghh!" she vented. "My nose won't stop running!"

Ben took a seat on the only open space at the foot of the bed. "Colds aren't any fun. At least you don't have a fever." Sarah didn't appear ready to focus on the bright side. "Looks like you'll be staying home from both practice and school tomorrow. I'll text Amber and let her know. I'll also give Grandma a call and ask her to come over in the morning after I'm gone."

"Yeah, there's no way I could do speedwork tomorrow or maybe even Tuesday," she agreed. "I'm so glad I didn't get this Friday or yesterday before the race."

"Me, too! It's never a good time to get sick, but that would have been terrible timing. Another silver lining." He rose, but Sarah spoke again before he could take a step toward the door.

"I hate to think of Amber being at practice by herself. Workouts are hard enough even when you're running with someone else; it sucks to do it all alone." After another moment's thought, she added, "Do you think it's even safe to be by herself in the dark?"

Now it was Ben's turn to do some thinking. "Good point. I didn't really think about that. Maybe I'll stop by and check on her in the morning. I'll also check with your teachers to see what you're missing if they don't post your homework online. OK?"

"Yep!" Sarah nodded despite her new preoccupation with tearing open the box of lozenges.

Turning to leave, Ben looked once again at the clothes on the floor and halted. "Speaking of Amber, this will all need to be cleaned up if she's going to come over next weekend and help you get ready for the dance. Even if you don't care, it's embarrassing to me."

"I will," Sarah assured him in a weary voice.

"Yes, you will," he persisted with a direct look. " . . . Goodnight, Sweetie."

"Goodnight, Dad."

With matters settled, Ben plotted the safest path out of the room before starting his trek.

*****

She first spotted him upon reaching the back stretch. Over a hundred meters distant in the pre-dawn duskiness, Ben, his back turned to the track, was busy setting up his grading post in the bleachers at the start of the homestretch. As Amber jogged the balance of the straight, her initial confusion was quickly replaced with curiosity. However, by the time she approached the next curve she had guessed Ben's intentions, and, in a word, she was moved.

Almost silently, Amber drifted into the outer lanes while rounding the curve, slowing her pace until she eased to a stop below Ben on the edge of the track. Sliding her slender fingers through the gaps and gripping the chain-link fence, she called up to him. "Hi, stranger."

Ben turned towards her, the first stack of papers ready in hand. "Good morning!" he replied. Setting the stack aside, he placed his hands on his hips. "Hey, now that I'm seeing you in person, congrats again on your race this weekend! A two oh three? Wow!"

Amber wondered whether Ben could detect her bright, wide smile despite the fence and the dimness of the hour.

"Thanks! I'm thrilled! That will definitely get me into the invitational heat at Western Relays, which sets me up well to make a run at a Trials qualifying time."

"That's close to your PR, right?"

"Yeah, just a few tenths off."

"And your PR was set how long ago?"

Amber did not need to pause even a moment to calculate the answer. "Almost seven years."

Ben, sinking his hands into his jean pockets, shook his head in disbelief. "Seven years? If I could whistle, I would. That's *amazing*, Amber!"

This time Ben couldn't see Amber blush. Then she caught herself. "Congrats to Sarah, too. She killed it!"

"She really did," agreed Ben, unable to suppress a smile of his own. "Despite her nerves, she ran smart and surprisingly aggressive. I'm really proud of her . . . and thankful to you."

"Well, thanks," said Amber, bashfully dipping her head. "I'd be stunned if a two fifteen doesn't get her into the high school division at Western, maybe even the invitational heat since they only take times run this season . . . It will be wild running at the same meet together."

Ben nodded vigorously. "We're certainly looking forward to it. It should be incredible!"

Amber nodded as well while debating whether to excuse herself and continue the workout. After a pause, she instead asked the obvious question that, as yet, had remained unspoken. "So, what are you doing here? Is Sarah feeling OK?"

Ben casually addressed only the second question. "She wasn't awake when I left; I wanted her to sleep. She seems to have gotten through the night fine. My mom should arrive at the house before she gets up. Hopefully, she'll just be out a day or two."

"That's great. We have three weeks before the meet, so it's as good a time as any if you have to be sick." But noting Ben's evasion, Amber persisted. " . . . Why did you still come if she's not here?"

Ben finally obliged. "Well, we didn't want you to be alone, especially before it's light at this time of day. Who knows who could show up here. Besides," he continued, gesturing to the stack, "I have to grade papers anyway! May as well be here as anywhere, and offering a little moral support couldn't hurt either, right?"

Amber withdrew one hand from the fence to tuck a few strands of hair behind her studded ear while swiveling a trainer on its toe. "Thanks. That's really sweet, but you didn't have to."

"Are you kidding?" countered Ben, his eyebrows raised. "You've already done much more for us. It's the least I could do."

"OK," Amber relented. "Well, I guess we both have some work to do. Bye for now." With a wave and another smile, she returned to her workout.

*****

With his satchel in one hand, the empty thermos and stadium chair looped in the fingers of the other, Ben stood waiting for Amber as she stepped off the track. As she approached, he admired the vivid contrast between her blonde locks and the snug, black sweat jacket to which they fell.

"So, how was it?" he asked as she neared the gate.

"Solid!" she replied. Reaching him, she stopped for a second to readjust the gear bag slung over her shoulder. "No hint of cramping . . . something I'm sure we're both happy about." Both grinning, they began strolling on the familiar walkway leading out to the parking lot. "The day off after the race helped, too, but I think I'm just still pumped from running the two oh three; that really provided a boost today." She looked over, her green eyes intent. "Thanks again for coming. It helped me to relax and focus on the workout. It was very thoughtful of you."

"Really, it's my pleasure," he reassured, briefly meeting her eyes. "So, are you traveling for Easter in a couple of weeks?"

"No. Since my mom passed away, I don't see my dad much. He lives too far away to drive, and we're not particularly close. I may see him at Christmas or if one of us happens to be traveling in the other's area."

"I'm sorry on both counts. How long ago did your mom pass?"

"Thank you...About four years," she answered. Neither commented on the coincidence of the timing. "And let's just say my father would prefer to see me in a more prestigious career and running after his grandkids, not 'pipe dreams', as he calls them."

Ben didn't attempt to hide his surprise. "Hmm. I gather he hasn't seen you in action either in the gym or on the track lately."

Amber flashed him an ironic smile. "That would be a definite 'No.'"

They drew near their cars, parked side by side in slots bordering the stadium. Amber fished out her keys from the bag, and Ben placed the chair in the truck bed, but neither moved to leave; instead, they lingered, facing each other between the vehicles.

"Well, if you don't have any plans for Easter, Sarah and I would like to invite you to attend our church's sunrise service in a couple of weeks."

Amber seemed amused. "Easter service? Thanks," she gently scoffed, "but I'm not much of a church-goer. I don't really see myself as religious."

"Yeah, I get what you mean," nodded Ben, assuming a knowing smile. "But fact is even the most seemingly secular person is actually still religious."

"And how is that?" Amber's skeptical expression was hard to miss.

Unruffled, Ben answered without missing a beat. "It's simple. We all hold to a set of beliefs that guides our moral values and the goals we pursue in life. We all worship something; it's just the way we're wired."

Amber's eyes searched the cloudy sky while she mused over his words. "OK. I guess I'll give you that," she conceded. "I've never really thought about it in that way."

"Look, I'm sure we both have to run—pun not intended," chuckled Ben, checking his watch, "but before we do, can I ask *you* a personal question this time?" Each regarded the other with a wry smile.

Amber didn't take long to surrender. "Sure, I guess it's only fair."

Ben wanted to preface things first. "Don't answer me now; think about it, and we'll talk more about it some other time if you feel comfortable with it."

Though grateful for Ben's sensitivity, Amber struggled with the suspense. "OK . . . But what's the question?" Ben's tone turned sincere when he posed it.

"What do you worship, Amber? What are you spending your life pursuing?"

Amber took in a deep breath and exhaled slowly. Then her lips tightened into another ironic smile. "That is personal! Nothing like a small question."

Ben nodded again, this time sympathetically. "Our lives aren't a small matter." Before continuing, he assumed a lighter note. "Just think about it, and we can talk whenever you like . . . or not at all, if you prefer."

"OK, I will," Amber replied firmly.

"I've really got to go," apologized Ben. Stepping around the hood of his truck, he waved on his way to the driver's side door. "Have a great day, and I'll see you tomorrow!"

"You, too. Bye!"

While Ben climbed in, started the engine, and pulled out, Amber unlocked her car door and stowed her bag. But before stepping in, she gazed back over her shoulder at the truck swiftly receding in the morning light and let out a sigh.

CHAPTER 24

An array of cosmetics crowded the sink counter, competing for space with a collection of brushes and the curling iron. Reflected in the hallway bathroom mirror, Sarah had reached the home stretch in getting ready for the spring dance.

With arms folded over an open olive cardigan and solid white tee, Amber leaned a shoulder against the doorframe, her legs crossed in a pair of distressed skinny jeans and suede booties. Her eyes followed Sarah's fingers, which held a lip gloss as she shaded her lips. The pink hue complemented her eye shadow and blush-colored dress, a sleeveless, high-neck jacquard that fell above her knees and offered a fit and flare silhouette that flattered her lanky figure.

"What do you think?" Sarah asked, turning to Amber.

"You look adorable! Now the final touch." Unfolding her arms, Amber picked up and shook the hairspray cannister. Guarding Sarah's eyes with one hand, she swirled the nozzle around the long, bouncy curls draped over her shoulders in one long burst. "There!" She stepped to the side before pronouncing the final verdict. "Perfect!"

Sarah, admiring herself for a moment, smiled her agreement. "Thanks, Amber," she said, wrapping an arm around Amber's waist in a side-hug and squeezing. "I appreciate this so much."

The unexpected gesture warmed Amber's heart. It took a moment for her words to catch up. "Sure thing! I wouldn't have missed this . . . When will your friends arrive?"

"They texted a few minutes ago and said they're on their way."

Amber promptly unhooked a pair of rejected dresses hanging from the shower rod. "Then let's take these and put them back." She walked across the hallway into Sarah's room and replaced them in her closet. Turning, she was drawn to an arrangement of framed photos on the near wall. When her protégé clip-clopped into the room in her heels, Amber pointed to one in which Sarah was missing a tooth. "Ah, this is cute. Tell me about this picture."

"That's me and my mom on a family vacation to Hawaii. I think I was six. We took a class on how to make leis, so we're wearing them."

"I can see where you got your long, dark hair from," noted Amber, studying the image for a moment. " . . . And this one?" she asked, drawing attention to a photo of Sarah with Ben and Joy.

Sarah faintly smiled. "That was taken at my eighth birthday party. My mom planned a backwards party, so everyone wore their clothes backward. We even had an inside-out cake."

"She seems like she was fun," chuckled Amber.

"Yep. She was always making plans to do something . . . until she got sick." Sarah picked the next photo. As she touched it, her tone grew subdued, her face blank. "This is the last picture I have of her." A candid portrait, it presented a more haggard Joy wearing a brightly-colored scarf over her head. "Her hair had fallen out from the treatment," she explained.

Amber's eyes welled. "What a terrible loss," she commented quietly, her voice suddenly hoarse.

"Sorry to interrupt," Ben apologized. Surprised, they turned to find him leaning against the door jam. His face lit up as he gained a full view of Sarah. "Is this my little girl?! You look amazing!" Sarah beamed while Amber wiped her eyes. Then he announced, "Marcie and Tiffany have arrived. They're waiting for you in the front yard."

"Let the party begin!" Sarah declared, shooting both hands above her head. "Amber, will you take pictures on my phone?"

Amber pointed her finger at Sarah with a slight tilt of her head. "Only if you promise to send me a couple when we're done."

"Deal."

*****

Ben could have sworn a professional modeling shoot required less time than Sarah's dance pictures. The three girls documented every possible combination of friends and family and captured every pose imaginable. Pictures with silly expressions. Pictures while leaping in the air. Pictures acting like hip-hop stars and so on. Then, of course, every shot had to be viewed in real time and retaken if not acceptable. When the shoot finally drew to a close, the three girls delicately entered the back seat of a parent's sedan, which chauffeured them through the twilight to the event. With only his truck, Ben had managed to avoid pick-up duty as well.

After waving goodbye to the final car, Ben sank his hands into his pockets and turned to Amber, who stood with one boot crossed over the other, hands clasped in front. "Thanks for taking the time to come over and be a part of this. I know it meant a lot to Sarah."

"You know, I had a really good time," she said pensively. "It brings back so many high school memories. And it was fun to do something with her off the track or outside the gym. Just seeing her with her friends . . . I've never quite seen that side of her. She can be so goofy! I love it!"

"Yeah," Ben nodded, "her personality can shift with the environment, that's for sure. Sometimes I feel like I live with a teenage chameleon." Amber grinned as they fell silent. "Hey, are you hungry?"

"Actually, I'm starving!" she replied with imploring eyes.

"Wanna grab dinner somewhere?"

"As long as it's not greasy fast food."

Ben playfully put a finger to his lips and made a show of thought. "Well, let's see . . . That eliminates about ninety percent of my favorite places, but I think I might still know a place that meets your standards."

Laughing, Amber deferentially extended a hand toward Ben's truck. "Lead on!"

*****

"Well, it's been over a month now since we met at the coffee shop," noted Ben, laying his silverware on his empty plate.

Leaning back in her chair, Amber looked at him across the table with a curious expression. "And . . . ?"

"You made it clear that our contract must be renewed on a monthly basis," he answered, an ironic grin creeping across his face. With mock severity, he touched his pointed index finger to the table to emphasize the last two words. "Can we negotiate a mutually beneficial agreement to move forward, or should Sarah and I seek an alternative arrangement?"

Amber rolled her eyes. "Please . . . That's not even funny!" she replied, shaking her head but smiling despite herself.

"I'll take that as a 'yes.'" Ben chuckled. The waiter arrived to take away their plates, and during the break in conversation, Frank Sinatra could be heard softly crooning "My Way" throughout the restaurant. Amber seemed to hum along as she dropped her napkin on the white tablecloth. Once alone again, Ben grew more earnest. "So, what's the latest on Kiana and her family?"

Amber, playing with an earring, hesitated as she recalled the latest update. "Well, her dad is making some progress, and he's going to be discharged from the rehab center soon. But, he's still having problems with his speech and motor skills. They're still trying to figure out how to handle the prospect of live-in home care. It seems her mother is overwhelmed with the idea of becoming a nurse and physical therapist."

"I don't blame her," Ben commented, his face sober, as if speaking from experience.

"At least Kiana's still been able to work," Amber continued more hopefully, "since she can do her graphic design pretty much anywhere with her laptop."

"So, when will she be coming back? Will she still be competing?"

"We'll see. She's working out as best she can, and she's got some connections to facilities in her old hometown. But she's still probably a couple of weeks away from returning." After a moment, Amber admitted, "Honestly, I don't know how she's going to stay competitive, physically or mentally, with such a major disruption in her life."

Ben looked down at his hands, folded on the table. "I feel badly for you both."

"Yeah, I miss having her around . . . " The conversation stalled as Amber stopped playing with her earring and started picking at a loose thread on her napkin. Just when Ben was about to ask for the check, Amber's wistful features turned playful. "So, about that personal question you asked me."

"Really?" asked Ben, looking up.

Amber nodded. "Well, as an honest man I know once noted, I said you could ask, and I should have the courage to answer."

Sitting up, Ben crossed his legs and settled back in his chair, clasping his hands over a knee. "I'm all ears. What did you come up with?"

"OK, so what do I worship?" she began, her eyes briefly searching the vaulted ceiling. "Most obviously, my primary goal, dating at least back to college, is to make the U.S. National Team, which would be the Olympic team this year. However, that quest has definitely suffered from a few setbacks along the way." Her fingers found their way back to her ear, but this time fingered a strand of hair after it was tucked behind it.

"I know a little bit about those setbacks," Ben admitted in the gap that followed. "I confess I've done a little cyber spying on your running career."

Amber tilted her head and raised an eyebrow, pretending offense. "Oh, I see . . . Then you know that after placing at the NCAA Championships my junior year, I had a string of injuries that I couldn't shake with even a fifth year of eligibility. At least I succeeded in getting a master's degree in Exercise Science," she noted with a touch of sarcasm.

"Wasn't it a stress fracture?"

"In the foot," she nodded. "That was senior year. Then came the Achilles and shin splint issues that started my graduate year and continued to plague me for a couple of seasons even after I left Arkansas. I've only been healthy again for the last couple of years, and it's taken that long to get back to the elite level." Her words began to waver with emotion. "But time is running out: I'm almost twenty-nine."

Ben had to resist an impulse to reach across the table and touch her hands. Instead, he met her eyes and struck his most compassionate tone. "You've devoted yourself to a long, tough road with quite the passion."

"And plenty of heartbreak." She sighed.

Ben uncrossed his legs and leaned forward, placing his thick forearms on the edge of the table. "Boiling it down, then, what do you think is at the heart of your pursuit?"

Looking back down at her napkin, Amber answered in fragments. "Personal achievement. The thrill of the experience. Perhaps recognition from others. Maybe even five minutes of fame. I certainly wouldn't mind the financial security of a sponsor either." There was a long pause. "So, if you drill down deep enough, I guess you could say I'm 'worshiping' myself in a sense." Her eyes popped up to meet Ben's. "And that probably makes me a bad person in your eyes." She was surprised by Ben's smile.

"First, let me say how much I admire your insight and honesty. That's a rare combination in this day and age. But as for the 'bad person' part," he began to chuckle, "I say welcome to the club—one that very much includes me!" Amber looked dumbfounded. "The Bible makes clear that 'All have sinned and fall short of the glory of

God.' Face it, we may like to think of ourselves as 'good' people," he claimed, using his hands to make air quotes, "but, in reality, we can't even keep the rules we set for others and ourselves, let alone God's perfect moral law. Churches are filled with nothing but 'bad people' in need of God's grace. And it doesn't end there. Even after coming to faith, Christians like me struggle to keep the things we pursue in our lives from becoming more important than God Himself."

Amber's shock gave way to confusion. "Really? Am I missing something? Where's the fulfillment in all that?" she asked, her palms upturned. Ben held up his hand in a gesture for her to hear him out.

"If that were the end of the story, I'd agree, but that's only the bad news. The good news is that Jesus won the battle for us by doing for us what we could never do for ourselves: perfectly obeying God's law in our place and defeating sin and death. When Jesus died on the cross, He restored my broken relationship with God by paying my penalty. Then God went a step further and changed my stubborn heart to accept His forgiveness by faith."

"So, what, do Christians give up all their goals and things they're passionate about to worship God instead?"

"Not at all! It's not an either-or proposition," he answered patiently while shaking his head. "Look, I'd like to think that my role as father and my drive to reach kids in the classroom are lofty aspirations worth pursuing."

"Well of course they are! Absolutely!" Amber agreed, her face intent.

"And Sarah is certainly seeking to be the best runner she can be, with a good deal of help from you I might add." Amber smiled. "But God's great love for us, which was shown at the cross, turns our hearts toward Him. Out of gratitude for God's grace, we align our individual pursuits with the primary goal of bringing honor to Him, the very purpose for which He created us in the first place." Ben slowed down and took a breath before summarizing his point. "So, yes, being a father, a teacher, and a runner remain important quests, but we find deeper and lasting fulfillment in them only when they serve God's higher purposes."

Amber, looking a bit overwhelmed, sat silently trying to process it all. "Well, that's a lot to take in at once. You've given me a lot more to think about."

"I hope I didn't drown you." Ben smiled sheepishly. "I wrestled with these ideas little by little for years, so I can sympathize." Grabbing the dessert menu on the table, he studied it. "I'm guessing a Hot Fudge Brownie Fantasy isn't on your menu during the season?"

Amber shook her head with a frown, then smiled after recalling the banquet. "But I wouldn't deny myself just a couple of bites."

"Now that's what I call a win-win proposition."

CHAPTER 25

Beep! With a jab of her slippery thumb, Sarah cleared the time of her tenth two-hundred-meter repeat. Her ninth success in a row, she welcomed the news, helping her tolerate the fiery heat in her legs and lungs. Still, she could kick herself for missing the thirty-three to thirty-four second time goal by a single second on one attempt. And of all the ironies, it had been on the first repeat.

"Thirty." Like a robot, Amber notified Sarah that thirty seconds remained of their sixty-second standing rest between repeats. Sarah swore they got shorter and shorter the more exhausted she became. She inhaled deeply a couple of more times, banking the oxygen for withdrawal in the very near future. "Fifteen." They both shuffled in a circle to a point five meters behind the start line, preparing for number eleven. When Amber spoke next, they would time their rolling start to coincide with crossing the line. "Three, two, one!" Beep! Beep!

Sarah thrusted through the line and accelerated into the curve. Once Amber gained a step on her, Sarah ducked in against the rail, leaning into it, her eyes locked on the driving legs ahead of her. Half-way around, she attained eight-hundred-meter race pace; the challenge was to maintain it for the next one hundred and fifty meters. By the time she straightened out on to the back stretch,

Amber had pushed a step further ahead, and Sarah's legs again began to feel as if they were filling with liquid cement, which hardened a little more with each stride. She focused on driving with her arms, but found them, like her legs, locking up earlier and earlier with each repeat. With fifty meters to go, Sarah exhaled like a steam locomotive, determined not to allow Amber, yet another step ahead, to extend that lead one foot more.

Beep! She lurched to a stop near Amber and denied herself the urge to bend over or fall on all fours. With hands on her hips, Sarah looked to the sky and spent precious seconds sucking in the air. At length, she turned and edged towards Amber, far past the point of conversation herself, who methodically checked her watch. Timing her breaths, she managed to get the word out. "Thirty."

Sarah did not think it possible; she had just finished. With procrastination no longer an option, Sarah braved a glance at her watch, relieved to see another thirty-four, high as it was, and cleared it. "Fifteen." Mechanically, they circled behind the two-hundred-meter line. Sarah thought to herself that the only reason she could toe the line again was the knowledge that this was the last one. She clung to the hope that one could endure almost anything for thirty-four seconds. "Three, two, one." Beep! Beep!

For the last time, the seemingly endless cycle began: accelerate; change lanes; lean in; reach race speed; ignore the searing coals in the legs and lungs; feel the limbs stiffen; strain for breath; hold on until the line; beep! Inching toward the infield, chest expanding and contracting like a frantic accordion, Sarah wondered if she could drain the lactic acid pouring into her legs by inserting a spigot in her calf. Checking her watch, her eyes grew wide upon seeing a thirty-three. Somehow the last one always clocked in a little faster. Spying Amber still on the track, Sarah remembered Amber, running sixteen, still had four repeats left. Amber allowed herself a few extra seconds before giving Sarah some instructions.

"Go ahead and rest . . . You can start your cool down after I finish my next two . . . and then I'll join you on the cool down . . . after my last two." Sarah nodded, feeling a bit guilty at being granted parole while Amber still had a longer sentence to serve.

*****

With her bent knee lying flat on the ground, Sarah, her hips facing down towards the grass, leaned forward and pressed her chest to the knee, the other leg straight behind her. Holding the classic "pigeon" pose, she could feel the tension in her glutes and I-T band. At length, she rose back up and seized her nearly empty water jug to greedily consume a few more gulps before switching legs. Amber did the same.

"I can't believe the repeat I missed was the first one!" Sarah complained. "That's so lame!"

"It's actually pretty common," Amber advised. "It's part trying to conserve energy at the start of a long set you know will be hard and part getting re-acclimated to your eight hundred race pace . . . But it's not something to get upset about. You went on to hit eleven in a row. That's a great workout in anybody's book. I missed a couple today myself."

"Yeah, but you were running thirty-one's and had four more!"

"The workout was still set for my race goals . . . but I'm not going to cry about it. When you push your limits, it's not always going to be perfect."

As they switched to the pretzel stretch, Ben walked up and set down his grading paraphernalia. Now a daily ritual, no greetings were necessary. "Looks like you guys went pretty heavy today."

"It's that time of the season," Amber replied, looking in almost the opposite direction on the stretch. "Everything from here on out is for keeps." She took another swig between reversing positions. "We'll lighten up the rest of the week to taper for Saturday. Tomorrow we'll run a three-mile tempo, and Thursday and Friday will be short, easy runs."

"Do you recommend another ice bath?" Ben inquired. He half-expected a snarky comment or look from Sarah, but from her expression she seemed open to the idea.

"Sure wouldn't hurt. I may take one myself." The runners finished their cool down routines with butterflies.

"Well, a couple more things," Ben said. "First, Coach Sutherland wants to come on Saturday, and he's offered to drive the four of us."

Amber approached the prospect cautiously. "What time is he leaving? It's a two-hour drive and we're running around one. We'd need to leave by nine-thirty at the latest."

"I don't think that will be a problem. I'll let him know."

Amber hesitated a moment before continuing. "OK, but you should know that I'll be focusing on my race all the way there. I'm afraid I'm not going to be very sociable, probably even have my ear buds in."

Ben dismissed Amber's concern with a wave of his hand. "No worries. Believe me, I'm used to the silent treatment with Sarah."

"Yep!" Sarah confirmed.

"And I got ready for a wrestling match or two myself in high school," he resumed. "At least be glad you're not also trying to make weight before competing. I'll be happy to chat it up with Coach in the front seat while you two stew in your nerves together in the back."

Amber ceded the point as she rose from the ground and dusted off her rear. "All right. And the second thing?"

"My mom is coming over to cook the family specialty for our pasta party on Friday night: lasagna."

"Yay! Grandma's lasagna is the best!" celebrated Sarah.

"You're invited," Ben added with a nod in Amber's direction.

"Well, that's quite an advertisement," Amber admitted, glancing over at Sarah. She picked up her water jug and shook it, but finding it empty, she tossed it back down on her gear bag in disgust. "Will there be plenty to drink along with the lasagna?"

Ben grinned. "Actually, we're serving Gatorade, on the rocks."

Amber's face lit up with a smile as she wagged her head. "I am so there!"

CHAPTER 26

"So we've been sitting there for almost an hour, and all this geyser cone does is smoke and gurgle." Three sets of eyes around the dining room table stared intently as Ben told his story. "It's getting darker and darker, and we're a mile from the lodge in some remote part of the geyser field. Looking around, I see everybody has left except us. Turning to Joy, I say, 'We gotta go; it's not gonna blow.'"

Sarah interrupted the tale, grabbing Amber's forearm. "Rangers can only give time estimates for when geysers go off; they can't know for sure." Amber nodded, and when Ben continued, the exasperation grew in his voice.

"Then it begins to rain. So, we get up, and, of course, Sarah starts crying."

Looking back at Sarah, Amber laughed. "I wanted to see it so bad!" Sarah grinned.

"Well, we haven't gone more than a hundred yards, dragging Sarah with us, before we hear this violent spewing sound, and Sarah screams, 'It's going off!' We turn . . . and see this huge fountain shooting up into the sky so high it dwarfs Old Faithful!" Shaking his head, Ben chuckled. "Of course, we went back to watch, but by the time we reached the lodge, we were soaked from head to toe."

"It was awesome!" Sarah confirmed, slapping her hands down on the tabletop.

"Yeah, I love Yellowstone," agreed Amber, a smile lingering on her lips. Then a hint of mischief crept into her voice. "Where else can you watch a momma grizzly and her cub out your car window while drinking coffee . . . along with a hundred others jamming traffic on the road." All four burst out before Ben and his mother rose from their side of the table to start clearing plates. "That lasagna was hands down the best I've ever had, Mrs. Turner," complimented Amber. "There was a hint of something I can't put my finger on."

Ben's mother stopped on her way to the kitchen, her apron still tied around her stout figure. "Please, Amber, call me Janet. And thank you." Then she assumed a conspiratorial expression and tone. "It's nutmeg, part of an old secret family recipe dating back to the Old Country."

"Really!" Amber looked impressed. But Janet broke character with another laugh.

"The nutmeg, yes. The Old Country, no: I got the recipe out of a magazine somewhere a long time ago." The rest of the table laughed with her.

While Ben and his mother carted the dishes into the kitchen and Sarah checked her phone, Amber admired the Craftsman-style hutch standing directly in front of her, behind Ben's seat on the other side of the table. In one compartment, protected by a pane of glass, her attention was drawn to a wedding photo of Ben and Joy, just out of college. Ben paired a muted faux hawk hair style with a classic tux, and Joy, in a strapless gown with a beaded bodice, wore her raven hair regally in an updo accented with a tiara. They looked adoringly into each other's eyes. The image made Amber feel unaccountably sad. When the current version of Ben returned to the table with his mother, the photo vanished from view behind him as he sat.

"Well, both Sarah and I have a big day ahead of us," began Amber, addressing all present, "so I think my evening better end early."

"Probably a wise idea," agreed Ben with some reluctance.

"But before I go, I'd like to make sure Sarah understands a few important things about tomorrow." The mood turned serious as Amber became the focus.

"Sure. Let it rip!" encouraged Ben, and Amber shifted in her chair to face Sarah.

"First, understand that the atmosphere at Western Relays can be a little intimidating. Not only will there be large crowds, but a bunch of vendors in a merchandise area, a sea of team pop-ups from colleges all over the country, and TV cameras surrounding the track because the meet is live-streamed nationally on the web." Ben, Sarah, and Janet looked at each other with surprise. "You'll even see adults competing, like me. But don't get psyched out. Only twelve girls are in your race, all of them high schoolers just like you. Nothing is going to change that." Sarah nodded with trusting eyes.

"Next, we're both in the invitational, or fastest, eight hundred heat of our respective divisions, scheduled in a special afternoon session. Only one race separates our heats, the boys high school invitational heat. So, our races may be as little as six minutes apart. That's almost perfect, because we can go into the staging area and warm up at the same time together."

"Awesome!" Sarah exclaimed at the prospect. Ben and her grandmother clearly shared her enthusiasm.

"Now, you'll have to be fully loose and ready to race by the time they lead your heat into the tunnel, because it runs from the staging area straight to the start line under the stands. It's really quite a dramatic entry into the stadium," Amber added, briefly looking at the adults across the table before returning her attention to Sarah. "But they may not allow you a practice start before they line you up."

"Got it."

"Wow!" Ben commented. "Sounds like an even more controlled environment than the Rodeo."

"Yes, very much so," Amber nodded with a glance in his direction. "Finally, as the last runner to qualify for the invitational heat, you're seeded twelfth. Now, you may think that's bad since you could place higher or win a slower heat in the morning session or even Friday night, but it's actually great. Remember: your race is all about time, not placement; the faster the race, the more the runners will pull you to that time. Potentially, you can place last and still run faster than winning a slower heat. So, if you find yourself at the back of the pack, don't panic!" Amber pointed at Sarah to emphasize the last two words. "You can still PR."

"That's good to know," Sarah said, taking in a big breath.

"I'd say so," Ben chimed in. "For all of us!"

"Just know it's a huge honor simply to run at Western Relays, let alone in the invitational heat as a sophomore with relatively little experience. This meet draws high school runners from a few states, and for the college/open division it's one of the premier meets in the country."

Amber's tutorial left the table in silence, which she took as her cue to excuse herself for the evening. Standing up in her sandals and T-shirt dress, she unhooked her purse and denim jacket from the chair and thanked Janet again for the delicious meal before saying goodbye to Sarah. As Ben walked Amber out to her car, parked along the curb, she located her keys. But rather than walking straight to her door, she turned, pushed the cuffs of her denim jacket further up her forearms, and looked up into his face.

"What, no sermon tonight?" she asked with a smile, tucking a blonde lock behind her ear.

Ben matched the smile while folding his arms across his sturdy chest. "Oh, I think I've already given you enough to chew on. Besides," he added with a tilt of his head back towards the house, "you always know where I live if you want one."

"Well, I've been thinking about accepting your invitation to the Easter service next weekend. I figure, if nothing else, it may offer a unique cultural experience. Would I have to wear gloves and a bonnet?" she inquired with facetious eyes.

"Only if you want people to think you're auditioning for a period movie," replied Ben with equal sarcasm. Amber laughed before Ben grew more sincere. "The sunrise service is held at the regional park at dawn, so, I'd suggest something comfortable and warm. If you're going for your long run that day, you might think about wearing your workout clothes and start from there."

"Really?" Amber suspected another joke.

"Really. And if you do come, don't worry about things like reciting prayers or singing songs you don't know . . . just as long as you don't make fun of my singing."

"I'm definitely coming now." Amber grinned widely.

"Good! We'll just be glad you're there, and that includes Cathy and Jack." Amber nodded but remained silent. "Hey, you need to get out of here," Ben remembered, sliding his hands into the rear pockets of his jeans. "Thanks so much for all you've done for Sarah in preparing her for this moment. You'll both have a rooting section." He paused, briefly looking down at the sidewalk before meeting her eyes. "Listen, I know we joke around a lot, but I also know just a little of how hard you've worked over a really long time for this chance to qualify for the Trials. And I wish you all the success in the world tomorrow."

Amber wasn't prepared for that. She swallowed back the knot forming in her throat, her eyes suddenly moist. After floundering for a moment, she found some words. "I wish I had a witty comeback," she almost whispered, "but I don't. Thank you. Good night, Ben."

"Good night, Amber. See you soon enough. With your ear buds in, of course."

A smile returned to her lips. "Well, I may pull them out just long enough for a quick 'hello.'"

Peeling her eyes away from his steel blues, she entered the car, turned over the engine, and pulled away from the curb with a wave. Ben waved back, his eyes following until he faded in the rear-view mirror.

CHAPTER 27

Ben counted six television cameras, though he guessed he may have missed one or two. One pair covered the home and back stretches, and two more were mounted above each end of the home straight, including the finish line. But the two cameras he found most interesting positioned themselves inside the curves on opposite sides of the infield. Suspended beneath the long arms of rotating cranes, they panned the curves in a wide arc, hovering just inside the rail. Head-phoned cameramen, seated at the cranes' bases, rotated with the cameras, their eyes riveted on screens before them. The complement of cameras provided not only the feed for the national live-stream broadcast but also the images projected on a jumbo screen above the scoreboard, delighting the five-thousand sun-drenched fans who had shown up for the invitational session of the Western Relays.

"I'm so glad Sarah has Amber to show her the ropes and keep her company today," said Ben, breaking a comfortable silence as he and Jack took in the spectacle near the two-hundred-meter clock. It was about the least-congested section of the stadium, but they still had to sit several rows up.

"Yeah," agreed Jack. "This is brand new territory for little Montevallo Christian Academy. She is definitely the first and likely the last of our students to run here."

Ben was proud of himself for remembering to bring a hat for the cloudless, mid-April afternoon. The day remained temperate, partially due to the persistent breeze that rippled banners and pop-ups around the track. Jack pondered the fact while smoothing his mustache. "I wonder how much the wind is going to affect times today. In the distance races, that may penalize the leaders here on the back stretch and alter some runners' tactics."

Ben turned to his friend and grinned. "I have a hunch that's a problem Sarah won't be in a position to worry about." Then, after thinking about it further, the grin faded. "But for Amber, that may be a different story."

*****

Amber, ear buds in, and Sarah returned to their gear bags with silent intensity, their shake-outs and dynamic stretching complete. As usual, Sarah suffered from nerves, but today her quietude had an added component. She did not want to be a distraction to Amber, preparing for her own big race. The last thing the protege wanted was for her mentor to regret her presence. Picking up their jugs, they took a couple of gulps before shedding their sweat jackets, revealing customized racing bibs boldly printed with their last names in all caps. Sarah planned to keep hers as a prized keepsake.

They dropped to the grass along the edge of the fenced-in practice field, which served as the warm-up area behind the home stands and progressed through their routine of static stretches to the muffled sounds of the public address system echoing incoherently in the stadium. Team tents and banners representing each of the Power 5 college conferences bordered the rectangular space, with athletes stretching, jogging, and striding as their races approached. Sarah was still trying to adjust to preparing for her race beside fully grown men sporting beards.

The tunnel entrance loomed near the busy clerk's tent on one end. Gazing over, Sarah observed a string of high school sprinters disappear into it, and several seconds later small clumps of collegiate runners exited, some staring blankly and others unable to contain their joy. Regardless, Sarah was jealous of them all. They were on the other side of the ordeal. She wondered what her emotions would be in twenty minutes. Her stomach tightened even more when the speakers in the staging area, the volume set too high, abruptly blasted.

"First call for the open division men's and women's eight hundred meters invitational heats; second call for the high school division boys' and girls' eight hundred meters invitational heats; last call for the men's and women's open division one hundred meters invitational heats." That seemed to be the signal for Amber to remove her ear buds, and, wordlessly, they switched out their trainers for their spikes. When finished, Amber deemed the time right to deliver her eleventh-hour set of instructions in a manner that was all business.

"Do everything you can to stay in contact with the pack, even if the pace seems too fast. Approach the race almost as if it were six hundred meters, not eight hundred. If you've got anything left, try to make a move with two hundred to go; otherwise, just try to hold on. And remember, even last place may still net you a PR here." Sarah took in a deep breath to try and calm her pounding heart. "It's time for you to hit some strides."

Sarah unzipped the ankle zipper and removed her sweat bottoms as Amber continued. "I'll try to watch your race from the end of the tunnel if they let me through. If not, you've still got this." Amber made a point of catching Sarah's terrified eyes. "Don't forget, you qualified for this heat. You've earned this chance; you belong here." Sarah nodded with as much confidence as she could gather.

Without a word, she stood up and departed for a brief rewarming and a few short practice starts until the distorted speakers blared to life again. "First call for the high school boys and girls division three hundred meter hurdles invitational heat; second call for the open division men's and women's eight hundred meter invitational heat; final call for the high school boys' and girls' eight hundred meter invitational heat." Sarah rejoined Amber with trembling legs.

"That's your cue!" directed Amber with forceful eyes, her jaw set. "It's go time!"

They faced each other and clasped hands above their heads, foreheads touching. Sarah spontaneously closed her eyes. "Lord, I'm so nervous," she quivered. "Give us both the strength and courage to run these races."

Amber separated from her pupil with a serious look. "You've trained for this. You're ready!" With a pat on her back, she sent Sarah on her way.

Sporting a pair of number twelve stickers, Sarah jogged weak-kneed over to join the group of invitational heat runners milling outside the mouth of the tunnel. An awkward minute of avoiding the eyes of her opponents ended when an official, wearing an embroidered Western Relays baseball hat and polo, strolled over from the clerk's tent to line up both the boys and girls in seed order with the assistance of heat sheets. When all checked out, she led them in past another meet official stationed at the tunnel entrance, girls followed by boys. For better or worse, the wait was finally over.

It took a few seconds for Sarah's eyes to adjust to the dimness as the metal spikes of two dozen runners reverberated loudly against the concrete walls. Midway, a string of women sprinters, still panting, passed them going the other way. At the end, the tunnel mouth opened, and they emerged, blinking, back into bright daylight before the line stalled. Only a fragment of the crowd was visible from Sarah's position well back, including many fans peering down as they pressed up against the railing that encircled them above. Directly across the track, Sarah spied a television camera mounted on a platform. Standing behind it, the cameraman wearing headphones gripped a long pair of handles to direct the lens toward the unseen finish line. To her right, against one wall, another man with a shoulder camera filmed an interviewer with a microphone in the face of a smiling runner. Sarah presumed she had just won the women's one-hundred-meter race.

The crack of a gun sent the stadium into a roar. Soon, Sarah thought, that would be her race. The roar reached a crescendo several seconds later, and a group of braking male sprinters suddenly burst into her narrow field of vision. A couple of finishers proceeded to jump ecstatically, while others crouched in disbelief or simply walked with their hands on their hips, eyes fixed on the scoreboard towering above.

A meet official continued to hold the heat for another agonizing minute or two while the sprinters were slowly ushered off the track and another crew of red coats set up shop at the eight hundred start-finish line. Meanwhile, the girls bounced up and down, squatted, and rocked back and forth; anything to try to stay loose. Sarah worried if she would have any adrenaline left by the time the race started. She swallowed hard, or at least she tried to. Given her cotton mouth, she wished she had been allowed to bring water with her.

Finally, after the last sprinter left the track, Sarah followed the string of girls released on to the track and quickly copied them in taking a forty-meter sprint down the straight, stretching out her legs. Slowly, she doubled back to the start line, her heart beating like a triphammer. She saw herself surrounded by an ocean of spectators while the jumbotron replayed the finish of the men's one-hundred-meter race in slow motion, to yet another roar, and the public address speaker highlighted the official results posted on the scoreboard. "Next up is the Invitational heat of the high school girls eight hundred meters!" the announcer eventually boomed and began introducing the entrants.

Sarah met her competitors standing on the starting arc just as a plump woman in a red hat and coat addressed them. "Number twelve, where are you?" she called, scanning the numbers on their chests. Startled, Sarah raised her hand. "Over here," the woman beckoned, pointing to the position against the rail. "Eleven?" Another girl soon arrived a foot to her right. The process continued until all twelve girls stood in descending order. Just as Sarah prepared herself for the final instructions, bobbing on the balls of her feet, she was puzzled to see the top four seeds escorted by another red coat several meters forward to a separate arc marked by an orange cone in Lane Five. Amber hadn't mentioned a staggered start, and Sarah wondered if it would give that group an advantage. At least it meant more room to maneuver within her own group.

"Spread out!" directed the red coat, and the line of eight lengthened a little but not much. "Now take two steps back from the line!" After complying with the others, Sarah heard her name.

"You've got this, Sarah!" She stole a glance at the mouth of the tunnel, where she saw Amber, hands extended, give her a nod with two thumbs-up. Sarah returned the nod while blowing out a huge sigh.

Turning her head back to the red coat, Sarah saw that she had already stepped off the track and now stood with one arm held straight out to the side a few meters in front of another, elderly red coat standing atop a short ladder. When he raised his gun in the air, the crowd noise dulled, and Sarah's heart skipped a beat. Then he delivered his command deliberately into the microphone: "On your marks." Twelve runners stutter-stepped up to the lines, bent, and froze with one arm cocked. A second of silence. "Crack!"

Immediately, Sarah's world transformed into a movie punched on fast-forward. The seven other girls in her group bolted forward, leaving Sarah to feel like she was stuck in slow motion despite a supreme effort to crank up her almost gangly arms and legs. By the time she reached mid-curve, she was already a couple of steps behind the nearest runner, and by the end of the first curve, where the higher seeds broke for the inside rail after passing another cone, Sarah found herself alone in the rear by at least five meters, more than ten behind the leaders. Watching the pack pull away, Sarah fought the sense of desperation that gripped her, propelling her legs to race speed. But it only succeeded in keeping the pack from slipping any further ahead by the end of the back stretch.

Sarah leaned into the curve after seeing the clock flash by, unsure she had seen the numbers correctly. She could swear she had passed at a low thirty-three at worst, a high thirty-two at best; either way, she knew it was a great start for her, and it took the edge off her fear. She called to mind Amber's words: even last place could still bring a PR.

Extending her stride with increasing confidence, she pulled around the second curve, determined to play to her strong suit: outlasting her rivals. She focused on setting a breathing pattern, driving her legs with knees high, and achieving a full range of motion while pumping her arms. By the time she straightened out on the home stretch, she was sustaining a steady rhythm and holding good form; yet it seemed to yield minimal results. As the clock at the start line drifted into view, the rear of the pack still eluded her five meters ahead, her link to it tenuous. It almost felt like she was running a solitary time trial in front of thousands. Crossing the line, she glimpsed a sixty-six and change.

"You're on PR pace, Sarah! Push! Keep contact!"

Even though Sarah didn't see Amber, she heard the excitement in her voice. And it fueled her. Leaning into the third curve, she saw the trailing runner start to labor. Slowly edging closer, she reeled her in a little more with each stretch of her legs. Drawing almost even by the end of the curve, Sarah briefly kicked out into Lane Two to face the breeze as she dumped out on the straight. With a few more vigorous strides, she forced her way past and slipped back into Lane One, where she immediately set her sight on the next girl, breaking the wind for her just a couple of meters further ahead. The familiar burning in her legs and lungs began to set in, but her forward progress numbed the pain.

Sarah exhaled forcefully, almost in a trance. Nearing the end of the straight, Sarah had caught her prey, and she popped around with a last burst as they passed the clock. Ducking back into Lane 1, and leaving the headwind behind, Sarah regretted missing the time, but she was certain it had to be good.

While rounding the last curve, Sarah felt the fire, having fully engulfed her legs and lungs, spread to her arms. Oxygen became an increasingly scarce commodity no matter how disciplined her breathing. To distract herself, she focused on the pair of girls yet another few meters ahead and decided that was her race for the last one hundred meters. Inching forward, she was determined to bag two at once this time. Executing a slingshot off the curve, she drifted almost even with them with sixty meters left. Just as she drew alongside ten meters later, the pair responded. A three-way battle ensued all the way to the line despite each of them locking up like rusty robots. Sarah guessed she out-leaned them at the tape before careening to an inelegant stop to avoid finishers who had ill-advisedly halted in their tracks. Due to the last-second drama, Sarah had again missed the clock.

Chest heaving, she at first bent over at the hips with her hands on her knees, her body at last allowed to rebel with a fury. But Sarah forced her hands first to her hips and then behind her head as she stood up. Resisting the fatigue, she looked up to the scoreboard and spotted it: 8th / Sarah Turner (Montevallo Christian): 2:14.06. The toll of the race collided with the immensity of the result, and Sarah turned numb. Vaguely aware someone was shepherding her off the track, she felt like she was sleepwalking while shuffling back into the tunnel. There, Amber awaited her, shaking her head with a pursed-lipped smile and open arms. She wrapped them around her pupil's still-contracting chest and held her close before speaking into her ear.

"You are an amazing young woman. Brave. I am so, so proud of you." When Amber released her, Sarah wiped her eyes and found her tongue, a crooked smile on her face.

"Thanks! Can't wait to watch you kill it!"

*****

Amber shifted back and forth, shaking out one leg and then the other in a constant cadence while the red coat reloaded his gun. She stood two steps behind the starting arc, her cropped racerback top exposing a washboard stomach. The racing briefs she wore proved so narrow over the hips that the number five sticker didn't fit; instead, like several fellow competitors, she had slapped the sticker on the outside of her upper right thigh. Standing inactive in the tunnel for an extra race had been far from ideal, so she was glad to have inserted an extra stride after stepping on the track: a long one away from the start line followed by another, shorter one on the way back.

Amber didn't hear the introduction of the invitational heat entrants and their PR's bounce around the stadium. She stared straight ahead into the curve from her position on the outside edge of the rear group. It was a good starting position, she thought. Now it was all a matter of execution and quick response if things went sideways. The plan was not overly complicated: reach the one-hundred-meter break point ahead of the merging, higher-seeded group to seize a position on the rail for the second curve and then draft behind the leaders on the windy back stretches whenever possible. That and sling-shotting into the straights at the three hundred and five hundred marks while ducking back to the rail before reaching the curves. The last two hundred meters couldn't be scripted. She would have to wait and see.

The red coat, his reloading complete, climbed back up the ladder. Amber instinctively tightened her ponytail, shook out her arms, and sucked in one last deep breath. 2:02.50. The number was fixed in her mind like an impenetrable wall. After a decade-long journey, she was two minutes away from discovering if she would breach it at long last or languish once again in its shadow.

The gun rose in the air, and the same deliberate words pierced the hushed air. "On your marks." Twelve women stutter-stepped to the lines, bent and froze with one arm cocked. Silence. "Crack!"

Unlike Sarah, Amber had no problem powering off the line. While some runners inside her chose to cut towards the rail almost immediately, she avoided the commotion by charting a course that placed her on the inside edge of Lane Three coming off the curve, two lanes inside the higher seeds, when they broke for the rail. With nothing in her path, she accelerated swiftly, extending her stride and reaching race pace. At the eighty-meter mark, though, she gauged that the outside group still had half a step on her. Surging just in time, she drew even with them at their break point, providing a clear path to the rail inside them while gliding to the front of the inside group. Or so she thought. While slanting into position, Amber realized one runner from the inside-starting group had sprinted a few meters ahead of the pack. By the time three members of the merging group had charged past her on the shoulder, she found herself against the rail with four runners in front and another pacing to her side. All was going according to plan.

Content to settle in after the opening sprint, Amber drafted off the leaders down the balance of the back stretch, clocking a thirty-second first two hundred. The pace was world class. Maintaining her position around the second curve, she prepared to slingshot into the straight. With the three hundred mark quickly approaching, however, the two runners immediately ahead of her had the same idea, so Amber went with them until she found a crevice just wide enough to slip ahead of the runner beside her into Lane Two. Pressing the pedal down the home stretch, she kept pace with the pair ahead and, along with them, passed the initial leader, whose pace had slackened. Amber cut back into Lane One just as she was passing the clock to spy a high sixty. A jolt of electricity hit her as she did the math, propelling her forward.

She leaned into the third curve, three runners still ahead and at least one literally breathing down her neck. While rounding it, she noted that the fuses in her legs and lungs had been lit, but they had not yet detonated. Chiding herself for mind drift, Amber forced herself to focus on the next move. As the five hundred mark neared, she began to pick up speed again, even as the rival huffing behind her tried to get the jump on the outside. Keeping a step lead, Amber chose to stay in Lane One to draft behind the leaders for most of the backstretch until her acceleration brought her up on the heels of the third-place runner, who was buffeted by the wind. With an added flurry, Amber popped out into the breeze and around, dodging back against the rail a step past the clock, missing the time. But she had a bigger issue to deal with: the fuses throughout her body had detonated from the effort.

While recovering from the surge, Amber leaned into the last curve and noted one co-leader, having separated from the other, seemed out of reach. Swiftly, she plotted a two-fold end game: catch the runner directly ahead while defending her flank. And sensing the stampede already charging from behind, that push had to start instantly, despite her now-searing limbs and lungs.

Launching her final offensive while still not half-way around the curve, she matched the unseen threat from behind, angling to the outside of Lane One as she approached the straight to avoid getting boxed in and creating space to pass the runner ahead. For the last one hundred meters, she punished her body with granite resolve despite the pain, demanding it not merely sustain her pace but increase it. Like a laser, she fixed her eyes on the clock, which stood tantalizingly in the distance. One forty-seven. One forty-eight. One forty-nine. She thrusted. She extended. She pumped. She exhaled. Amber's body raged, but her desire raged more. One fifty-six. One fifty-seven. One fifty-eight. The final thirty meters passed in surreal slow motion; the harder she strained the more time seemed to stand still.

Only after a few stumbling steps across the line, every part of her body throbbing as one, did her world return to real time. Amber did not know whether she had won or lost the razor-thin placement battle for second. In truth, she didn't really care. What meant everything was her glimpse of the clock, which left her almost certain that the wall had at long last been scaled. But she didn't dare let herself celebrate until it was official.

She staggered forward a few steps further, the adrenaline of hope blunting the pain, before the confirmation flashed on the scoreboard to the approving roar of the crowd. Throwing her arms above her head, hands clenched, Amber gazed across the stadium, triumph and elation lighting up her face. She checked a second time just to make sure she had seen the numbers correctly. She had: 2nd / Amber Jones / Unattached / 2:02.37.

Amber yearned to run into someone's arms. To celebrate with another in a swirling embrace. But there was no someone. No mother. No father. No Kiana. Not even a teammate. Just a couple of gracious competitors with a congratulatory pat on the back and a few kind words as she lingered in the finish area. Then again, she remembered, there was her new rooting section. Escorted slowly off the track by a complimentary red coat, she searched the thousands for three now-familiar faces but located none of them. Entering the tunnel, Amber found herself unexpectedly determined to find them.

*****

Back in the staging area, Amber's spikes crunched their way across the concrete. She wavered between choosing a quick detour, to retrieve her sweats and switch out her spikes, and heading directly to the warm-up area entrance to check if her rooting section had shown up. Though hedging towards the former, and therefore not setting herself up for disappointment, the decision was made for her the moment she passed the clerk's tent when she heard her name called.

"Amber!" A breathless Sarah, in sock-covered feet, bounded a few steps past the official monitoring the entrance, spikes in hand. She almost knocked Amber over, jumping on her with an over-enthusiastic hug. "You made it to the Trials! That's crazy! I can't believe I even know you!"

After recovering her balance, Amber returned the embrace. "It's a little hard to believe myself," she admitted with a dubious smile. Together, they retraced Sarah's steps to the entrance, where Ben and Jack awaited to the side with broad smiles.

"I'm a believer!" Ben declared as Amber shyly approached, pulling an invisible lock of hair behind her ear. "I've watched you crush it in practice every day!" He stepped forward without hesitation to offer a warm hug. "So much for a 'pipe dream'," he spoke softly in her ear. "I couldn't be happier for you." Amber squeezed back. When they parted, she wiped away a mascara-stained tear as Jack stepped forward to grasp her hand with both of his.

"Congratulations, Amber!"

"Thank you, Jack." She smiled appreciatively. Amber took a deep breath before addressing them all, the emotion causing her smile to wrinkle. "Honestly, I didn't know if this day would ever come." Her faltering voice steadied as she continued. "Thanks for all your support! Believe me, it means more than you know." Her eyes lingered on Ben for a moment before her demeanor shifted, her tone becoming upbeat, her smile unbridled. "But today isn't just about me." Amber turned to face her pupil. "Sarah, you did awesome! You didn't panic on that first lap and let them come back to you. What a huge PR! And you placed four spots above your seed!" Looking at Ben and Jack, she predicted, "I think some college coaches probably took note of our not-so-little sophomore!"

"Yep! We're very proud of her!" agreed Ben, placing his arm around Sarah's shoulders, adding, "And she had some great coaching to pull it off."

"You keep breaking your own school record," Jack noted with a chuckle. "And at this point, that might count for both boys and girls; I'll have to check!" They all laughed.

"Hey, let's get some pictures," Ben suggested. "Sarah, stand next to Amber."

She posed with Sarah for a couple of takes before making an offer of her own. "Let me get some of you and Sarah." Nodding, Ben readily handed his phone over and traded places for a couple more.

Then Sarah spoke up. "Amber, can we get one of you with us, too?"

Pausing, Amber shot Ben a questioning glance before he waved her forward enthusiastically. "Yes! Absolutely!" With a grin of her own, Amber handed Ben's phone to Jack and hurried over to stand with them, both draping their arms over Sarah's shoulders in the middle. Jack, after a few questions, eventually figured out which buttons to push.

"Make sure you send these to me," instructed Amber as the photo shoot broke up.

"Of course!" said Ben. "Now let's go out to lunch to celebrate! I'm starving."

"That sounds great," Amber concurred, "but not until we girls finish our cool downs and stretch." Half-sarcastically, she cautioned, "Injury prevention comes first!"

Ben sighed at the inevitable delay, but Sarah had a great idea to keep him occupied. "Dad, can you get me a t-shirt while you wait?"

Ben's head and shoulders sunk in mock defeat. "Yes. But I may have to take out a second mortgage."

CHAPTER 28

"Take my life and let it be consecrated, Lord, to thee. Take my moments and my days; let them flow in endless praise, let them flow in endless praise. Take my hands and let them move at the impulse of thy love. Take my feet and let them be swift and beautiful for thee, swift and beautiful for thee."

Four hundred voices blended with a pair of acoustic guitars, the hymn wafting over the hills of the regional park. Blankets and lawn chairs stretched across the grass amphitheater like a patchwork quilt, while the musicians, perched on stools, strummed on a simple concrete stage equipped with a portable sound system at its base. The glaring sun had already risen above the ridges on the horizon, casting long shadows but not yet drying out the dewy grass or providing much warmth.

Ben and Sarah sat lightly bundled with Amber on a large blanket as they sang, with Cathy and Jack butting up next to them on their own blanket. While those around her joined the chorus, Amber, in calf-length leggings and layers under a sweat jacket, listened quietly to the songs she did not know. With her arms hugging her knees to her chest and her eyes scanning the crowd, she found the singing strange, intriguing, and beautiful at the same time. She had joked with Ben about coming to the sunrise service in order to add a new cultural experience to her resume, but it was true. Outside of a funeral here or there, she had never sat amidst a congregation of children and adults praying and singing, let alone by heart and many with their eyes closed or their arms upraised. In truth, she was a little shocked. She had never really considered that such gatherings were a weekly aspect of life to otherwise seemingly normal, intelligent, and even admirable people she rubbed shoulders with every day—people like Ben, Sarah, Cathy, and Jack. If nothing else, Amber had to admit that she lived in a bit more insulated bubble than she realized.

At length, a middle-aged pastor in jeans and a windbreaker took the stage, speaking without a podium and holding a Bible in one hand. Amber had expected something a little different. Her attention weaved in and out of the sermon he delivered, and she often had to reposition herself to keep her limbs from falling asleep. But when the pastor announced his closing summary, she checked back in. After all, she thought, it would be embarrassing not to have something to say in the conversations with Ben that would inevitably follow.

"So, the message of Easter is simple," the pastor continued. "The perfect Lamb of God, Jesus, mercifully took our place and was sacrificed for us. But Christ did not only died, He rose again on the third day. In doing so, He defeated sin and death, and by faith we can share in those priceless blessings. That's why we're here on this most special of days, Friends. So, what should be our response to this most gracious act? The Apostle Paul puts it well in the book of Romans, writing, 'I urge you, brothers and sisters, in view of God's mercy, to offer your bodies as a living sacrifice, holy and pleasing to God—this is your true and proper worship.' Paul is saying that we, given what Jesus has done for us, should no longer live for ourselves, but for God's glory. And that is my prayer for all of us today . . . "

*****

"Good seeing you again, too, Jack," said Amber. "And I'll see you at work tomorrow, Cathy. Bye!"

With a final wave to all three, the Sutherlands began the hike to their car, joining the caravan of worshipers carting their chairs and blankets home. The sun, now high above the horizon, warmed both the departing pilgrims and the crew breaking down the sound system.

"You ready?" asked Ben, the folded blanket bulging under his arm. Amber nodded, and they started their own journey toward a lot in almost the opposite direction from Jack and Cathy. "We can at least walk with you out to the truck," he noted, knowing Amber was parked further away in the same lot.

"Thanks for inviting me," Amber said. Then, sending a knowing look towards Ben, she added, "It seems like I'd heard the end of that sermon somewhere before."

"So you did stay awake," joked Ben. Amber playfully punched his arm, almost causing him to drop the blanket. "Hey, remember that you practically live in a weight room," he chuckled. "You're going to leave a bruise."

Amber rolled her eyes. "Hearing all those voices was moving," she conceded. "And you both don't sing that badly!"

Sarah protested with feigned offense. "Hey! That doesn't sound like a compliment to me!"

"Thankfully, you guys didn't get the chance to hear me." Amber grinned.

"Well, then, I think we should add a sing-along to our workout routine!" suggested Sarah. "Then we could compare."

"I think not, and my vote is the only vote that counts," countered Amber.

"Dictator!"

Ben redirected the conversation, and Amber was happy to oblige. "So what's next for you today?"

"Actually, I'm using your idea of going for my long run now, since I took yesterday off. One of my favorite trails leads through the park and out into the canyons."

"Then I guess it's a good thing you decided against the bonnet and gloves," quipped Ben.

Amber played along, smiling. "Oh, I still brought them. I'm heading to my audition after the run."

"What audition?" asked Sarah, thoroughly confused. Ben and Amber laughed.

"There's no audition," Ben assured her. "It's just an inside joke." Sarah didn't see the humor.

They reached Ben's truck and Amber paused long enough to say her farewells. But just as Ben opened the door to throw in the blanket, she stopped and spun around excitedly. "Oh! I can't believe I almost forgot to tell you!" she said, a finger pointed in the air. Ben and Sarah looked at each other with curiosity and then back at Amber. "Kiana called. She's flying home tonight!"

CHAPTER 29

By the time Amber and Kiana dropped their gear bags on the infield, the sun had already risen. On one hand, Amber always welcomed the calendar's march towards May. Not only did rolling out of bed and running prove less difficult in the light of day, but the mornings were also generally more temperate. However, in the week since Western Relays, Amber noted it also meant casual runners starting to show up earlier at the track. Rather than arrive during their cool down or post-workout stretching, Amber spied one already plodding along in Lane One before she had even started her shake-out. More often than not, Amber found joggers ignorant of track etiquette that called for leaving the inside lanes open for faster runners.

Taking her eyes off the runner, Amber turned to Kiana and sighed. "Well, we may have to barn-storm some joggers today, but it's still great to have you back, hopefully for the rest of the season."

"Believe me, it's great to be back," Kiana said, taking in the stadium as if seeing an old friend for the first time in a while. "I can't wait to get into a normal routine again . . . I hope it's not already too late."

Reaching up, Amber placed an arm around Kiana's bony shoulders. "Me, too."

"Kiana! Welcome back!" Sarah shouted and waved her greeting while still thirty meters away as she crossed the track. Kiana broke into a smile as Sarah approached and plopped down her bag beside theirs. "How is your family?"

"Thank you for your prayers," she said with a nod. "Things are stable for the moment. My dad will never quite be the same, but at least he can talk and perform some basic tasks. Having live-in care for the next few weeks should help with his transition back home. They may switch to day care after that."

"I'm so sorry," offered Sarah, more subdued, "but glad to hear that at least he's back home."

"Thank you. And congratulations to you, Sarah," Kiana declared with a raise of her eyebrows. "A low two fourteen at Western Relays?! Wow!"

"Yeah, it's been crazy," Sarah admitted, shaking her head in disbelief. She joined Amber in putting up her hair, and they all took swigs from their water jugs before stepping on the track, where Amber decided to get down to business.

"We actually have a lot of housekeeping to take care of today, so let's run the shake-out together. I'll be doing most of the talking, so you should be able to keep up, Sarah, especially with your recent progress." Sarah smiled shyly at the compliment as the three set themselves in motion.

"OK, let's start by previewing the week ahead. Sarah, your season is down to, hopefully, three meets: the small schools regional, the regional finals, and the State meet. At both of the first two meets, you must qualify to move on. At this point, you're the clear favorite to win the small schools regional this weekend."

"Yay!" celebrated Sarah.

"Only the top three will go on to the regional finals the following week," Amber resumed quickly. "That shouldn't pose a problem, especially since you placed third there last year. Honestly, if you can't make the top three in the small schools regional you really have no business going to the regional final against the bigger schools. But you'll have a target on your back. After Western Relays, you won't be sneaking up on anybody."

"There are no do-overs!" cautioned Kiana.

"Got it!" confirmed the pupil. The three bounced around the jogger huffing slowly away in Lane One before Amber, frowning, continued.

"Meanwhile, Kiana and I will be out of town for a tune-up meet. We'll be leaving Thursday right after the morning practice."

That announcement caught Sarah by surprise. "Leaving town again? Kiana just got here!"

"Living out of a suitcase, Baby!" confirmed Kiana, half-laughing.

"So, Sarah," continued Amber, "you'll be on your own again Friday for an easy thirty-minute run." Ben looked up from his papers as they passed, and Amber shot him a smile and a wave, which he returned. "Last, I'm not going to taper you for the meet this weekend but train you right through it to peak when it really matters next week and, hopefully, the following week at the State meet. Like we did last week with your one thousands, today we'll be bumping up your four hundred repeats while keeping the same rest and time goal. So, that means you'll be adding two more, to make seven, at a seventy pace."

"Sounds fun," responded Sarah with obvious sarcasm.

Kiana replied before Amber had the chance. "Fun doesn't get you to the State meet."

*****

Sarah, stripped down to her racerback top, happily stepped off the track. She wondered how she could be sweating as much after her cool down as she had after completing her four hundred repeats. At least that's what it felt like. The weather was definitely getting warmer, earlier. Another ice bath might be in the works, she thought, feeling her dead, throbbing legs. Still, she took satisfaction in the fact that she had hit five of the seven times and missing only by a second or two on those two despite increasing the workload and having to avoid a pair of clueless joggers. Thankfully, they had finally got the message and moved into the outer lanes as the workout progressed. She seemed to have been a step or two closer to Amber on her repeats, too.

Sarah guzzled down what was left in her water jug before settling down on the ground to stretch beside Kiana and Amber, who had cut her work out a couple of repeats short. Ben soon joined them.

"Welcome back, Kiana," he greeted.

"So good to be back! Even if I am a little rusty." She continued chatting with Ben and Sarah about her past several weeks until Amber's silence drew her attention. Looking over, Kiana noticed she was rubbing her ankle with a concerned look on her face. "Something wrong?"

After a moment, Amber replied, a trace of fear in her voice. "My Achilles is not very happy right now," she said, starting to massage it. "I started feeling it on my long run yesterday, and it's worse today; that's why I cut the workout short." She decided to stop rubbing and changed her stretch. "I'm gonna keep an eye on it, but I may be cross-training the rest of the week at the gym."

Sarah's eyebrows narrowed. "What does that mean?"

"Instead of running, I'll probably substitute working out on the stationary bike or aqua jog in the pool between clients. That and avoid lower body lifting for a while. Don't worry," she assured Sarah, looking over at her, "I'll still be here each morning."

Sarah sighed. "After today, I don't know if that's a blessing or a curse!"

CHAPTER 30

Amber walked through the open door into Kiana's room, an ice pack wrapped tightly around her ankle. She sat down beside the open suitcase at the foot of the bed and watched passively as her training partner zig-zagged between her dresser, the bathroom in the hall, and her suitcase, preparing for their departure in the morning.

"How's it coming?" asked Amber, her mind half-elsewhere. Kiana was too busy to notice.

"Pretty well. I've come and gone so many times I've got packing down to a science."

"I hear you on that."

"Still, I have to say that coming back this time has been a little different."

The comment broke Amber's train of thought, and she refocused her attention on Kiana. "Really? Why?"

"I may have been out of town for a little longer this time, but it feels like I'm stepping back into a time warp."

Amber tilted her head with curiosity. "And how's that?"

Kiana paused for a moment to figure out where to begin. "For starters, boy has Sarah come a long way since I last saw her!" she noted, resuming her dizzying task. "Watching her in practice the last few days, I had to do a double take. Her speed, endurance, form—you name it—have taken a giant leap forward. Even her confidence. I guess I shouldn't be surprised. She did come within an eyelash of running a two thirteen at Western. Amber, that's almost four seconds better than her PR last year, and you haven't even pulled back on grinding her yet!"

Amber's eyes looked up to the ceiling, as if checking her memory. "You're right. She's gone to a whole new level, and I think she is poised to go even higher. I guess since I see her almost every day it hasn't been as obvious."

"'Whole new level' is right. Especially for her age. Were you knocking on a two thirteen when you were a sophomore in high school?"

Amber looked towards the ceiling again. "Actually, she's just about exactly where I was at that point."

"But didn't you also run club a few years before high school?" asked Kiana, pausing just long enough to point a finger.

Amber pushed out her lips as she added that fact into the equation. "Point taken."

When she continued, the respect in Kiana's voice suddenly dipped. "And then there's 'The Hermit.'"

"His name is Ben," Amber clarified with a direct glance and tone. She reached for one of the pillows on the bed and hugged it.

"Whatever you call him, he's not only migrated from his car into the stadium but even entered the 'No Parent Zone.'"

Amber had to grin before breaking into an outright smile. "Yeah, I tweaked that rule. Actually, that's just the half of it." Kiana stopped in her tracks and stared at Amber in confusion. Amber shrugged. "Kiana, you've been gone the better part of two months. After you left, Ben helped fill the gap. When I had car trouble, a terrible leg cramp and couldn't drive, he was there to help. You'll probably be shocked to know that they invited me over to their house for a pasta party the night before Western, then to help Sarah get ready for a dance a couple of weeks ago, and also to an Easter service last weekend." Then Amber put up both hands. "Full disclosure—I even went with Ben to his school banquet so he wouldn't feel awkward going alone." Kiana's confusion morphed into disbelief as she folded her arms across her chest.

"A dinner party, a church service, and a banquet? With 'The Hermit'?"

"The former 'Hermit,'" Amber again clarified, her features growing softer. "He's come out from under his rock. He's actually quite funny and incredibly supportive."

"You haven't been seduced by his muscles, have you?" Kiana asked a question but posed it more as a benign accusation.

"We've just become good friends," Amber replied dismissively. "That's all we are."

Kiana looked as skeptical as her tone. "Umm hmmm."

Amber closed her eyes and waved her hands back and forth. "Enough of that. Honestly, what concerns me more right now is my Achilles," she asserted, turning abruptly somber and looking down at the pillow. "I shouldn't have done speedwork on it Monday. Even with cross-training the past few days, the tenderness isn't going away."

Kiana succeeded in regaining Amber's gaze. "Which means?"

"It means I still plan on going with you, but I don't think I should race this weekend." She sighed. "I hate missing a chance to tune-up, but it's just not worth the risk of damaging it further at this point.

The Trials are just a month away. If it flares up big time now, another season is over, and this is an Olympic year! Will I have any other chances? I'll be almost thirty-three next time around!" Hearing Amber's voice about to crack, Kiana unfolded her arms, sat down next to her, and put an arm around her shoulders. Then Amber's voice did crack. "It seems like every season is Ground Hog's Day."

"Hey, it's going to be OK," Kiana soothed, patting her back. "You're right. You should rest it this weekend and probably cross train all next week, too." Then she adopted a more hopeful tone. "But there's still plenty of time for it to settle down. Who knows, getting off your legs for a bit may actually keep them fresh going into the Trials."

Wiping her eyes, Amber sucked in a long, deep breath. "Thanks, Kiana. Let's hope you're right."

CHAPTER 31

Another Montevallo Christian Academy assembly was well under way, this time to celebrate the spring sports teams. With smiles pasted from ear to ear, the song leaders held their poses well after the thunderous strains of hip hop had stopped echoing throughout the gym. When the applause died down, they bounced up and over to the base of the stands, where they sat clustered on the hardwood floor. Two hundred teenagers, the entire high school student body, crammed themselves into the pull-out bleachers on one side of the basketball court, sandwiched between their teachers, who lined the walls on both sides while keeping an eye out for mischief.

When not chatting softly with Marcie, who sat between her and Tiffany, Sarah passed the time smoothing the pleats on her navy and gold plaid skirt, which she had paired with the approved navy school polo. She was glad she had chosen to wear no-show socks with her Adidas; the gym was hot in winter, let alone early May. Sarah gave her attention to the pep commissioner for a few moments as she interviewed the tennis coach and a pair of team captains at half court. A themed backdrop painted on towering cardboard panels, created by the ASB, accented the scene. But an easel with a sheet thrown over it lurking to one side kept catching

Sarah's eye. What surprise lay beneath? They were going to milk the suspense by waiting until the end of the assembly to reveal it.

Then things started getting weird when Marcie elbowed her ribs. "Isn't that your grandmother standing with your dad?"

Sarah's eyes darted over to the wall, where her dad leaned next to a few other male teachers. Sure enough, there stood Grandma, a bit dressed up, too, standing among them. Not only that, but she noticed Mr. Sutherland dressed uncharacteristically in a necktie and button-down shirt.

Sarah's heart began to pound. "Yep!"

"Why is she here?"

"I'm not sure I want to know," replied Sarah, keeping an eye on the wall.

After the tennis team left the floor to cursory applause, the cheer leaders took their turn in the spotlight, performing the competition routine that had earned them an honorable mention in the District Finals. But the team couldn't hold Sarah's focus despite its creative formations or the gravity-defying acrobatics of its flyers.

Then she saw Amber. She slipped through a side door, acting a little lost and looking as if she had come straight from the gym. Spotting her dad and her grandmother, Amber slid along the wall and joined them, her face animated while exchanging pleasantries.

Sarah's heart had leapt up to her throat well before receiving another elbow from Marcie. "Isn't that your coach?"

"Yep!" Sarah gulped.

Once the cheerleaders had scurried back to their seats next to the song leaders, the pep commissioner again took center stage with the microphone, her perky voice making clear why she had been elected to the post. "Thank you, varsity cheerleaders! Let's give them another round of applause!" She glanced down at her agenda while the audience politely complied before looking over to Coach Sutherland and nodding. He nodded back. "Now we'd like to call up the track coach, Mr. Sutherland, for a special presentation!"

Coach Sutherland's tall figure ambled out from against the wall while motioning for a pair of ASB boys to bring the easel forward. Sarah was now officially nauseous. Once the pep commissioner handed off the mike, Coach Sutherland turned to the student body and smiled before speaking the dreaded words: "Sarah Turner, would you please come down to the floor and join me?"

With Marcie and Tiffany looking like they'd seen a ghost, Sarah had an out-of-body experience as she stood up and somehow wiggled herself through a few rows of students to reach the gym floor. She vaguely heard students clapping as she made the interminable journey to the side of Coach Sutherland, who looked as though he was thoroughly enjoying himself. Heat rising up her neck and face, Sarah clasped her hands in front and looked down at the floor, worried she might faint.

"Earlier this month," began Coach Sutherland in his deep bass, "Sarah became the first runner in the history of Montevallo Christian Academy to run at the prestigious Western Relays, placing eighth in the invitational heat against elite runners from multiple states. And now, just last Saturday, Sarah again became the first student in school history to be crowned champion at the small schools regional track meet!" A generous round of applause followed, punctuated by a few hoots.

Sarah sneaked a glance over to the wall to see a couple of teachers patting her broadly smiling father, no longer leaning on the wall, on the back. "But she's not done. This coming Saturday Sarah will attempt to make more history by becoming the first runner from Montevallo to qualify for the State meet at the regional finals. Only the top four girls will advance." Another round of applause forced Coach Sutherland to wait before resuming. "Many of us know what verse Sarah has chosen for the back of her letterman's jacket, but for those who don't, it's First Corinthians chapter ten verse thirty-one: 'Do all for the glory of God.'" He turned and faced her. "We will be praying that you may do just that this weekend at the regional finals."

Just when Sarah thought she would be released from the public eye with a last batch of applause, Coach Sutherland resumed speaking. "But wait . . . there's more!" he joked with a pointed finger. He smoothed his mustache and smiled sheepishly when it was greeted with silence. "Sarah's historic accomplishments this season have made her eligible for the honor of adding her portrait to the MCA Athletics Wall of Fame in the foyer. Today we're going to unveil that picture, and to help make this special presentation, I'd like to invite her event coach, Ms. Amber Jones, to join us, who I might add has herself qualified for the U.S. Olympic Track and Field Trials later this month!"

Amber walked out to renewed applause and more than one whistle, blushing almost as much as Sarah by the time she reached her on the other side of the easel. Coach Sutherland ramped up the drama. "Here we go; on the count of three: one, two, three!"

On the last number, Sarah and Amber gently pulled off the sheet to reveal a large, framed photograph taken just three days prior while she posed at the top of the podium at the small schools regional. A gold medal hung from a wide blue ribbon around her neck. Sarah was too stunned to smile, but not Amber.

Stepping over, she embraced Sarah and spoke in her ear so she could hear over the robust ovation. "This is what happens when you work hard day after day while nobody's watching."

CHAPTER 32

Clank! Steel met steel as Kiana stepped forward and guided the barbell resting on her shoulders back into the reinforced hooks of the squat rack. Kiana released her grip and stepped out from under the bar, catching her breath. By the time she exited the cage, Sarah had already stepped over to one end of the barbell to slide off a couple of plates and rack them. Kiana did the same on the other side.

"I heard you got a little surprise today at school!" Kiana grinned, a sparkle in her eye. She had to speak up to be heard above the classic Aerosmith streaming from the speakers spaced around the weight room.

"Not just a little one," admitted Sarah, allowing herself a small grin of her own. "I thought I was going to pass out in front of the whole school."

After checking to ensure the weight on each side of the bar was balanced, she took Kiana's place in the cage. Ducking her head under the barbell, she adjusted her neck, so it was comfortably centered on the pad that was attached around it and squared up her body. After a lunge forward and a quick dip of the hips, she stood up to her full height, freeing the barbell from the hooks' grasp. Kiana, spotting only a step away, kept a watchful eye as Sarah carefully edged back and again squared her feet, shoulder-width apart. With her eyes focused straight ahead and her back straight, Sarah lowered her hips. When her legs reached a ninety-degree angle, the bar hovering just above the safety bars, she thrusted back up through her heels with a forceful exhalation.

"Eyes up!" Kiana reminded as Sarah's head slightly sagged. Five squats later, she was done with the last set of her last lifting session of the week. Possibly of the season, depending on Saturday's outcome.

The pair racked the remaining weights until the barbell was bare. Grabbing her nearly empty bottle, Sarah left to refill it just as Amber dismounted a stationary bike on the far side of the room. When Kiana joined her, all Amber could offer her was a frown.

"Not going well?" asked Kiana.

"No," Amber confirmed, gazing down at her ankle as she tested it. "I thought that sitting out last weekend would do the trick, but it hasn't. And it's still not improving even though I've been cross-training all week."

"I'm sorry."

Amber was thankful her training partner knew better than to offer an optimistic platitude. But then she caught herself and looked up at Kiana. "Hey, I feel stupid complaining about this when you're dealing with your own lost season on top of family issues. I so wish you'd been able to come back strong on Saturday."

"Yeah. I was hoping for a muscle memory miracle. Instead, I got slapped with reality." Kiana shook her head with a sober face, her eyes growing distant. "You can't patch together almost two months of training and compete at this level, let alone make the Trials. And with only two weeks left to qualify, it just won't be enough time to get me there." Kiana shrugged, her eyes returning to Amber. "It is what it is. There wasn't really an alternative; my family needed me. I just have to face it and start setting the groundwork for next season." Kiana stopped to dab her brow with her towel. "But you're having a career year. You've already made the Trials. If I were you, I'd be upset, too."

Amber reached out and touched Kiana's arm. "Well, I really appreciate that you're still coming with me up to the mountains next week . . . I just hope there's still a reason for me to go." Taking her own sweat rag and phone out of the bike's cubby hole, Amber began to wipe down the bike. "By the way, Ben kind of panicked when I told him I'd be gone if Sarah made it to State. But I think he was OK with it when I explained I'd give him the workouts and join them at the meet on our way home."

"Hmmm . . . From 'The Hermit' sentenced to the 'No Parent Zone' to being appointed 'Coach Ben' in one season! Now that's a story." Kiana chuckled. Amber couldn't agree more.

Sarah, taking a swig from her bottle, walked up and joined them by the bike. Amber took an extended look at her watch and then stared towards the door by the front desk. "I think I'm gonna skip stretching with you guys today and head out a few minutes early. I'd like to get ice on this ASAP," she informed them, adding, "Sarah, I'll see you in the morning. It will be your last tempo run before backing off Thursday and Friday. I want you fresh for Saturday."

Sarah looked surprised by the announcement. "OK. Hope you feel better."

While Kiana and Sarah retired to the empty dance room, Amber collected her things from a day-use locker and headed purposefully toward the front door. But once alone outside she immediately stopped, her eyes scanning the parking lot. It didn't take long to spy Ben's truck parked nearby at the curb in the loading zone, waiting to pick up Sarah. After a moment's hesitation, she walked over from behind the bed to find his head bent over a paper. She tapped on the driver's window, a forced smile on her lips. Slightly startled, Ben rolled down the window.

"Hi there! How are you doin'?" he asked, returning her smile just as Amber's dissolved.

"Hi . . . Honestly, not so well."

Ben's mood shifted immediately to match Amber's. "What's going on?" His soft tone helped Amber to blaze ahead despite the awkwardness.

"I'm kind of struggling with this injury thing." With imploring eyes, she tucked a wisp of hair behind her ear. "Could we meet to talk sometime this week?"

"Of course! I'm free later tonight if you like. We could grab some coffee."

"That would be so great. Thank you," Amber replied with a faint smile, this time genuine.

Ben filled the gap that followed. "Eight o'clock? Where we met last time?"

"That's perfect, but only if that works for you," she quickly added.

"It absolutely does," he assured with a firm nod. Amber seemed uncertain of what to do or say next, so Ben finished the conversation for her. "I'll see you there. Looking forward to it."

"OK. Thanks again. Bye." Leaving Ben with a puzzled expression, Amber turned and disappeared among the cars just as suddenly as she had appeared.

*****

It was almost a case of déjà vu. When he walked through the coffee shop door, Ben again found Amber perched on a tall chair wearing the fitted Arkansas tee and a pair of neon orange trainers, though they seemed to be a newer version. But on the mild spring evening she had ditched the jacket and substituted a pair of capri-length leggings for calf-length. More important to Ben, the blonde in the back corner, waiting at a high table reserved for just the two of them, waved him over with a smile rather than lurk behind a coffee cup at a congested barista bar. In fact, Amber had even bought him his own cup of Joe.

"Hello!" said Ben, sliding up on the chair across from her.

"Hi! Thanks for coming. I hate to impose on your evening with Sarah."

"It's no big deal. Sarah has plenty of homework to do. Besides," he pointed out with light irony, "friends do things like this."

"That's sweet of you to say." Amber watched Ben take a tentative sip from his cup. "I didn't know what you would like, so I just got you plain old coffee. I also mixed in a little cream and sugar," she noted, as if hopeful that was OK.

Ben grinned at the gesture. "Perfect. Thanks! So, what's up?"

Amber paused and struck a more subdued note before answering, talking mostly to her cup. "Right. Well . . . I know we've only known each other for a few months, but we've already been up front with each other about some pretty deep and personal issues." Ben nodded ever so slightly. "I've found that openness remarkably refreshing."

"Me, too."

Looking up, Amber caught his eye. "I could really use adding a chapter to those conversations tonight."

"By all means!" he encouraged with an understanding expression.

Amber's voice and features started to waver. "I'm really struggling right now . . . You know my dream of running at the Trials and making the Olympic team . . . It's taken six years to claw my way back . . . with countless sacrifices . . . and just when that goal is within reach, along comes another injury to rip it away. You know my history. This may well be my last chance . . . It's devastating." A hand covered her face. "I'm sorry!"

"No worries at all, Amber," Ben calmly responded. " . . . But it's not over yet, is it? The Trials are still, what, almost three weeks away?"

"It's possible," admitted Amber, carefully wiping her eyes with a thumb, "as long as I can keep up my cardio with cross-training . . . But I'm trying to figure out how to deal with it if it really is over, you know?" Her eyes cautiously angled toward Ben's again. "That brings me to you." If possible, Ben grew even more curious at Amber's statement. "I know you've suffered a deep loss. How did you deal with that? And as a Christian, why didn't that turn you against God?"

Ben, stroking his chin, thought for several seconds before responding, and even then only after taking a deep breath. "I'm not going to lie to you, Amber. There were some very dark days . . . and, as you already know, there still are, though not as bad." It seemed to Ben that she was weighing his every word. "But pain is part of our world, whether you're a believer or not."

"True."

"So, I would turn the question around: as hard as it has been, how could I possibly deal with Joy's death if I wasn't a Christian?" Amber, sitting back, looked intrigued by the reversal. "First, I would have no understanding of God's enduring goodness. My breaking God's moral law deserves punishment, even death, so the last thing God owes me is an ideal life. Still, He has not only saved me for eternity at a massive price, but He gives me daily blessings. The time I shared with Joy was a gift, not a right. So, my response to that love is to become a 'living sacrifice,' regardless of outcomes."

"Like we heard on Easter."

Ben couldn't help grinning while nodding. "Exactly. You were listening."

Amber mirrored his grin. "You didn't hear me snoring, did you?"

Conceding the point, Ben turned serious again. "Secondly, without God I would have no confidence that Joy's death and my pain serve a higher purpose; instead, her death would merely be a random, and therefore meaningless, event. Christians stand on the promise that somehow ' . . . All things work together for good . . . for those who are called according to His purpose.'" A trace of emotion crept into Ben's voice as he held Amber's eye. "The story of my life has not been fully written, so I can't see all that God has intended from Joy's death right now. But I can tell you it has already enabled me to come alongside others who are hurting, and if God were to use it to redeem even one soul, that would give it a priceless value."

Amber remained silent for a moment. To Ben, the signs of her former turmoil had ebbed. "This is exactly why I wanted to talk with you. You always seem to provide perspectives I just wouldn't have thought about on my own."

"Amber, I don't pretend to know how things are going to turn out for you this season, and please know I'm praying for your recovery."

"Thank you."

"But most of all, I want to assure you that there is no 'failure' in God's economy for one pursuing His purposes." Ben took another sip of his coffee before continuing. "I'm starting to suspect that God is at work in your life. And your pain may well be His way of getting your attention."

Amber's eyebrows raised. "Well, that's encouraging . . . but, honestly, a little scary, too."

CHAPTER 33

The irony was thick. After waking up, Ben had checked his traffic app to discover the one-hour trip to the regional finals site had ballooned to two due to a major accident on the interstate. Moving up their departure, they had picked up Jack and hit the road an hour earlier than planned. But halfway to the meet the accident ahead on the map suddenly cleared. Now, setting up camp in the bleachers, they found themselves an hour early for Sarah's warm-up. An extra hour for Sarah to stew silently in her nerves.

While Jack started thumbing through the heat sheets, Ben and Sarah settled in to watch the preparation for the boys' heat of the 4 x 100-meter relay, the meet's opening event, as the girls vacated the track. It was the first time they had arrived early enough to see the relay all season. Nine teams had dispersed their runners to the four corners of the track, with one runner from each team setting and testing his block in the staggered starting area. Meanwhile, the runners in each of the passing zones walked off and marked their personal starting points with pieces of tape on the track's grainy surface before completing a couple of test runs. When receiving the baton, gauging the timing and distance of the start wasn't the only key factor in a fluid, full-speed hand-off within the zone, but certainly the most critical one. Especially when it was done blindly without looking back. Executed correctly, the baton exchange was artistry in motion, but when not it could quickly turn to comedy or, at worst, tragedy.

After a few minutes, the lead-off runners finally froze in their starting blocks, and a crack of the gun triggered the rapid-fire drama with a flash of speed. As nine sprinters converged on the first passing zone, their batons glinting in the sun, another nine timed their take offs and punched the blast-off button. Six teams emerged from the ensuing flurry without a hitch, while three others survived with a hiccup, falling off the frenetic pace. The second exchange proved harsher to the six teams still in contention. To the collective groan of the crowd, one team dropped the baton; the receiver left too early, leaving his teammate unable to place the baton securely in the back-stretched hand no matter how far he stretched. Meanwhile, the runner of another squad started his take-off too late; not only did his teammate have to brake to avoid running him over, but he received the baton at half-speed, losing more precious time.

Then tragedy struck again in the third and final passing zone when the anchor runner of the second-place team made the same mistake of starting too early in the tight race. Though his teammate wisely held on to the baton until he finally reached him for a secure exchange, they failed to complete the hand off before crossing the zone's furthest border line, earning the red disqualification flag from an official. Just like that, the State dreams of three competitive teams lay in ruins as the culprits stared wide-eyed in disbelief, hands to their heads. Ben and Sarah gave each other a disconcerted glance, glad her destiny would not be determined by teammates' performances or such precise mechanics.

His review of the heat sheet complete, Jack's voice brought them back as he stuffed the packet back inside the manila envelope. "Sarah is seeded sixth out of fifteen. I'm not surprised since seeding is based on last weekend's times, not season PR's. She wasn't pushed at the small schools meet either, so her mid-2:15 doesn't really mean much when girls in the other divisions probably had to run PR's in highly competitive races to get through. And they ran at three different sites, too, so who knows if the conditions were similar."

"Why fifteen?" questioned Ben, turning to face Jack. "What happened to twelve runners in a race?"

"It's political. Each division has a set allotment of qualifiers: the small schools three, the mid-sized schools five, and the large schools seven."

Ben looked confused. "Is that fair?"

"Actually, yes, more than fair to the smaller schools," he answered, smoothing his mustache. "Of course, it depends on the specific year and event, because in any given year an elite athlete like Sarah can pop up in the small school division. But the small schools have a hard time competing against schools sometimes ten or more times their size. Occasionally, the seventh-place qualifier from the large school division can be faster than the small school champion. Small school athletes don't typically make it through to the State meet. We've never had one do it at Montevallo." Ben bit his lip at the news, hoping Sarah, on her phone, wasn't listening too closely. "Anyway," Jack resumed, "Sarah should start away from the rail, probably somewhere in the middle of the pack. If they have a staggered start like they did at Western and last week, she'll be near the outside edge of the inside group. That shouldn't be too bad."

Ben looked at his watch and pondered whether he wanted to sit for an hour and a half before Sarah's race. He decided he didn't. He had his own set of nerves to deal with. "I'm going to stretch my legs," he informed Jack.

Standing up, he made his way to the aisle and walked back down the bleacher steps. Reaching the concessions and merchandising area behind the home stands, he was glad to see Amber and Kiana strolling in from the direction of the entry gate and waved. "Hi, Guys!"

Spotting Ben, they altered their path to join him.

"Hi!" said Amber from behind the reflection of her aviator sunglasses. "Is the meet running on time? Where's Sarah?"

"We're all a little early. They were just lining up the girls sixteen hundred when I left a minute ago. Sarah is up in the stands with Jack near the far twenty-yard line, a little up." He motioned in the general direction.

"Oh, OK." With time not an issue, Amber seemed content to delay her search for Sarah.

"So, altitude training," mentioned Ben, slipping his hands back into his pockets. "Sounds like fun . . . You're leaving for the mountains straight from the meet?"

Smiling, Amber placed an arm around Kiana. "Yes. Kiana's being a real pal and keeping me company for the week."

"I'm not gonna say 'no' to a free vacation!" Kiana chuckled, flashing a smile. "If you call running at eight, nine thousand feet a vacation." She shrugged. "My competitive season may be over, but, moving forward, I can still build my base back up. And I'm fortunate; with my laptop, I can take my design work almost anywhere. But I'll be sure to take some time to relax."

"So how hard is it to run at that elevation?" inquired Ben.

Amber frowned. "We'll do our speedwork on a track a bit lower, around six thousand feet," she clarified first. "But it's definitely an acquired taste. The first day or two are the worst, but once you get acclimated it gets better. And you really have to be careful about drinking plenty of water, because it's so dry at that elevation."

Kiana nodded her head in confirmation, but, having spotted a bathroom nearby, she cut in apologetically. "Excuse me; I'm going to run to the restroom."

Once Kiana left, Amber assumed a more confidential tone. "She's being a sport about not qualifying for the Trials. She just wasn't able to stay focused on her training with all she had to deal with."

"Emergencies are never convenient, that's for sure," Ben sympathized, but then turned upbeat on a dime. "I didn't want to mention it in front of Kiana, given her disappointments, but I'm just so excited to hear that your Achilles seems to finally be clearing up! What a relief!"

"Yeah! Knock on wood," agreed Amber, a smile returning to her face. "Thanks for your prayers. Just to be careful, I've kept it to cross-training only and still may until Monday. I want to give it every day I can to fully heal before I really push it again." She paused long enough to pull a breeze-blown wisp of hair from the corner of her mouth. "I'm hoping that I've succeeded in maintaining my fitness. I've hit the bike, aqua jogging, and even the elliptical hard, and though it seems like a lot longer, it's been less than two weeks since I stopped running. I still have two weeks to tune up."

When the conversation paused, Amber checked the direction Kiana left before continuing. "Hey, before I go find Sarah, I want to thank you again for our talk the other night. It was very calming."

"Seriously, it was my pleasure. I'm glad you found it helpful."

"So, I've been thinking." A subtle grin formed on her lips. "If I have some free time this week while lounging around our mountain chalet, would you recommend reading anything to follow up on our talks?"

Ben masked his surprise well. "Hmm . . . Well, it's not the simplest book of the Bible, but you'll find many ideas we've discussed in Romans. But if you find that a bit too heavy, perhaps the gospel of John. I can text you a link to an easy-to-read version online—assuming you have wi-fi!"

"Great! Send me the links. Maybe I'll check them out."

"Only if you text me Sarah's workouts. If she gets through to State, that is."

"Yeah, I'll be sure to do that. They'll be pretty easy. I'll pull her way back to peak next weekend with fresh legs."

"Sounds good!"

Kiana approached, still waving her hands to dry them. "Well, I better check in with Sarah."

"Yeah, you probably should." Ben nodded.

"See you in a bit!" said Amber, offering a smile.

Ben waved and continued on his way, looking for nothing in particular but with plenty to ponder.

*****

Sarah stood race-ready in her uniform, the bib safety-pinned to the front of her jersey and a pair of sixes pasted on her chest and the right hip of her spandex shorts. Hands on her hips, she robotically shook out one foot after another as Amber, arms folded, kept company beside her. Filled with far fewer athletes than normal, the warm-up area seemed a little strange. No frosh/soph. No JV. Only Varsity, and the remnant of the Varsity elite at that. After the bustling activity of the Rodeo and Western Relays, the relative scarcity of athletes seemed a little anti-climactic; yet one could cut the tension with a knife. Every soul on the fenced field knew the dream of reaching the State meet would be realized or crushed in a matter of minutes. For some, it would even bring the unceremonious end of a running career.

Amber turned her aviators toward Sarah. "How you feeling?"

"Nervous."

"Everybody's nervous. You belong here. You've put in the work. This is why we ran you at the Rodeo and Western Relays, so that when you got here, to today, you'd be facing nothing new. You've already faced the big schools and had success. You're absolutely competitive here." Sarah nodded. "So, no slipping to the back of the pack. Always stay within striking distance of the leaders. And remember, it's all about placement now. Your time doesn't matter in this race; either you're in the top four and move on, or you don't. Be sure you're counting."

Sarah quickly glanced over at her friendly rival from Arroyo Hills, wearing a pair of threes on her silver and royal blue uniform. She avoided eye contact with Sarah as well. It wasn't the time to be renewing acquaintances. Sarah noticed the girl's teammate from the Rodeo was absent.

"Coach says there are fifteen girls in your race," resumed Amber, breaking the renewed silence. "So things will be even a little more crowded than usual. All the more reason to stay on the edge of the pack and give yourself options. Don't get boxed in. If they don't call you soon, take another stride or two before reporting. Otherwise, you'll have time to get a couple in on the infield."

Just then, the speakers in the warm-up area crackled to life, almost on cue. "Last call, girls eight hundred meters!"

That finally made Sarah talk. "My heart's about to leap out of my chest."

"Focus on what you can control. I know you'll give this everything you've got. As your dad once said to me: 'All things work together for good . . .'" Amber left the verse incomplete, but Sarah finished it. And made it her prayer.

"'. . . For those called according to His purpose.' Amen."

"You've got this!" They performed a double fist bump, and the protege left for the staging area, unaware that her mentor's concerned eyes followed her. With her heart pacing faster than she would have expected, Amber turned to rejoin the rooting section.

*****

Fifteen girls hovered impatiently behind the starting arc, lined up in seed order, as a pair of red coats finished lining the inside of Lane Five with a string of cones that stopped at the end of the curve. When done, one returned to lead the top four seeds to the forward starting arc. That left Sarah second from the outside edge of the rear group of eleven, and when the second red coat arrived, she instructed Sarah's group to take a step back from the line. Sarah worried that her group was too tightly bunched, but the official didn't seem to notice or care enough to tell them to spread out. Both red coats then retreated to the infield, leaving the girls to bounce up and down or rock back and forth until a third red coat with a headset mounted the ladder.

Meanwhile, the four adults had moved to a position near the start-finish line a bit further up in the bleachers, enabling them to sit together. They shouted words of encouragement down to Sarah, with her father sitting on his hands, his knee jiggling incessantly. Next to him, Amber bit her lower lip. The entire stadium seemed to be watching the red coat on the ladder as he pulled back one side of his sports jacket, located the handle of the pistol holstered on his hip, and pulled it out.

As the gun rose in the air, the spectators grew quiet. "On your marks!" Fifteen runners stutter-stepped to the lines, bent, and froze with one arm cocked. Silence. Crack!

Sarah drove off the line, beginning the process of cranking up her lanky legs. Unsurprisingly, the girl to her right surged a step ahead almost immediately, and Sarah, as if anticipating the move, slid behind her with only the slightest hitch as the girl cut towards the rail. Once on the outside edge of the rear group, with plenty of space, Sarah accelerated to race pace without further hindrance. The trade-off of adding a couple of extra meters was worth it.

At the break point, the top four seeds, a few steps ahead, angled towards the rail far enough ahead to allow Sarah's stride to remain constant while also pulling her forward as she strove to match their pace. Halfway down the back stretch, Sarah was satisfied to drift to a position in the middle of the pack on the shoulder. But the pack remained unusually compact, with the leaders less than ten meters ahead of the caboose. Some girls in the middle ran three or even four abreast, including Sarah, who found herself just over the line in Lane Two astride two others inside her.

But just as the race seemed to be settling into the routine, all chaos broke loose. While approaching the second curve, the jostling began anew as some runners sought to improve their positions by moving closer to the rail for rounding the curve. The ensuing commotion seemed like a replay of the opening sprint, with too many runners maneuvering in too small a space. Suddenly, a girl in the thick of things, directly ahead and to the left of Sarah, pitched headlong, sprawling to the track.

The pack shattered in an instant as the entire stadium groaned. While the girls behind tried to leap over the fallen runner, Sarah instinctively lunged to her right to escape the hazard, as did the girl directly in front of her. The double evasion caused Sarah to careen almost into Lane Four, her stride severely disrupted, but she somehow managed to stay on her feet. Behind her she heard a second competitor go down as well in a failed bid to evade the fallen runner. An extra shot of adrenaline abruptly charged through her veins, and Sarah veered back towards the inner lanes just as swiftly as she had left them, trying to process both what had just happened and assure herself that all her limbs were still intact.

But the situation was dire. The front cluster of runners, unaffected by the crisis behind them, had continued on at full speed, while Sarah spent the rest of the curve resuming her race pace and then sprinting beyond it down the home straight in an attempt to link back up with the lead pack. By the time she neared the start line, she succeeded in closing the gap and reconnecting with the rear. Sarah had been faced with no alternative but wondered at what cost the extraordinary effort would come.

Amber's voice pierced the air as Sarah crossed the start line. "You're back in it, Sarah! Dig down!"

As they rounded the curve, Sarah counted herself in eighth place, with one girl close behind. Most important, the fourth-place girl, wearing silver and royal blue, was still conceivably within striking distance less than ten meters away. But she knew she had used up a lot of energy and oxygen to give herself a chance. She strove to rein in her breathing and reset.

The runners held their positions through the third curve and Sarah, fueled by anger and desperation, kicked out on the straight, closing on and passing a couple of girls laboring even more than she before tucking in against the rail to enter the final curve. She didn't bother to look at the clock; it no longer mattered. Sarah counted again to be sure: five runners remained ahead with the sounds of another still on her heels. Passing at least two of them while letting no one pass her became her obsession.

Every runner left in contention was elite, and all knew the stakes at hand. Accordingly, each started her final surge sooner than later while rounding the curve. Despite the bodily deficit caused by simply getting back into the race, Sarah willed herself to hold her position, extending her stride, as those ahead tried to pull away. Nearing the final straight, she sensed the girl behind attempting to slingshot past on her shoulder. Sarah succeeded in heading her off by slanting to the outside of the lane and then, once off the curve, drifted into Lane Two to create a potential path around the runners on the rail in the final stretch. Two girls had pulled away, leaving behind a five-girl trail pack, including the insurgent still on her shoulder, all converging within five meters of each other. But one, near the rail, sagged back, leaving the remaining four girls strung out across the first three lanes in a sixty-meter duel that brought the crowd to its feet. Sarah and the insurgent caught the other pair with forty meters to go, but the two redoubled their effort at the challenge. Beyond strategy or feeling,

Sarah simply set her eyes on the finish line, summoned every fiber of her being to get there first, and leaned.

To Sarah, all four seemed to cross as one, but the computer, aided by the camera mounted at the finish line, calculated their separation to hundredths of a second. Two collapsed to the track, the trailing runners narrowly avoiding spiking them. Sarah, meanwhile, stumbled forward several more steps, her hands behind her head, chest heaving, legs pulsing, eyes locked on the scoreboard. Then, growing light-headed, she took a knee. As interminable seconds passed, with the technicians huddled in the timing tent to confirm the data against still images from the finish-line camera, Sarah tried to steel herself for the news. Finally, with a nod of the lead official's head, another official clicked a mouse and made the results public above Sarah's head. She had eyes for only one: 4th: Sarah Turner / Montevallo Christian / 2:14.57. Two one hundredths of a second separated her apart from fifth place.

The flood of tears came without warning. Bleary-eyed, Sarah jumped up and turned towards the unbridled screams in the bleachers to make out Amber and Kiana bouncing up and down, their arms wrapped around each other. Next to them, Ben and Jack bearhugged, pounding each other on the back, the surrounding spectators grinning at the sight.

After she had caught her breath, Sarah turned her eyes heavenward and uttered a prayer. "Thank You, Lord, for one-thousand-meter repeats."

CHAPTER 34

The overcast Monday morning did not reflect their mood. The glow from Saturday's epic performance still hung in the air as Sarah stretched on the infield, Ben standing beside her. As her 'coach' for the week, he had opted to leave his dwindling paper load at home.

The race was only two days in the past, but it already seemed much longer ago. Another week had arrived with another meet to prepare for. This one was different, though. Only the highest caliber track and field athletes in the state still soldiered on in relative anonymity. Now mid-May, the rest had been released back to finishing term projects, preparing for final exams, and making graduation plans. But Sarah had been blessed to reach the ultimate end of the seasonal road. Especially as a sophomore, she had already succeeded simply by earning the opportunity to pull on her spikes for the State final. Now it was a matter of having her cake and eating it, too.

"You did a great job recovering from that girl's fall," Ben commented, staring down at the field while replaying the scene in his mind. "I don't know how you avoided going down with her."

Sarah shot him a glance. "I do." Ben met her eyes, momentarily confused, then grinned. "But now the State meet looks a lot like the Western Relays. I may be the last seed."

"Maybe on paper," scoffed Ben. But you and I both know that's totally misleading." He decided to take a seat with Sarah on the artificial grass, deeming it sufficiently dry. "You still ran a mid-two fourteen while almost getting taken out! That cost you at least a couple of seconds, possibly more. Otherwise, you'd have come away with a huge PR and been right up there with the leaders, who were untouched by the whole thing. You were the only runner to make it through to State that was affected by it, and you still almost beat that Arroyo Hills girl."

"Her name is Eva. Eva Espinosa," informed Sarah. "We've talked a couple of times now. She's nice. After the race, we joked that every time we race each other we have a photo finish. We follow each other on Instagram now. I'm glad she got through, too."

Ben didn't know which he found more interesting: knowing the girl's name or that Sarah had talked with anyone at the meet, let alone a rival. Then he remembered the point he was making. "So, a low seed at State may actually end up being a big advantage to you, because the other runners probably aren't going to know what happened at your regional Saturday. It kind of keeps you under the radar, if that's possible after Western. Or maybe they'll think you've already peaked." Nodding silently, Sarah seemed to see her dad's point. "Not only that, but Amber's aim all season has been to tailor your training to peak at the State meet. So after tapering you this week," Ben shrugged, "who knows what more you'll be able to do?"

"True. I never tapered like this last season. Actually, I'm not sure there was anything to taper me from!" She grinned while Ben chuckled.

An affable silence fell on them as Ben mused privately. Then he felt compelled to speak. "You should know that I'd be proud of you whether you had moved on or not. So would your mom." Sarah swallowed hard. "You did the absolute best given the circumstances, both in training and in the race. That's all anyone can ask of you or you can ask of yourself. God's in charge of the rest, and whatever He intends is for His glory and your good, even if we may not see it right away."

His final comment broke Sarah out of her silence. Her stretching complete, she stood and unzipped her sweats. "It's interesting that you mention that. Before my race, Amber said you told her that 'All things work together for good.'"

"Did she." Ben stated it more as an observation than a question. "Did she, really," he repeated.

"Yeah. I had to finish the rest of the verse that she didn't include. But what have you been talking about with her?"

Ben massaged his chin with a thumb and forefinger before answering. "Our conversations occasionally drift into spiritual topics," he admitted. "I keep putting the ball in her court, and, sooner or later, she keeps hitting it back . . . I think God's using us to work in her life." After a pause he added, "And the other way around, too."

Sarah looked up to the sky as she considered the news. "She's definitely been a blessing to me," she began before her eyes strayed to Ben. "And to you, too, I think."

"Didn't I just say that?" he said, giving her a knowing look as he stood up.

Squelching a grin, Sarah changed the subject. "So, when are we leaving for the meet?"

"Amber insists we travel Friday following your morning easy run to keep you fresh for Saturday and your legs loose. She doesn't want you getting up before dawn and crawling out of the truck after a three-hour drive the day of the race. I can't say I disagree with her. So, we'll both be missing some school. Your workouts will be light all week, and on top of that no more lifting. The heavy work is done."

Sarah smiled. "I'm down with that!'" Then she abruptly turned to business. "All right, Coach. Let's get things rolling."

CHAPTER 35

"The wrath of God is being revealed from heaven against all the godlessness and wickedness of people, who suppress the truth by their wickedness, since what may be known about God is plain to them, because God has made it plain to them. For since the creation of the world God's invisible qualities—his eternal power and divine nature—have been clearly seen, being understood from what has been made, so that people are without excuse. For although they knew God, they neither glorified him as God nor gave thanks to him, but their thinking became futile and their foolish hearts were darkened."

Amber sat reading on her cell, pillows propping her up on one end of the sofa. Her sock-covered feet, tucked under a velvety blanket, almost touched the other side. Pausing, she laid the phone in her lap and reached for the mug of coffee resting on the edge of the coffee table. Then, holding it with both hands, she turned her head to ponder the majestic mountain view through the rental's picture window. In the distance loomed a snow-laden peak with a granite face. An endless, light blue sky soared above it, and below sprawled an emerald carpet of pines. If looking closely enough, one could glimpse the darker blue patch of a lake through the trees.

While Amber absorbed the sight, a blue jay alighted on the rail of the deck outside. She studied it as it cocked its head in a variety of directions. Eventually, the bird dipped its beak to grasp a tiny nugget, its long, stained tail feathers slanting up behind it. With a couple of deft movements of its jaw, the morsel disappeared into its mouth, and after a few more rotations of its dark, lidless eye, it darted back into the forest from which it had appeared.

Amber's solitude was interrupted when Kiana walked by and suddenly backtracked to stand behind the couch, looking down at the phone in her lap with a furrowed brow. "That's not Insta or the news. What are you reading?"

"Romans," answered Amber, taking a sip in as nonchalant a manner as she could muster.

"As in the book of the Bible?" asked Kiana, her voice raising an octave.

"Yes."

"OK, 'The Hermit' and Sarah aren't the only ones who've changed lately. Three months ago, the Amber Jones I know would not be casually scrolling through Scripture in her free time." Kiana expected a defensive or dismissive response, but she received neither.

"You're right," Amber conceded without protest. "Probably not even a week ago."

Kiana tilted her head as she gave Amber a questioning look. "Does this have to do with Ben?"

Amber considered the matter for a few moments before replying. "Yes . . . and no."

Kiana had heard enough. Striding around the couch, she swatted at Amber's feet to make her move them before sitting down. "OK. Spill it."

"Look," she said, suppressing a smile while putting her mug back down, "I won't deny that I'm becoming more and more attracted to

Ben, and I'm not just talking about physically . . . The more I've come to know him, the more impressed I've become with him as a person. At first, I admit, I was kind of freaked out by his faith, but he's down-to-earth, not pushy or judgmental." Amber's eyes began to search the ceiling. "Not to mention intelligent. Caring. Funny. He can be so funny!" She smiled before shrugging. "I simply like being around him. And he's been tested by some pretty huge challenges in his life."

Kiana looked as though she was trying to give Amber the benefit of the doubt. "Losing a spouse and raising a daughter on your own is no cakewalk, that's for sure."

"Yes, but he still managed to hold on to a peace and hope through all of it that, I admit, I just don't have." Amber paused. "Some of the guys I've dated have been so shallow. Remember Doug . . . and Scott? I don't think they were capable of discussing anything deep or personal. All they wanted to do was talk about work or their latest diets and then jump in the sack."

Kiana's eyes grew wide. Amber had never been so transparent with her. When she continued, a new sympathy tinged Kiana's voice. "Well, aren't you an open book today. Go on!"

"So, yes, it partly is about Ben," Amber repeated, her eyes seeking the ceiling again, "but it's not all about him. Knowing Ben has forced me to confront some questions about myself and the world that, frankly, I've spent my life avoiding."

"Such as?"

Both Amber's tone and expression abruptly turned ironic. "Oh, nothing major. Just little things like is there a God? And if so, what does it expect of me? Is there any lasting purpose to my life? And what actually is success?"

Kiana looked like she had been bowled over. "And have you come up with any answers?"

Amber looked at the view outside again before responding. "Not yet. But I'm starting to wonder why I resist the idea of a god when so much evidence of design surrounds us day in and day out." Her gaze, more earnest, returned to Kiana. "Wouldn't common sense conclude that there is a Creator behind the universe? I mean . . . Kiana, you're a designer. Isn't it a much bigger stretch to believe it all came from nothing by chance? And if we really are all living in a random world, if we're merely accidents of Nature, then why does anything you or I do even matter in the end?"

"Well, that's beyond my pay grade," Kiana replied, shaking her head. "Good luck with that. When you find the answers, let me know!"

Amber rubbed her eyes, suddenly tired. "I admit, I've never really wanted to think about these things either. But if I'm honest with myself, what does that impulse say about me? And how do you keep pursuing and sacrificing for goals without knowing if they have any lasting meaning or value?"

"You're starting to depress me!" Kiana laughed nervously, placing a concerned hand on Amber's knee.

Amber assumed a wry smile of her own. "I guess that's why we spend so much time finding ways to not think about it."

CHAPTER 36

Amber, phone to her ear, stood alone, leaning with her elbows on the wooden rail of the deck. The chill of the alpine night had settled in, though she remained toasty in a sweatshirt beneath her quilted ski jacket, zipped to the chin. While looking up at more stars than she thought the sky could hold, she watched her breath as it wafted into the darkness.

Each time she replied to Sarah, a hundred miles away, her voice interrupted a perfect stillness. "Well, I'm glad to hear that things are going well, and your legs are feeling good."

"Yeah, I think I'm as ready for State as I'm ever going to be. My new coach is way less demanding than my old one, though."

Amber chuckled. "Well, you couldn't pick a better time to peak. There will be plenty of college coaches there; this will be a great opportunity to get noticed. Have you given much thought to where you want to go to college?"

"Not much," admitted Sarah. The connection muffled for a moment as Amber heard Sarah reposition herself on her bed. "I'm not sure what I want to study yet. Or how far away from home I want to go."

"You've still got some time to figure that out, but those decisions will be coming faster than you think. As a junior, coaches will be allowed to contact you through the school, and I can assure you that you'll be getting plenty of mail. So, by this time next year you'll want to have narrowed down the top schools you want to visit. Speaking of college, how is school going?"

"Same old. I'm excited about missing classes tomorrow for the trip. That's another good thing about making it to State! But I'll be bringing homework to do in the car and the hotel, so it won't really be much of a vacation."

Amber switched her phone to the other hand, stuffing the cold one in her jacket pocket. "I can't tell you how many papers I wrote on long bus trips while traveling to meets in college. Or the exams I had proctored by coaches in hotel conference rooms. That comes with the territory."

"Sadly."

"Well, it's good catching up with you! You have a couple of long days ahead and should be heading to bed. If there was ever a time not to stay up scrolling Instagram, this is it."

"OK."

"And be sure you're drinking your protein shakes and taking your iron."

"Believe me," Sarah said with some exasperation, "my dad won't let me out the door each day until I do."

"Good man! . . . Hey, before you go, can you put him on for a minute?"

"Sure," agreed Sarah, sounding sleepy. "I think he's in the study. I'll go get him. See you Saturday."

"Bye!"

Amber could hear Sarah's voice calling for Ben as she walked down the hall. "Dad! Amber wants to talk to you!" While waiting, she stood up and turned to spy on Kiana through the picture window.

Her laptop open, she was working on a design project at the dining room table. Amber strolled a few steps further away to the far end of the deck and resumed her former pose by the time Sarah tracked down her dad.

After another muffled exchange, Amber heard him come crisply on the line. "Hey, hello! So, how are things going with you and Kiana?"

She switched ears again, with the cold hand pulling a blonde lock behind her ear before it found her pocket. "We're doing well! Kiana's a lot of fun, and I owe her big time for coming. But I miss you guys." One of her trainers tilted on a toe and wiggled as she hesitated. "I miss you. I wish we could have spent a night or two up here talking over hot cups of coffee. It's still pretty cold after the sun goes down even though it's the middle of May."

After a brief pause, Ben replied. "I have to confess, that sounds like it would have been wonderful, as long as you duplicated your cream and sugar recipe." Amber laughed. "But believe me, you'd have grown tired of my sermons."

"Never!" she replied, still laughing.

"It's been odd here, too, with just the two of us at the track," Ben confessed, sounding more serious. " . . . So, how is your Achilles holding up?"

"So far so good," she answered, her tone growing earnest as well.

"That's great to hear!"

The relief Amber heard in Ben's voice warmed her further. "Yeah, with some fear and trembling I've been putting a little more stress on it each day this week, and it hasn't flared up. I'm starting to trust it again. I have my last long run tomorrow morning and then a light recovery session in the afternoon. I'm keeping my fingers crossed."

"Well, I hope it turns out to be a best-case scenario, and all this will allow you to go into the Trials both conditioned and with fresh legs. That's certainly what I'm praying for."

"Thanks, Ben." Amber stood up and paced back to the window. Kiana's eyes were still locked intently on the laptop screen. Leaning her back against the rail, Amber crossed her feet. "Hey, I'm rethinking leaving early Saturday morning for Sarah's race. I guess I'd rather not take a chance with bad traffic and miss it. So, what do you think of our arriving late tomorrow night instead?"

"Fantastic! I'd really rather not make my coaching debut at the State meet." Amber grinned. "I can text you where we're staying if you want. It's not the Ritz but it has good reviews and a free breakfast."

"Perfect! I'll text you when we get in if it's not too late."

"Sounds good . . . I Hope you have a healthy last day of training, and I look forward to seeing you."

"Same here . . . Bye, Ben."

"Bye, Amber."

Amber punched the end call button and slid her phone into the leg pocket of her leggings. Then, turning to gaze back up at the stars, she saw her breath as she blew a sigh.

CHAPTER 37

Kiana had opted to take the last morning off, and Amber was perfectly fine with that. Frankly, the prospect of a little alone time sounded refreshing after six full days together. Amber arrived at the trailhead early enough to grab one of the few parking spaces. That boded well for a lack of foot traffic, she thought. Four miles up and out and four miles down and back: that was the plan.

Slipping the car key into the rear zipper pocket of her shorts, Amber scanned the sky with trepidation. A low-pressure system had begun to roll in overnight, and rain was forecast. In the distance, she could already see a threatening bank of dark clouds advancing over a ridge. She hoped the storm would hold off for another sixty minutes, but just in case, she was glad to have brought the hat, her ponytail pulled through the back, and the rain slicker worn over a long-sleeve tee.

After checking the settings on her GPS watch, Amber set herself in motion, taking the first mile a bit slowly before picking up speed. The trail had been chosen because it was sufficiently flat and wide enough to pass others, at least in most spots. Cut into the side of the mountain canyon, it generally twisted above and parallel to a large creek teeming with the spring runoff, the raging cascade crashing into and churning around sometimes enormous boulders. Against the backdrop of the creek's constant roar, the sound of her footfall was barely audible when crunching on sandy stretches or those strewn with pine needles and relatively silent when running over powdered or compacted dirt. She found a few sections of the trail damp, even muddy from melting snow or hidden springs seeping out from the side of the slope, causing her to tread carefully or lunge over a rivulet. And here and there patches of dirty snow still bordered the path. For the most part, though, the footing was suitable as she threaded her way ever deeper into the scent of fir and pine.

Amber relished the calming solitude, disturbed only when easing past a few hikers with a smile and a wave. The open space and fresh air allowed her room to think, to reflect, to muse over the future. Dotted with sweet ferns, blooming wildflowers, granite outcroppings, and the decaying hulks of fallen giants, the landscape occasionally dazzled with a lifting mist or a dappling of shadow and light. She found herself content to let the sublime setting wash over her without the distraction of conversation. But as she neared the turn-around point, Amber was unprepared for an entirely different conversation that began to brew in her mind, even as the storm clouds began brewing high above her head.

It started with a drip. As she soaked in the inspired beauty enveloping her, she heard a whisper, the whisper of her own reading voice: "For since the creation of the world God's invisible qualities—His eternal power and divine nature—have been clearly seen, being understood from what has been made, so that people are without excuse." Amber pondered the recollection of the prior day's text as the towering trees parted before her on each side. But that thought was just the beginning. It was followed several moments later by another whisper, this time Ben's voice, stealing into her mind from a conversation now weeks in the past: "All have sinned and fall short of God's ideal perfection." Amber's pulse quickened, and not just from the demands of the trail's incline.

As the path continued to unwind before her, the dripping turned into a trickle. The voices kept coming, increasing in frequency and volume. Next, she again heard the words of the pastor on Easter Sunday: "The perfect Lamb of God, Jesus, mercifully took our place and was sacrificed for us," followed by his biblical exhortation: "I urge you, brothers and sisters, in view of God's mercy, to offer your bodies as a living sacrifice, holy and pleasing to God—this is your true and proper worship." Then Sarah's voice, vulnerable and trusting, took a turn: "My grace is sufficient for you, for my power is made perfect in weakness." Without realizing it, Amber picked up her pace.

Then, somewhere inside her soul, a dam burst, and the thoughts began to flood her mind faster and faster, so rapidly that they could not be staunched: "Even the most seemingly secular person is actually still religious . . . We all hold to a set of beliefs that guides our moral values and goals in life . . . The wrath of God is being revealed from heaven against all the godlessness and wickedness of people, who suppress the truth . . . We can't even keep the rules we set for others and ourselves, let alone God's perfect moral law . . . But Christ did not only die—He rose again on the third day . . . He defeated sin and death, and by faith we can share in those priceless blessings . . . All things work together for good, for those who love the Lord and are called according to His purpose . . . "

The cacophony of voices overlapped and even repeated themselves, racing to a climax even as Amber, her jaw clenched, accelerated to a sprint. But try as she might, she couldn't outrun them. The voices ceased only when she halted abruptly in the middle of the trail. All except one. In the silence, broken only by her own strained breath, a voice she did not recognize asked once more: "What do you worship, Amber?"

Thunder clapped across the horizon, and Amber fell to her knees, her face seeking the stirring clouds above. "It's true," she confessed, her eyes unveiled. "It's all true." The raindrops started softly at first, a delicate patter on the tree branches and light sprinkles upon her upturned cheeks, mingling with the tears that began to stream down them. Steadily increasing, the shower soon turned into a downpour as heaven seemed to empty itself. Amber's grimace relaxed into a grateful smile. Her pulse slowed, and her mind stilled. All she heard was the pelting rain set against the incessant rumbling of the creek.

Amber did not know how long she knelt. Standing, she turned and resumed her run in the opposite direction, the trail already turning into mud. By the time she sloshed up to her car, caked with mud to the ankles, she was sopping wet.

CHAPTER 38

The blackout curtains had been pulled all the way across the window, leaving Ben and Sarah's room in almost total darkness. The only exceptions were the sliver of light cast from the bathroom, the door of which they had left cracked open, and Ben's phone screen, which glowed below his face. He scrolled through his favorite news sites, propped up in bed by a small mountain of pillows. He had always wondered why hotels placed so many on the beds and usually tossed all but one on the floor. Tonight, though, he was glad for them. He wore long sleeves and sweatpants, since he always considered the thin top sheet alone insufficient to stay warm. He never wanted to touch the comforter, which he guessed seldom saw the inside of a washing machine.

Sarah, meanwhile, slumped in the queen-sized bed beside his, trying to fall asleep on the eve of her big day. They had set the AC at a comfortable seventy degrees, but the vent on the wall was pointed directly down on them. Ben worried that the constant draft would leave them both with dry mouth, and he didn't want Sarah waking up dehydrated. Taking a sip from one of the complimentary bottles of water, he made a mental note to turn the fan down before he went to sleep.

Halfway through an article expounding on the latest political outrage, a muted text message notification popped up on his screen. Seeing it was from Amber, he tapped it. He had been expecting one.

"Just checked in. You awake?"

Ben glanced over towards Sarah's indistinct form before thumbing his reply: "Yes. Sarah's sleeping. Tired?"

The answer arrived just as he found his place again in the article, and he tapped once more: "Yes, but there's news I'd like to share. In person. Too late to meet in lobby?"

Ben was a long way from falling asleep at ten o'clock p.m. and spending some time with Amber certainly sounded more appealing than continuing to read the news. The cryptic nature of her message only increased his curiosity. His thumbs went back to work: "Give me five minutes." Ben climbed out of bed, groped for his duffle bag, and changed into some jeans while speaking to Sarah just loudly enough to be heard over the AC. "They're here. I'm gonna go say hello. I'll be back in a bit."

He heard Sarah, far from slumber herself, roll over. "OK," she softly replied. "Say 'hi' to them for me."

"Will do." After Sarah rolled back over, Ben slipped on a pair of trainers, grabbed the room key, and headed quietly for the door, which opened and latched behind him all too noisily despite his best effort. He tried the handle and pushed on the door before leaving just to make sure it was shut and locked.

Ben took the elevator down to the first floor, and after rounding a corner stepped out into the recently renovated lobby. Brightly lit, the check-in area was vacant at the late hour, but he saw Amber standing amidst an arrangement of new Modern furniture in the furthest corner. Wearing skinny jeans and a long-sleeve Henley, tucked behind her belt buckle in the front and left out in the back, she gazed at the abstract décor on the wall with folded arms while biting on a nail. Ben strolled toward her across the pristine tile, and, seeing him approach, she faced him with a smile.

"Hello! How was traffic?" asked Ben as Amber accepted his hug with open arms.

"Well, besides crawling half-way down the mountain behind an RV, it was pretty smooth sailing."

Ben winced about the RV as they parted and set his hands on his hips. "I hate that! You wonder why they don't pull over when there's a dozen cars stacked up behind them! But otherwise that's great . . . I hesitate to ask, but how's the Achilles?"

Amber, with one booty crossed over the other and her hands clasped in front, nodded affirmatively. "Solid! By the end of the week, I wasn't holding anything back. A little stiff and sore the day after a workout, but nothing out of the ordinary."

"Awesome!"

There was a gap as Amber, simmering with excitement, seemed uncertain of how to steer the conversation to the matter at hand. "Hey, sorry to drag you down here this late, but I really didn't want to wait until tomorrow. It's going to be a busy day, and we wouldn't have any privacy."

"You have to stop apologizing," Ben insisted. "I'm glad you texted. But you certainly have piqued my interest." His tone turned ironic. "Did you win the lottery? Are you going to share it with me?" He chuckled.

"In a way." Amber grinned even as Ben noticed her jade-colored eyes begin to water.

Leaving off with the joking, he gestured to the couch. "Let's sit down," he suggested gently.

Amber readily agreed, and they stepped over to sit down facing each other, their knees almost touching. Belying his eagerness, Ben casually leaned back and crossed one leg over the other, stretching one arm along the back of the couch, while Amber leaned forward with her elbows resting on the fashionably frayed knees of her jeans. Her blonde tresses almost veiled the hands folded beneath her chin. Looking down, she took a moment and silently gathered herself before raising her eyes back up to meet Ben's. When she began, her tone suggested she had reflected on the topic many times over and reached a firm conclusion.

"Ben, something incredible happened to me this morning on my long run up the mountain. When I started the run, I can say that I was interested in your views on faith and God . . . intrigued by our conversations and the Bible reading you gave me . . . and maybe even a little jealous of the peace and purpose you have found as a Christian." She paused. "Still, despite my own inner restlessness, I was resisting all of it. I didn't believe." Amber slowly shook her head to accent the last point, while Ben shifted his own head with increasingly widening and intent eyes. When she continued, Amber, shrugging, acted as if the reality of what she was about to say was hard for even her to grasp. "But by the time I finished my run . . . I did believe. Something happened inside me." Amber stared blankly ahead, as if reliving the moment. "I don't really know how to describe it other than to say it felt like the walls that I had put up around my heart were torn down, and God's truth rushed in. All at once, I saw God's . . . " For a moment, Amber searched for the right words before finding them, " . . . holiness and my sin, and I gladly accepted His mercy." Her gaze returned to Ben, her face radiant. "Suddenly, I don't want to live for just myself anymore. Now I want something more . . . to live for God, even—and this is the scary part—not knowing where it may lead."

"Amber!" Ben leaned forward and enfolded her, pulling her head close to his shoulder. When he finally spoke again, his voice was choked with emotion. "Words can't describe my joy . . . What a gift!" He felt her arms tighten around him.

When they separated, Amber peered up at Ben with dripping eyes and a skewed smile. "I must look like a mess!" she said, half-laughing at herself. Already pulling a tissue from a pocket, she began wiping her face.

"That makes two of us," Ben assured her, gently wiping away a missed tear from her cheek with his thumb. He took in a deep breath and let it out slowly as they stared at each other in rapturous disbelief. "Wow! So, you had some news you wanted to share in person. I'll say! You really did win the lottery, so to speak. Thanks for sharing this with me . . . I'll wait to let you tell Sarah. To say she'll be thrilled is an understatement."

Amber, still dabbing under her eyes, nodded and cleared her throat. "Well, I'm not sure that's going to be tomorrow. She has plenty to focus on already."

CHAPTER 39

The pickup followed the orange wand as the parking attendant pointed left. Sarah and her dad then passed at least a dozen rows blocked off with lines of orange cones before they reached the end of the lane, where another attendant waved them to the right. This lane stretched for a few hundred meters, past several lots already full, until it reached yet another orange wand waving them to the right. Finally, they arrived at the lot furthest from the stadium, already half-full, where one last attendant motioned them into a parking space next to the car pulling in ahead of them. Amber and Kiana soon slipped the silver sedan into the slot on the other side of the truck. The parking ordeal served as a vivid reminder not only that the State meet was already well under way but also that Sarah had joined the ranks of the state's track and field elite.

All four gathered by the tailgate of the truck to double check that they had everything they needed. Due to the warm day, Amber and Kiana wore t-shirts and running shorts, while her dad debuted a pair of cargo shorts and a baseball-style cap purchased as a memento at the regional finals. Sarah, shouldering her gear bag, had still chosen to wear a pair of calf-length leggings over her shorts and her letterman's jacket over her jersey despite the balmy weather. Her decision was part practical and part mental. The compression tights would ensure a quick and thorough warm-up with some protection while stretching on grass, but there was also something about shedding layers of clothing that made her feel lighter and fresher for her race. And she didn't want to mess with a proven routine now.

Standing next to Sarah, Amber looked down at her dad's pale legs, and grinned.

"What?" He shrugged.

"I don't think I've ever seen you in shorts before. Did you bring sunscreen?"

"No."

"You're going to burn!" She laughed. "I've got some in the car if you want some."

He shook his head with a frown. "I'll be fine! We're not going to be here for more than a couple of hours. This isn't Hawaii."

"OK," relented Amber, putting up her hands. "But just remember I offered."

Sarah led the way as they embarked on the almost quarter-mile journey into Veterans Memorial Stadium. Situated between a large regional park and the city's newest high school, the municipally-owned stadium was used by all the high schools in town for football games and graduations. However, it had been designed specifically with track and field in mind, one reason it had hosted the State championships for the last ten years. Not only did it accommodate an official capacity of eight thousand, but it uniquely offered a throwing ring for shot put and discus in the infield rather than a remote location. As they drew closer, the muffled echoing of the PA system grew more distinct, and the double-decked home bleachers began to loom large, the sprawling press box perched above the top deck.

The four briefly split up at the admission gate. Amber stayed with Sarah as they headed towards the team entrance on the left, where Amber picked up the team packet with the heat sheets and her bib, while her dad and Kiana merged into the ticket lines on the right. A few minutes later, they reunited with her dad and Kiana by the entrance on the broad concourse that wrapped itself behind the stands on each side in a cement oval around the entire stadium.

The spot afforded an impressive view. Only then did Sarah realize the track sat down in a bowl, almost doubling the size of the stands as seen from outside the stadium. The monolithic home bleachers on the right, packed with fans almost to the top row, proved three times larger than those on the visitor side, less than half-full. Arced slopes of grass linked the two sides around the curves, where hundreds of spectators, some equipped with beach chairs and blankets, could get close to the action by leaning on the waist-high portable iron barriers that lined the edge of Lane Nine.

Spread out below her, the competition zone pulsed with activity. She watched as a crew busied itself on the home stretch, setting up flights of hurdles on the light blue track stylishly inlaid with burnt orange relay exchange zones. In the infield, jumpers sprinted down a pair of runways before leaping into the sand pits along the home stretch, while vaulters, bending fiber glass poles like rubber, launched themselves heavenward before falling into two padded pits along the back stretch. Meanwhile, boys in the near corner grunted in the shotput ring, and girls attempted to soar over the high jump bar in the far corner.

In the midst of it all, at midfield, stood the elegant awards stand crafted from hardwood and presided over by a professional photographer.

Sarah observed the end of the award ceremony honoring the six medalists in the boys sixteen hundred meters, narrated by the voice of the PA announcer, which bounced around the stadium. At its conclusion, the crowd erupted into applause. Sarah's heart rate quickened at the sound and the thought of earning a spot on that podium.

"Quite a set-up," commented her dad.

"Wish my State meet could have looked like this," Kiana concurred.

"It's nice," Amber allowed. She looked back over to the track to see the hurdle crew had finished its work and nine girls setting their starting blocks. "Well, they're about to begin the girls one-hundred-meter hurdles, so Sarah and I better get going if we're not going to rush her warm-up."

"Where is the warm-up area?" asked Sarah, scanning the stadium.

Amber pointed a little more than fifty meters to their left on the visitor side, past the line of merchandise tents. "It looks like it's over there." Sarah glanced down the concourse to see a trickle of athletes entering and exiting a gate in the chain link fence that led to an open field. Directly across from the gate, the staging area consisted of a corridor cordoned off by a pair of lines with small, triangular flags strung from the edge of the concourse all the way down the grassy slope to the edge of the track. The clerks sat at tables set beneath a long canopy stretching half the length of the corridor, providing shade. A moment later, an official began leading the boys hurdle finalists down the passageway to the track while stragglers made their way back up after their events, a few gleefully clutching medal cases.

Her father turned and gave Sarah a hug while Amber and Kiana looked on behind their sunglasses. "I'm so proud of you. Try to enjoy this moment!"

She rewarded him with a faint smile. "Thanks. I'll try."

Suddenly, she realized that she had been less anxious than normal all day. She chalked it up to her reaching the last race of the year, for better or worse, and the privilege of having made it there at all. With one last look up into his beaming face, Sarah turned and walked away through the milling crowd with Amber at her side.

*****

Her last stride complete, Sarah slowly ambled back toward Amber, on the other side of the field, who was leaning against the chain link fence with one knee bent. Stripped down to her spandex shorts and racing jersey, Sarah had never felt her legs so light and energized before a race. There really was something to this tapering idea, she thought. While reviewing the competition, she recognized not only the three girls from her regional final, including Eva, her friendly rival from Arroyo Hills, but also a few others at Western Relays and another at the Rodeo. She guessed that she had already run against over half the field.

At length, Sarah reached Amber's aviators, and her coach leaned forward, placing both feet on the ground, before launching into her last advisory session. "You've had an incredible season, especially for a sophomore. The heat sheet shows you're one of only two underclassmen to make it to this race."

"I feel like I'm walking in a dream," confessed Sarah.

"I get it. But there's a danger in being satisfied. Understand that many of these girls are seniors, and this is it for them. This will be their last high school race. They've worked longer for this than you, and they'll be hungry, even desperate, to go out on top with a medal and a spot on the podium. Only six of you will make it there. There are no do-overs. Don't make the mistake of looking back and wishing you'd matched their intensity level."

Sarah nodded, and Amber shifted gears. "OK, three tactical keys. One: do not lose contact with the pack at the start, but if you do, continue your opening sprint until you link up again. Two: always stay within striking distance of a spot on the podium. Know where you are. And three: if there's still a lot of traffic at the end of the race, and at this level there very well may be, don't get boxed inside for the last two hundred meters. Keep your pathway options open by running the last curve on the shoulder of the pack, even in Lane Two, if necessary. The flexibility is worth the extra distance." Sarah nodded again.

"Last call, girls eight hundred meters," crackled the loudspeaker at the entrance to the warm-up area.

"That's my cue," Sarah noted stoically. Her features tightened up.

Setting her sunglasses on top of her head, Amber placed a hand on Sarah's shoulder and caught her eyes. "Can I pray for you before you go?"

Sarah did a double take. " . . . Sure," she agreed with a hint of uncertainty that she immediately regretted. Seeing Amber close her eyes and slightly bow her head, Sarah did the same.

"God, please let all of Sarah's hard work and the gift of running You've given her be displayed today." Surprised to feel a knot on its way, Amber fought hard to keep emotions from complicating the moment. "And help her to trust You no matter what happens in the race. Amen." Amber looked up again to see Sarah still staring at her, a stunned expression lingering on her face. When Sarah failed to move, Amber pointed towards the staging area with a wide smile. "Don't just stand there! Go! You'll miss your race!" Finally, with a smile as big as Amber's spreading across her lips, Sarah spun around and jogged off to do battle.

*****

The matter had been decided by text. Any decent seat near the start-finish line on the home side had been snatched up hours ago, let alone three seats together. Instead, Ben and Kiana had found room on the railing in the first row of the visitor stands just a few meters short of the two-hundred-meter clock, where Sarah's splits would be easy to see, and Sarah would be sure to hear them as she passed by at two key moments in the race. If she needed any encouragement or advice after the start or before the final push, they would provide it. Less than a minute's walk from the warm-up area gate, it would also prove convenient for Amber to reach.

Looking constantly over his right shoulder, Ben finally spotted Sarah report to the staging area, roughly fifty meters behind them at the top of the slope. Moments later, Amber arrived with Sarah's gear bag in hand. "Everything's in motion," she announced, as they made room for her to sit between them. "Time to sit back and watch it unfold." She took one glance at Ben's knees and cringed. "Ouch!" She covered her mouth in an unsuccessful attempt to disguise her amusement. Ben noticed.

"What?"

"If your knees are already that red," she answered, pulling her hand away, "you'll look like a lobster before we leave!"

Ben looked down and couldn't argue. "OK, you were right! Are you happy?" he asked with a hint of annoyance.

Amber, muting her expression, patted him on the back and assumed a more sympathetic tone. "Just be sure to get some aloe vera on that when you get home, OK?"

"I'll be sure to do that, Mom." He grinned despite himself. Amber grinned, too.

While they waited for the one hundred-meter finals to start on the far side, Ben tried to calm his nerves by observing those around them. Their section seemed to be a favorite for heat sheet-scouring and stopwatch-toting college assistants, conspicuous in their crisp school polos and hats. He noted multiple Big XII and SEC schools, among others. Ben was briefly distracted by the firing of the gun, followed by a twelve-second outburst from the crowd. Another rise came when the results flashed on the scoreboard, showing the top three finishers separated by five one hundredths of a second.

Between the girls' and boys' one hundred meter races, he spotted a camera positioned on the back stretch for the live stream. It reminded him that Jack and Cathy were watching. The production didn't seem as extravagant as that for Western Relays, however, as the only other cameras he could locate were of the mobile variety carried on shoulders to record field events and interviews. He assumed there was one or two more on the home stretch, too. Eventually, the gun cracked again, this time followed by an eleven-second outburst from the crowd.

The buzz in the stadium was still dying down when Ben heard Kiana's update. "And they're off!" Ben's heart skipped a beat as he and Amber turned to see an official leading Sarah's heat down the grassy corridor to the track. As the runners crossed on to the infield in front of them, with Sarah eleventh in line, they yelled to her. Turning her head, Sarah saw them but looked too embarrassed to acknowledge herself as the object of the cheers. The line proceeded across to the infield during the girls one hundred meter awards ceremony, careful to bend behind the podium on its way to the start-finish line on the far side of the track. At the same time, Ben observed eight track officials holding flags begin to space themselves out every fifty meters around the track.

"What are they doing?" he asked Amber, pointing.

"They'll be watching the race for any disqualifying actions. If they see any, they'll raise a flag to notify the red coats."

"Where were they last week?" he mused aloud.

He didn't receive an answer as the string of twelve runners had reached the starting arc and immediately scattered as each took at least a couple of strides. On the track, there was no hurry; a crew still worked on carting away the starting blocks of the boys one hundred meter race on one end of the straight while a set of red coats organized itself for the start of the eight hundreds on the other end. With the awards ceremony complete, the PA announcer launched into announcing the names and schools of the entire girls eight hundred meter final field. All three cheered loudly again at Sarah's name and school as it echoed throughout the stadium.

"They messed up the school pronunciation!" Ben complained.

Kiana laughed. "You'll have to forgive them; it's the first time they've ever read it here!"

Amber smiled at the thought. "I have a hunch they'll get it right before Sarah graduates. So will all the college scouts here," she predicted, motioning her head toward the rows behind them.

From Ben's distant position, Sarah looked like she was second from the rail in the rear group, though it was hard to confirm with the timing equipment and officials milling in the area partially blocking their view. That was right where the heat sheet placed her, too, as the eleventh seed. "She's in a terrible starting position," he worried. "She's going to get cut off by everybody."

Amber offered a different take. "In this race, everyone will be lightning off the line. Sarah may well be able to accelerate to her race speed without having to break stride or swing too far out to find the shoulder and move up. Let's hope!"

With the introductions at an end, a red coat mounted a ladder, and the top four seeds were led to the forward starting arc. Then all the runners received the instruction to take two steps back from the line. After the supporting red coats evacuated the track, the starter's gun pointed to the sky. Ben was too far away to hear the command, but when he saw twelve girls stutter-step to the line, bend, and freeze with one arm cocked, his heart tensed further. Then he heard the gun fire.

*****

Crack! The scene instantly blurred in Sarah's eyes as she strove once again not to be left behind. Eva, the tenth seed to her right, shot forward, along with the other lower seeds further down the line. As Amber had predicted, the sprinting cutters angled to the rail while far enough ahead that Sarah did not need to break her stride; while revving up her long legs, she forged almost straight ahead near the rail without adding extra meters. By mid-curve, she succeeded in trailing just a step behind a pair of girls who had sifted back to the rear of the pack, and she maintained that link to the curve's end. Meanwhile, Sarah watched the top four seeds merge with the pack ahead, tucking into a gap behind a pair of lower-seeded leaders that seemed determined on pulling away.

While the rest settled in, Sarah sustained her opening dash down the back stretch on the pack's shoulder. Less than halfway down the straight, she caught and then passed the rear pair, drawing even with another girl running against the rail. For a moment she considered trying to move up further, but after quickly assessing the swiftness of the pace, the distance to the next pair ahead, and the distance to the curve, decided against such an early expenditure of energy in favor of playing to her strength: the long game. Tucking into Lane One next to the girl on the rail, she enjoyed a splendid view of the mid-thirty-two on the two-hundred-meter clock as they clicked by. "Right where you want to be, Sarah!" Amber's voice confirmed her own thought. In fact, it was the fastest opening two hundred of her career by half a second.

Heartened by her start, Sarah focused on remaining even with the girl inside her around the curve and again succeeded. Anticipating the home stretch, she then attempted to slingshot past the next pair of runners, inching into Lane Two as the lanes straightened out. Suddenly, she recognized the runner directly ahead as none other than Eva. Sarah felt the adrenaline coursing through her veins as she extended her stride, powered her arms, and forcefully exhaled, blind to the thousands looking down from above. But all her opponents applied the same strategy, and as she neared the start line her reward for the exertion was merely maintaining her position. That and another PR split. She caught the clock as it whisked by: a mid-sixty-five, a full-second best four hundred. It provided some comfort to know she was on the top of her game, but Sarah knew full well time alone wasn't going to get her on the podium.

As she entered the third curve, Sarah marveled how she could be on such a PR pace without feeling much worse. Her arms and legs still felt capable of sustaining her pace a bit longer, and her lungs still detected the oxygen in the air.

Sarah ran the third curve like the second: matching stride for stride with the girl inside and at least sustaining her advantage over the girls behind; she couldn't hear them anymore. While counting the runners curving ahead, Sarah noted that all eight ran as pairs, with the lead pair still more than five meters ahead of the pack. She also quickly gauged the distance between herself and sixth place at roughly five meters, within striking distance. It wasn't time to panic yet, but she knew the number of meters left to catch them was shrinking by the step.

The curve wound to an end, and Sarah surged on to the back stretch, again edging slightly out in an attempt to pass Eva and her inside partner. But despite another supreme effort, the four pairs of runners ahead drew no closer, with the co-leaders holding on to at least a five-meter lead in front of the pack. However, this time her burst came at the expense of igniting the ever-familiar burning in her legs, arms, and lungs. She immediately focused on regulating her breathing before it spiraled out of control.

Approaching the six hundred meter mark, Sarah, deflated, drifted yet again back into the outside of Lane One, her position unchanged and her body aflame. She paid no heed to the clock now. Panic officially set in as she realized she had no alternative but to try and extend her final surge for the last two hundred meters of the race. "Keep your options open!" Amber's reminder penetrated the fog of her mind, but she doubted if it would end up mattering.

Just when it seemed Sarah's search for opportunities had failed, opportunity found her. As she entered the final curve, she gazed helplessly at the arced column of pairs she could not reach until noticing the co-leaders, now visibly laboring, had started to sag slowly back to the pack, which strode purposefully on. Having taken the race out too fast, whether in an ill-fated gamble or an inability to harness their nerves, both were now paying the price in spades. As the co-leaders' collapse accelerated, the rate at which the pack closed the gap increased, too. Sarah immediately perceived a traffic jam would form as the runners at the front of the pack would be forced to swing around them to pass. The window would close fast, but if she could just get on Eva's shoulder before Eva and her partner tried to pass, it could change everything. If she possessed another gear, the time to discover it was now.

Sarah shifted into overdrive and drifted into Lane Two just as the front of the pack caught the co-leaders at mid-curve. The third-place girl on the outside easily slid into Lane Two, maneuvering around them to take the lead, but the fourth-place girl on the inside, following her, barely squeezed into Lane Two ahead of the fifth-place girl as she attempted the same maneuver. On cue, the sixth-place runner then made a move to squeeze into Lane Two ahead of Eva and her partner. But just as Eva looked to angle outside and beat her to the spot, she discovered it was too late: Sarah had already drawn even on her outside shoulder, boxing her in and causing both Eva and the runner on the rail inside her to break stride rather than run up the backs of the former co-leaders. Sweeping by unimpeded, Sarah not only passed four runners in one fell swoop but left her challengers frantically trying to regain their full stride after they finally managed to ease past the moving roadblock.

Breaking on to the home stretch, Sarah spied only four runners, also in full-sprint mode, still ahead. It took a moment for the magnitude of the reversal to register—she was suddenly one hundred meters from glory that just moments before seemed out of reach. But she was far from certain she could survive the final flight before lactic acid paralyzed her body; her early kick was already taking its toll. She barreled on as if the hounds of hell were nipping at her heels, and it wasn't far from the truth: three rivals just a few meters behind, including Eva, had indeed rediscovered their stride and strove just as desperately to run her down.

Sarah dared not turn her head, but she heard them coming. For her. First the striking of their spikes. Then the gasping of their breath. Every desperate stretch of her foot, swing of her arm, and gulp of air felt like throwing gasoline on the fire. Fifty, forty, thirty: she watched the yard-lines on the football field pass with agonizing sluggishness, the finish line unmoving. Then she saw what she had only heard: a runner edged into her peripheral vision, causing a final spasm of effort she didn't know possible.

Sarah wasn't sure her eyes remained open for the final twenty meters, but she did see the sheer mercy of the finish line flick beneath her. Staggering to a stop like a drunken scarecrow, she threw her hands behind her head, her first concern to force oxygen into her reluctant lungs. As she wheezed, her eyes seeking the scoreboard, she knew she had given everything and run smart. She had done her very best. She could live with that.

The results soon began to post in the order of finish. Sarah patiently continued sucking in air while the first four names appeared and then pumped a fist, her teeth clenched, as her name appeared next: 5th / Sarah Turner / Montevallo Chr. / 2:12.27. Eva's name immediately followed.

Euphoria expelled the pain. Sarah, still catching her breath, knew the letters and numbers were more than just pixels on a screen. Her two-second PR almost an afterthought, she had achieved what was seemingly impossible just three months ago. Spinning, she searched the crowd on the far side of the track near the two-hundred-meter clock and heard what her labored breathing had prevented: the uninhibited cheers from her rooting section. Bouncing up and down, she waved her arms in acknowledgement.

Sarah was still waving when a pair of slippery arms startled her as they draped themselves heavily over her shoulders, followed by an exhausted voice in her ear. "Congrats! . . . Smart race . . . You caught me sleeping."

Sarah wriggled around to find Eva, still heaving herself, with a fatigued grin on her face. She gladly returned the hug. "Eva! . . . Congrats to you, too! . . . I can't believe we're on the podium together! You were pulling and pushing me the whole way . . . You deserve it!"

Eva nodded. "I'm not gonna complain . . . A big PR for me . . . and a medal I've dreamed of for four years."

"Take it to the infield, Girls!" interrupted an approaching red coat, herding the contestants off the track. Looking around, they were surprised to find the boys eight hundred field already stepping on to start their strides.

They complied, with Sarah slinging an arm around her new friend's shoulders. And while half the field of girls, dejected, slowly started their trek back to the grassy slope, a giddy Sarah and Eva prepared themselves to make the coveted stop at midfield with the other half.

*****

Ben, Amber, and Kiana drew some curious glances as they jogged briskly down the concourse, chattering like little kids as they went. They couldn't have cared less. Sarah had just pulled off the improbable, and they were not going to watch the awards ceremony from the rear.

After rounding the curve, they made their way past the concession lines extending behind the home stands and chose a central portal leading into the bleachers. They popped out on the other side to find themselves on a wide aisle separating the two decks and surrounded by spectators on all sides. Ben felt like he had just parachuted into a professional sporting event. Finding three seats together was out of the question, so they contented themselves by standing back against the wall below the first row of the upper deck. They hadn't arrived a moment too soon.

The runners had already taken their places on the graduated stand, with Eva standing on the lowest pedestal to their far right and a delighted Sarah perched on a slightly higher step on the extreme left. Ben was surprised how small the medalists looked from that height and distance. They cheered for both girls' names as they bent down to receive a handshake and a case with a medal secured inside from a meet official. When all had been recognized, the photographer posed them with their cases, right side up, held with both hands at their waist. Dozens of flashes made the crowd sparkle.

After a final ovation, the girls stepped down, and Ben turned to his two female companions with reddened eyes. "I can't believe that just happened. Thanks so much for sharing this moment with Sarah and me. I really appreciate it," he said to both, and stepped forward to give Kiana a hug she gladly accepted.

"Believe me, it's my pleasure," she assured with a wide smile as they parted.

When Ben turned to Amber, she did not wait for him to initiate. With a look of deepest satisfaction, she stepped forward, and they held each other, neither saying a word.

CHAPTER 40

The strains of Guns 'N Roses wailed above the clanking of the weight room equipment as Amber worked with a client in front of the wall mirror by the dumbbell rack. The forty-something housewife, in capri-length leggings and a tank top, stood feet together, leaning over at close to a ninety-degree angle with a pair of five-pound dumbbells in her outstretched hands. Each loud breath marked another repetition as she persevered through her last set of bent-over back flies.

"Five, four, three, two, one!" counted Amber, supervising from behind. "Great job!" Setting the weights down on the rubber floor mat, the housewife placed both hands on her thick waist and sighed. "That's it for today," Amber announced, looking at her watch. "We went a little long with the lifting, so, if I could, I'm going to let you stretch out on your own today. My next client will be here in just a few minutes."

"Sure, that shouldn't be a problem," the housewife replied. "I remember what to do."

"Thanks, Jenny." Amber smiled appreciatively. "And remember, I'm going to be out of town again for the next two sessions, but I'll text you your workouts. I hope you still get in here while I'm gone! I know it's easy to let it slide when you're not meeting someone."

"I'm planning on it," said Jenny, wiping her brow. "I'm getting a lot more comfortable with the exercises and how everything works in here, so it's not so intimidating anymore." Stooping, she grabbed her water bottle off the floor by the mirror, groaning from the effort. Then she smiled. "Have a great trip! I'll look forward to seeing you when you get back!"

"Same here! Bye!" Taking a gulp as she went, Jenny strolled off toward the yoga mats in the dance room. While Amber squatted to pick up the weights and return them to the rack, she spied Cathy Sutherland near the front desk, dressed in a floral, short-sleeve blouse and crème-colored slacks, scan the room with searching eyes. Locating her target, Cathy confirmed Amber's attention with a wave, and Amber made her way toward Cathy with a smile while tightening her ponytail.

Cathy didn't wait for Amber to reach her. "Congratulations, Amber!" she half-shouted.

Amber's smile turned a little bashful as she approached. "Thanks!" She couldn't get out another word before Cathy continued, her hands and eyes doing half the talking.

"We watched the live stream online and were starting to lose hope near the end. But what a finish! Sarah was amazing!"

Amber's face lit up. "She sure was! A huge PR! I'm so happy she made the podium, and she's only a sophomore!"

Cathy gave Amber a knowing look. "Well, we all know she had a lot of help. You did a phenomenal job with her."

Amber reverted to bashful. "Thank you, I really appreciate that. But you set all of this in motion; none of this would have happened if you hadn't approached me." Cathy appeared flattered by the recognition. "I know I was hesitant about taking Sarah on at first but looking back now I'm so glad we did this." Amber took a moment to ponder. "I had no idea how satisfying coaching a runner would be, especially one as committed as Sarah. And not just that; It's been so great to just get to know her and Ben."

Cathy nodded more than understandingly. "Well, I know the feeling is mutual. Ben called us on the way home to celebrate Sarah's race, but . . . he also told us some wonderful news about you, too!" She gave another knowing smile while assuming a more discreet tone. "Frankly, I don't know which one he was more excited about."

Amber felt herself blushing. "Yeah. It's still sinking in," she admitted, her eyes suddenly seeking the floor. "It's all a bit surreal, but in a good way," she added, nodding.

One of Cathy's hands found her necklace and started rubbing it. "Well, you're not starting this new life alone. Please know we're all here for you any time," she assured, her voice even more subdued. "Take it one day at a time—which is good advice for all of us."

Amber's eyes rose to meet Cathy's. "Thank you."

"So, when do you leave for your big race?" Cathy inquired, perking up again.

Amber's voice grew more confident, too. "I'm flying out Wednesday morning. The prelim is Friday night."

Cathy's eyes tilted up while she calculated. "Wednesday is the twenty first, right?" Her face fell. "Sadly, I always remember that date because it's the day Joy passed away." She took in a breath and sighed. "So, I guess I'm doubly glad for all this good news; it's usually a tough week for Ben. Will your training friend be traveling with you?"

The question seemed to catch Amber off-guard, as if she had been thinking of something else. It took a moment for her mind to catch up with the conversation. "Uh, she was going to, but unfortunately her family needs her back home again. They're transitioning her dad, who had a stroke, from live-in care to just day care. She feels she should be there to help for the first several nights. I'm going to miss her, but, of course, I understand."

Cathy gave a sympathetic look. "I'm so sorry to hear that. Will the race be live-streamed?"

"Actually, it will be televised live on cable."

"Wow!" said Cathy, her eyes popping. "Then I'm sure we'll be watching with Ben and Sarah. We'll certainly be with you in spirit."

Amber's smile returned. "Thanks! I'm glad for the support, believe me!"

Spying her ten o'clock client waiting behind Cathy, Amber tentatively put up a finger. "Please excuse me for just one second." She then waved to an elderly gentleman who always wore a polo shirt and sweatpants to his sessions. "Hi, Joe! Good morning!" She smiled. "I'll be right with you. Why don't you warm up with a five-minute walk on the treadmill?" With a nod, he plodded over to the cardio section.

"Hey, I'll get out of your way," said Cathy, half-turning toward the hallway. "I just wanted to stop by and tell you how excited Jack and I are about how things worked out. And blessings on this weekend!"

Amber's expression indicated that she was touched. "Thank you so much for thinking of me. Bye, Cathy!"

With each offering a final wave, Cathy strode back to her office just as purposefully as she had arrived. Meanwhile, Amber inched over to the day use lockers with distant eyes and pulled out her water bottle before taking a couple of gulps. Cathy's visit had left her with much food for thought, but there wasn't time to digest it now. Joe was waiting for her at the treadmill.

CHAPTER 41

The longest day of the year was just weeks away. Though still early morning, the sun had already hovered above the horizon for an hour by the time Amber locked the apartment door behind her. Rolling a carry-on suitcase out to her car, she placed it in the trunk alongside her carry-on bag. She wasn't going to risk losing any of her running gear by checking a bag. The purse stayed with her as she scooted into the driver's seat with her sock-covered feet slipped into slides. Along with leggings and a cardigan over a tee, her travel outfit promised the most comfort for a day spent in airports and planes.

With a flick of a lever, Amber cleared the heavy dew off the windshield before rolling down her window to wipe the rear-view mirror and backing out from the carport. She had added an extra hour to her timetable just in case. After all, she thought, one never knew if the commuter traffic would grow particularly sluggish when entering the metropolitan area near the airport or if the shuttle bus would show on time at the long-term parking lot. Then again, maybe the security lines would be longer than normal. It was always better to be bored inside the terminal than panicked outside it.

Amber slogged her way through a myriad of stoplights until turning on to the four-lane highway. The road seemed all too familiar: she had just driven Kiana to the airport Sunday morning.

The suburban landscape soon gave way to a more rural one for several miles, a stretch usually relaxing and pretty, ideal for musing.

Amber had to remind herself that she really was traveling to the U.S. Olympic Trials. A life-long athletic journey had finally reached its intended destination. She would be pulling on the spikes and toeing the line with the biggest names in U.S. Track and Field. She imagined herself wearing the national uniform as a team member. But apprehension tempered her elation. The competition would be fierce, and her dream may prove all too short-lived. If only she could make it through the prelims and run in the final. Anything could happen.

Then a new thought penetrated her mind, one that would have been utterly alien just a week before: Amber began to ponder God's purpose in it all. The sense that there was a larger purpose added to the thrill, but at the same time it humbled her. She now knew too well that her accomplishment stemmed more from God's goodness than her efforts, immense as they had been. She had hit a wall with injuries she could not overcome too many times to think she was actually in the driver's seat. She hadn't healed her Achilles in time for the meet. What was God up to?

The thought lead into last night's phone call from Ben and Sarah. Their support and well-wishes had been so sweet. Now that was a God-send.

Amber's route skirted one of the valley's cemeteries, and as she neared it, she noted the sprinklers arcing their spray across the section nearest the highway, glistening in the morning sunlight. The scene triggered a new set of thoughts. Was Joy buried there? And just how hard would the day be for Ben? The thought depressed her. Should she have said something about it to Ben and Sarah last night?

She didn't know if it was her place. The last thing she wanted was to pry or bring any offense. As she passed the ornate gate, her eyes strayed to a lone figure standing at the top of a hill beneath a tree. It looked like a man slouched with his hands in his pockets. Sneaking a last glance before the highway rounded a corner, Amber felt her pulse jump. The man almost certainly was Ben.

As she continued down the road, her mind spun into a quandary. Checking the dash clock, she quickly ran some numbers through her brain even as another part debated whether stopping would be viewed as an invasion of privacy. A quarter mile further down the road, Amber's burdened heart made clear that the two other issues didn't really matter. Following her impulse, she clicked the turn signal and slowed to a stop at the next opportunity before turning around and hastening back to the cemetery entrance.

Passing the hill once again, Amber's gaze confirmed her suspicions, and with a now-thumping chest she took a left to pass through the massive wrought iron gates. It wasn't difficult to find her way to the base of the hill on the access road, where she pulled over to the edge and parked behind Ben's truck. She glimpsed the top half of his form just over the crest facing the opposite direction towards the highway.

Still battling a hundred reservations, Amber opened and closed her door with a trembling hand as quietly as possible before starting a tentative journey up the hill, her slides and socks far from ideal for navigating the slippery grass. Her stomach in knots, she succeeded in reaching the crest without drawing Ben's attention and stopped respectfully a few feet behind him to the side.

*****

Slump-shouldered, Ben stared blankly at the grave. For the last several minutes, a series of images had wandered through his mind. His courtship with Joy. Their wedding. The pregnancy. Their family. Her illness. Her death. Today, though, his eyes remained dry. The fact puzzled him for a moment. He assured himself he hadn't come to say goodbye. Never. The memories were too deeply ingrained. He would always cherish Joy. But then a second thought answered the riddle: his heart had at last been touched by another.

Ben became aware of a presence. Startled, he turned to discover Amber standing meekly, her feet together and hands clasped before her. Ben's shock quickly melted into gratitude, and he pursed his lips.

"Hi." Amber said it so softly it almost sounded like a whisper. "I didn't want to interrupt. Cathy told me about today."

Ben attempted a smile. He could only imagine how awkward she must feel. "Hi, Amber," he replied after clearing his throat. "I thought you'd be halfway to the airport by now. This is your big moment."

Amber nodded silently while studying the grass beneath her. When she raised her eyes again, there was no uncertainty in her voice. "If I miss my flight, there will be others . . . I didn't want you to be alone."

Her words found their mark. Ben widened his smile a little as he removed his hand from his pocket and extended it to Amber. Stepping, she grasped it, and when Ben pulled her forward to join him, she angled slightly into his side to cup his hand with her free hand as well. His voice cracked. "Thanks for coming."

"Absolutely." Amber read the inscription on the marker to herself and noted the fresh flower gracing the holder. "What a perfect verse. For all of us." Ben could only nod.

They stood without speaking for another couple of minutes before carefully walking back down the hill together. Amber had a plane to catch, and Ben had a final exam to give.

CHAPTER 42

Dirty plates and glasses cluttered the coffee table, the scent of Grandma's lasagna still lingering in the air. Jack and Cathy shared the leather sofa with Ben as Sarah, snubbing the matching love seat, opted for the rug on the other side of the coffee table. The eyes of each remained riveted on the flat screen tucked inside the living room's Mission-style cabinet, while Janet busied herself with clean-up in the kitchen.

"I admit," said Jack, sitting back and smoothing his mustache, "when Amber mentioned her goal of competing at the Olympic Trials, I never thought we'd actually be here watching her do it."

The authoritative voice of the broadcast's lead announcer interrupted Jack's confession. "This will be the third and final heat of the Women's Eight Hundred-Meter Preliminary Round. To repeat, the top two finishers in each heat qualify automatically for the final Sunday, and the next three fastest runners over all three heats will join them."

The announcer's English-accented partner jumped in with additional analysis. "It looks like it will take something better than a two oh one point sixty-three to get through to the finals on time, Marty."

Ben looked over his shoulder toward the kitchen. "Mom, they're about to start Amber's race! You're going to miss it!"

Janet returned to the room and stood behind the couch. Wiping her hands on her apron, she placed them on her son's shoulders just as

Sarah pointed to the screen. "There's Amber!" In the camera's panning shot, Amber could be seen shaking out her feet, her gaze distant and her jaw clenched, in front of a tall, yellow cone. The number seven stickers pasted to her cropped racerback top and on her right thigh below her racing briefs matched her lane assignment. Sarah marveled at Amber's customized Trials bib, with "JONES" printed boldly in all caps, and thought about how much most serious runners would give to have one.

"Interesting," noted Jack. "They're limiting each race to nine runners, each starting in their own staggered lane. That tells you everything you need to know about the stakes at hand. They're not taking any chances with an opening pile-up."

Next, a different camera focused on the number one seed in Lane Five, bouncing up and down while shaking out her arms. The announcer jumped back in. "Kendra Williams, the former University of Oregon standout, is the favorite in this heat, as well as with her home track fans at Hayward Field here in Eugene."

"Yes, Marty," concurred the Englishman. "She's run plenty of races on this track, so she's very comfortable here. Her season best is a two minute flat run at the Western Relays last month."

The announcers' voices hushed out of habit, even though they were probably seated in a press box far above the track. "The gun is up." The screen switched to another panned shot of the whole field, this one including the starter on his ladder.

"Come on, Amber!" muttered Ben, his heart rate spiking as they watched the runners stutter-step to the line. He couldn't believe how nervous he was for something happening so far away. He felt like he was there.

The gun cracked, and the competitors instantly sprinted into and around the opening curve. Upon reaching the one-hundred-meter mark at the end of the curve, the outside runners, Amber among them, broke toward the rail, aggressively converging with those in the inner lanes. The forming pack, remaining fairly compact, stampeded down the backstretch, where Amber's rooting section spied the only blonde ponytail in the race swishing back and forth just behind the leaders in the thick of the commotion.

"Some contact there in the pack," commented the announcer, "but still a brisk first two hundred here, similar to the first two heats, with the leaders just under a twenty-nine-second clip."

"Whoa!" exclaimed Sarah, her eyes wide. "They're movin'!"

"Sure are!" agreed Jack.

"The runners in this heat have the advantage of having watched the first two heats," the Englishman advised the viewing audience. "So, they know exactly how much they need to press the pace if they're going to get through to the final on time."

The runners wound into the second curve with the pack still somewhat bunched together, but it started to thin once they reached the home stretch.

"Williams looks smooth," said the announcer, "and she's deciding to push the pace here with a trio of runners going with her!"

"Yes," concurred his partner. "Williams is forcing the issue early."

The producer decided to ditch the panned shots of the whole field and began to focus exclusively on the leaders. The rooting section all glimpsed a grimacing Amber among them on the rail, a step behind the two others separating from the pack in pursuit of the leader.

"Amber's in that trail group!" Jack almost shouted. He lunged forward so suddenly he almost knocked over his glass. "She's in this!"

"Yep!" It was all Ben could say, as his knee shook incessantly. Cathy just sat quietly beside her husband with wide eyes, as if she couldn't believe what she was observing, either to her side or on the screen.

"Williams comes through four hundred at a sub-minute pace!" informed the announcer, a thrill in his voice.

"She's not taking any chances here!" commented the Englishman. "She's clearly seeking at least one of the two automatic bids, if not the victory outright."

The runners snaked around the third curve maintaining their positions, but upon reaching the back stretch the three women in the trail pack began straining to keep contact with the leader, who opened up a five-meter gap. Meanwhile one runner accelerated from the group behind to join them on Amber's shoulder by the time they passed the six hundred mark.

"Williams, extending her lead, looks firmly in control, and that's Valerie D'Agostino coming up from the rear group to join the trail pack," noted the announcer.

His partner laughed nervously as the four trailers entered the final curve. "Things are getting interesting for that second automatic qualifying spot!"

"Go, Amber!" Sarah shrieked, her hands over her mouth. "She's staying with them!"

"Come on!" Ben urged quietly but intensely. Unable to sit any longer, he stood, forcing his mother to step to the side to see.

Jack followed suit, his eyes boring themselves into the screen. "She could do it!"

The announcer cut Jack off again. "Yes, it looks like four runners will be dueling for the last automatic qualifying bid over the last one hundred and fifty meters!"

The camera showed the leader increasing the gap between her and the trail group to almost ten meters around the last curve. By the time the two pairs chasing her reached the final stretch, she was out of reach, but Amber followed the runner on her shoulder, angling away from the rail, as they attempted to slingshot past the pair ahead. Spread out across the first two and a half lanes, with Amber furthest to the right, the four-way duel over the last one hundred meters began. With her defined arms and legs pounding like a machine, her six-pack abs constricted, Amber inched forward ahead of two other runners to challenge the second-place runner striding just as fiercely inside on the rail.

"Amber's surging!" Sarah screamed.

Ben almost matched her volume. "Come on!"

The lead announcer took note, too. "Williams looks like she will cruise into the final, but there's a fight here for second! Amber Jones, the former Arkansas product, is challenging Shauna Hendricks, the NCAA champion from Michigan!" But Amber started locking up, preventing her from reaching the second-place runner ahead even as the two rivals launched their own last-ditch effort from behind, reversing Amber's forward trajectory as the finish line neared. "Now here come D'Agostino and Gina Herbert, battling back with those three at-large berths on the line!"

"Go, Amber!" Sarah was hysterical, pounding her fists on the floor.

"Come on!" yelled Ben.

But Amber's two challengers ran out of room. Though all three leaned at the tape, even a television audience could see that Amber had just held on to edge them for third. Still, no one in the living room seemed to know how to react. As the announcers expounded on the performance of the two winners, they awaited the final results in silence.

"Did she make it?" Sarah demanded, spinning toward the adults on the couch, her face distraught.

"We don't know yet," Jack answered cautiously, his eyes never leaving the flat screen. "It depends on her time." Even as he finished speaking, a graphic posted on the screen listing the nine Finals qualifiers and their times. Amber's name was listed eighth.

Jubilation erupted within the Turner household, momentarily drowning out the continued business-like voices of the announcers. All except Ben's mother, who smiled happily off to the side while soaking in Ben's delight.

"She did it! Two oh one thirty-three! That's a new PR!" Sarah proclaimed.

"No way!" stated Jack, shaking his head. "Unbelievable!" Still sitting beside him, Cathy just beamed. They all settled down long enough to hear the wrap-up commentary.

"So, Kendra Williams takes the heat with a no-nonsense one fifty-nine, a season best," recapped the announcer. "She'll be joined in the final by the second-place finisher, Shauna Hendricks . . . and it looks like Amber Jones and Valerie D'Agostino will join them on time, each coming through at two oh one, earning the last two at-large berths."

As the slow-motion replay of the finish rolled, the Englishman underscored the drama. "Jones and D'Agostino just do outlast

Gina Herbert, who misses out on a trip to the finals by just a few hundredths. She gave it everything she had but came up just short."

After a round of sighs, Amber's rooting crew watched as a camera, mingling among the runners milling in the finish area, showed some congratulating Kendra Williams, including Amber. Exhausted but with her glistening face aglow, Amber traded pats on the back with her, their chests still heaving as they briefly spoke.

Ben spun to face Sarah, his face set. "Sarah, there's no way we're missing Amber's run in the finals." Then he grinned. "What do you say we pay her a little surprise visit?"

Sarah simply squealed.

CHAPTER 43

"And for you, Sir?"

Taking one last glance at the well-used menu, Ben wished his palate was as narrow as his daughter's taste for cheeseburgers. Feeling the waiter's eyes on him, he decided to go with a budget selection. "I'll have the club sandwich on sourdough with the fries. Please hold the tomato." He doubted the baby back ribs would be worth the investment at a twenty-four-hour restaurant a block off the interstate.

The harried server swiftly scribbled the order on his pad and retrieved their menus. "I'll be back in a minute with your waters and some bread."

Thanking him, Ben settled back into his side of the booth. It felt like he was sitting in a hole, but he didn't dwell on the fact. He was simply happy to have reached the Portland suburbs with the flights and the rental car pick-up in the rearview mirror. He was ready for an early dinner. The two mini-bags of nuts on the planes had served as a poor substitute for lunch.

"Well, we couldn't have asked for a better time to take a spontaneous trip," noted Ben.

Sarah thought about it for a moment. "I didn't really think of that. It really is with school just out."

"Yep. You're completely done, and I have until Wednesday to submit final grades. I've already graded my Scantron finals. Now all I have to do is enter the scores into the grading program and upload everything to the school intranet." After second thought, he added, "I guess I also have to add citizenship and work habits comments, but I can do all that when we get home Monday, or Tuesday at the latest."

Sarah looked tired. "So, how long 'til we get there?"

"We've got about an hour and a half to go. We should arrive before eight."

The information seemed to enliven Sarah, who displayed an impish grin. "Us talking to Amber on speaker phone last night was so funny!" She laughed. "If only she knew I was packing for the trip the whole time we were talking! I wanted to tell her we were coming so bad, but it will be so awesome to see her face when we suddenly show up!"

"I know! I can't wait!" Ben agreed with a chuckle. "I just hope she's in her room when we get there."

Sarah suddenly looked puzzled as she realized she didn't know all the details of their plot. She hoped her father did. "How do we know where Amber's staying? . . . I assume you do?"

Ben grinned. "After the phone call last night, I texted her before going to bed. I told her we wanted to send her something special, so she had to tell me where it should be delivered. She replied this morning before we left for the airport."

"You liar!" Sarah accused, tongue in cheek.

"Not really." He laughed. "I'd like to think our showing up in person is more special than sending flowers or chocolates."

"True," Sarah conceded, "but she's probably been waiting for something to arrive all day. That's so sad!" Sarah frowned. "I hope she hasn't been too disappointed. We probably should pick up some flowers for her along the way."

"You read my mind." Ben nodded.

The waiter appeared with a pair of waters and a basket of bread lined with a paper napkin. "Thank you," Ben acknowledged, and promptly drank half of his glass almost before the server had stepped away from the table. The second half was gone a few seconds later. He pushed the empty glass towards the edge of the table to catch the waiter's eye on his next trip by. Meanwhile, Sarah had pounced on the bread and was in the midst of devouring her first piece.

Ben decided there wouldn't be a better time than the present to raise the delicate question that had been on his mind. "By the way, Sarah, I've been wanting to talk with you about something."

His words and cautious tone caused Sarah to refocus her attention away from her next piece of bread to him, her eyes widening warily. "If this is about the birds and the bees, we already had that talk a few years ago. And we covered it again in health class this year."

"No, it's not about that." Ben laughed nervously. His subsequent pause left Sarah looking increasingly alarmed. He knew he just needed to come out with it. "How would you feel if things between Amber and me became more than just friends?" Much to his relief, Sarah broke into a huge smile.

"Dad, I could tell you like her," she declared.

Ben stared back innocently. "Is it really that obvious?"

"Totally." Sarah giggled. "Believe me, I've lived with 'The Hermit' for years, and I've been glad to see him go." But then she grew more sincere. "Dad, I'm old enough to understand that mom isn't coming back, and your not dating isn't going to change that . . . I just want you to be happy, and I think Mom would, too."

Sarah stared down at her fingers and began to fidget with her fork. But just as Ben was about to respond, it became clear Sarah wasn't done. "Honestly, I can't imagine anyone I'd rather see you with than Amber. She's been an awesome mentor. She's helped me get ready for a dance. She knows what happened with Mom, and I can talk with her about it without it being weird . . . And now she's even a believer." Sarah looked up and met his eyes. "Seriously, what more could I want?"

Ben shook his head ever so slightly. "Teenagers are a curious breed. One moment they can be so clueless, and the next they surprise you with their wisdom." He reached across the table and grasped Sarah's hands. "I love you."

Sarah smiled. "I know, Dad."

CHAPTER 44

Ben left the luggage in the car, but he remembered to bring the hat. With Sarah holding the large bouquet of wildflowers, they walked into the hotel lobby just in time to observe the desk clerk turn away a potential lodger with the utmost sympathy. "I'm very sorry." Hearing there was no longer any room at the inn made Ben thoroughly glad he had called ahead to snag a cancellation during their layover.

Sarah hung back as Ben took his turn approaching the wholesome-looking young woman at the counter, her hair pulled up in a tight bun. Penny, the night clerk according to the tag on her fresh white blouse, pivoted cheerfully. "Good evening!" she chirped with a smile. "Do you have a reservation with us?" Ben confirmed, gave her his name, and waited as Penny pulled it up on her screen. "That's for two nights checking out on Monday?"

"Yes."

Seeing the reservation had been made just that afternoon, she affably added, "We usually do have a few cancellations each day during Trials week as guests' plans suddenly change." While handing over his requested credit card and driver's license, Ben admired her genteel manner of noting athletes typically checked out after the flames of their Olympic dreams had been extinguished.

Sarah stepped up to set the bouquet on the counter and give her arms a rest. Between clicks of the mouse, Penny peeked at the flowers. "Those are lovely! Are they for you?" she asked with a pleasant glance at Sarah.

"Oh, no," Sarah sheepishly replied, explaining, "We brought them for someone else staying here."

Penny tilted her head before continuing with her clicking. "That's interesting. I wonder if that's the same guest that stopped by on her return earlier this evening to ask if a delivery had been left for her. She didn't seem to know exactly what she was looking for, or that it would be delivered by anyone she knew."

Sarah raised her eyebrows. "We decided to surprise her. Was she a pretty blonde?"

"That would definitely be the one!" Penny confirmed with a firm nod and a laugh. "I'm so glad! She seemed so disappointed when I told her 'no.'"

Ben turned to look at Sarah, who was wincing at the news. "Dad, I told you!" she scolded.

"Well, I have a hunch she'll forgive us when we show up at her door," he reassured her.

Ever the professional, Penny politely ignored their exchange as she returned Ben's personal items and handed him the room keys. "Breakfast is served in the room behind you between six and ten am, and the elevator is right around the corner." She pointed to both. "Is there anything else I can help you with at the moment?" When Ben declined, she happily sent them on their way. "Well, please don't hesitate to ask. I hope you have a wonderful visit! And good luck on your delivery!"

Ben thanked her, and Sarah handed off the bouquet to him before they sought the elevator. Moving into their room could wait, they had decided; both wanted to get on with the surprise first, and Penny's story only strengthened that resolve. Beeping their way up to the fourth floor, Ben found himself more anxious than he had envisioned. But while he began to second-guess the wisdom of their ambush, Sarah seemed ready to bounce out the elevator doors the moment they opened. Following the room number signs to the right, they padded their way down the hall over the carpet's bizarre patterns and garish colors almost to the end of the wing before locating Room 431.

As they drew near Amber's door, Ben was relieved to hear the television inside. At least she seemed to be home and awake. Sarah huddled with him to propose a hushed, last-second refinement to the plan. "Amber's going to look out the peep hole, so we can't both stand in front of the door. She knows they wouldn't send two people to deliver flowers, and they're not big enough to hide both of us." Ben couldn't argue with the logic. "Hold the flowers up in front of your face, and I'll stand to the side against the wall, where she won't see me right away." That idea led Sarah to another. Already pulling out her phone, her face filled with mischief, she announced, "I'll take a picture of her reaction . . . I can't wait to see this!" Ben nodded.

Sarah hid herself from Amber's view, and Ben set himself directly in front of the door. First pulling down the bill of his hat, he held up the flowers to cover his face. Then, after taking a moment to gather himself, he knocked firmly and called out in his best fake deliveryman voice. "Delivery for Amber Jones!"

*****

The Trials broadcast droned on. Marty and the Englishman took turns commentating on the steeplechase as exhausted runners clambered over the barriers. But Amber wasn't paying attention.

Barefoot, she lay propped up in the unmade bed dressed in an oversized sweatshirt and running shorts, phone in hand. Yet again, she studied the picture of Ben, Sarah, and her taken at Western Relays. Then she scrolled to the more recent picture of all of them with Kiana taken at the State meet. She wished she had a picture of just her and Ben together as well, but it would have been too awkward to ask to take one.

Against all odds, Amber checked once more to see if she had received another text from either Ben or Sarah, only to find nothing newer than Ben's from last night. She reread it for the third time just to make sure she had read it correctly. She had. Ben asked for her address to send something special. She looked at the current time in the corner of her screen, seven fifty-three p.m., and sighed before glumly tossing her phone on the bedding. She didn't want to call the desk again. It was too humiliating. Then again, it wasn't like Ben not to follow through. Amber blamed either the weekend, corporate incompetence or a backlog of orders. After all, she surmised, there were plenty of athletes, and perhaps graduates as well, celebrating in Eugene. Or possibly Ben was sending it by overnight mail. Still, she hoped she hadn't somehow missed a delivery attempt.

A sudden knocking caused her eyes to dart to the door, dispelling her thoughts in a moment. Even over the television, she could swear she heard the voice that followed use the word "delivery." She hoped her mind wasn't playing tricks on her. With anticipation filling her face, she scrambled off the bed and hurried toward the door, smoothing out her clothes and sliding a quick hand through her hair. Peering through the peephole, she strained to see someone with a hat holding a bouquet of flowers. Her heart jumped.

"Yes?" she shouted through the door. "Who is the delivery for?"

"Amber Jones," came the oddly distant reply.

Despite the tingling running the length of her body, Amber forced herself to be cautious. "Who sent them?" A bored answer followed a brief pause.

"Let's see . . . Ben and Sarah Turner."

It had to be real. Wasting no further time, she swiftly unlatched the security bolt and pulled open the heavy door to find the source of the voice still obscured by the flowers. Then the bouquet abruptly sank, and she stood face to face with Ben's bright smile. "Congratulations, Amber!"

Disbelief ran through her before she caught her breath and pressed her fingers to her lips. This man had traveled a thousand miles to bring her flowers. Impulse took over. Lunging forward, Amber reached for Ben's face, and after grasping it, her lips sought his. Ben warmly welcomed them . . . until they both heard a shutter click. Startled, Amber pulled back to see a grinning Sarah, who had stepped out from against the wall, peer out from behind her phone.

"Surprise!"

"Sarah? You, too?" She squealed, her disbelief doubled. Amber felt the blood rush to her cheeks. But her embarrassment vanished when Sarah lurched forward to hug her from one side, and Ben wrapped his free arm around her shoulders from the other. Accepting the bouquet from Ben, she smiled, moisture already rimming her eyes. Looking at both in turn, she sniffled while gently shaking her blonde locks. "I can't believe you guys," she softly croaked. "I couldn't have asked for a more special gift."

"Neither could we," Ben replied. "And we didn't want you to be alone."

CHAPTER 45

The last thing Ben wanted to be was a distraction on the big day. Recalling Amber's mental approach to Western Relays, he had presumed they would wait to see each other until after she had run. So, last night it had come as a bit of a surprise when she told him she preferred to walk the mile from the hotel to the stadium together rather than alone. They had agreed to meet in the lobby, and Ben made sure he and Sarah arrived five minutes early. While they waited among guests checking out on the last day of competition, Ben, out of an abundance of caution, decided to give Sarah a bit of unsolicited advice.

"You probably already know this, but it won't hurt for me to say it anyway just in case. Remember what you're like on race day: you're so full of nerves that you're irritable and just want me to leave you alone. Today you're in a new position as a spectator, not a competitor, so do what I've done for you. Shift into response mode. Give Amber as much distance today as she needs and let her set the tone."

"I know," replied Sarah, sounding a bit irritated. "After all, I did sit in the back seat with her all the way to Western Relays and then warmed up with her. She had her ear buds in almost the whole time. I get it."

"Like I said," Ben repeated in a conciliatory tone, "I thought you did, but you're in a new situation today. I just wanted to be sure."

Their conversation ended when Amber, shouldering her gear bag, emerged from the elevator right on schedule, wearing a zipped sweat top and ankle-length leggings over her uniform. The ear buds plugged into her pierced ears were wired to the phone in her thigh pocket. Smiling nervously, she pulled out the ear buds as she approached. "Hi! Ready?"

Ben and Sarah nodded. "Would you like me to carry your bag?" Ben offered.

Amber shook her head. "No, but thanks for asking." It wasn't all that heavy, and she didn't want to admit the comfort it afforded when held against her body.

Ben noted that the eyes of one bystander, a woman standing nearby with her suitcase in a new Trials tee, had followed Amber from the moment the elevator doors opened. When the three proceeded to exit the lobby, she leaned forward and snuck in a quick wave to Amber as she passed. "Good luck today!" she wished with a thrilled smile.

Like a pro, Amber flashed one in return. "Thank you!" It wasn't the first time she had been greeted by a complete stranger.

As soon as the automatic doors closed behind them, Ben encouraged Amber to retreat to her ear buds. "Don't change your routine for us. You do whatever you need to do to get ready. We'll be totally fine." With a grateful smile, she pushed them back in and punched a button on her phone as they threaded their way through the busy guest loading area under the portico. But they hadn't gone more than a few steps further before Amber silently reached for Ben's hand and clasped it for the remainder of their journey.

They set out under a cloudy sky, the sidewalk damp with a smattering of puddles. Typical Oregon weather, Ben thought. While he and Sarah chatted about her season and summer plans, they crossed

Franklin Boulevard and headed south on Walnut Street for a block until it met East 15th Avenue. Turning right, they joined a steady stream of pedestrians headed to and from Hayward Field less than ten blocks away, a few giving knowing looks to each other while Amber strode past. Well before reaching the stadium, they arrived at the outskirts of the university campus, where they heard the PA system and outbursts from the cheering crowd waft through the grid of leafy streets.

Eventually, they arrived at Agate Street, across the intersection from the wrought iron gates and classic overhang bleachers of Hayward Field. Once they crossed the street, they would invade the hub of the festival atmosphere, where any chance for privacy would be impossible. Slowing her pace, Amber pulled out her ear buds again. "Hey, Guys, before we cross, I'd like to pray," she announced. "Can we walk over there?" She pointed to a paved plaza set off from the street in front of the law library, filled with shade trees and bike racks.

"Of course!" Ben affirmed while Sarah nodded. They sought out an empty space for themselves and huddled together. "Would you like me to pray?" Amber simply nodded as she grasped Sarah's hand, too. Ben gathered his thoughts before beginning. "Father, in your divine plan, You have brought Amber to this place and this moment. We give You the glory for what You have accomplished in her life and for this platform You have given her to represent You. We don't know where Your plan will go from here, but we do know that You promise it is both for her good and a purpose bigger than just herself. We pray that You would help her to trust You with that regardless of the outcome. We ask that You bless her with strength and peace as she uses the gift and opportunity You have given her in this act of worship today. Please let her sense Your presence in the midst of this spectacle, while warming up, while on the starting line, and throughout the race. We ask this in Jesus' name." They all joined in the "Amen."

As Ben and Sarah opened their eyes, they could see Amber's eyes welling even as she smiled. "Thank you so much!" Amber said gently. She looked across the street to the stadium in the short pause that followed before continuing. "You know, I've pictured this day in my head more times than I can count. And in all those visions I never saw you two. Or God! Funny how He works. He had something better in store for me that I couldn't even see." Ben and Sarah could feel their throats closing up as Amber's gaze returned to meet theirs. "I have to say that my biggest comfort is knowing that God is in control and has a plan for me." She nodded. "But a close second is knowing that you'll both be here waiting for me when it's over."

By the time Amber hugged Sarah, they were all sniffling. Then Amber turned to face Ben, and she buried her head in his chest while he wrapped his arms around her. When at length they parted, she took in a deep breath to regroup. With renewed vitality, Amber gave them an exaggerated smile and a double thumbs-up. "Let's do this!" Ben and Sarah laughed.

The three retraced their steps and crossed the street, where they parted ways; Amber headed to the athletes' entrance and Ben and Sarah in search of a scalper for tickets. But just before she slipped off into the milling crowd, Amber gave them a determined last look, already pushing her ear buds back in and setting her jaw. "See you on the other side."

*****

The sky had cleared, and a legion of fans basked in the early afternoon sun. Seemingly every one of the seats surrounding the track was filled, even in the temporary bleachers soaring around the curves. Drama hung in the air as the ultimate winnowing moment had arrived. Nine women stood in front of nine tall, yellow cones, each emblazoned with the lane number in black, staggered through the first curve from the rail to the edge of the track. Three would attain a lifelong dream, and six would go home.

Amber stood in Lane One, her figure pasted with number one stickers as well, not because she was the number one seed but because she had drawn Lane One as the eighth-fastest qualifier. It was better than drawing a position well forward in one of the outermost lanes, she thought. At least from Lane One she could see the entire field spread out before her. She preferred chasing the eight runners ahead, who would pull her forward, rather than running blindly while chased from behind.

A model of toned fitness in her cropped top and racing briefs, Amber waited with hands on hips for the introductions to begin. It was taking too long. Her glazed eyes stared out over the burnt orange surface of the track and followed the clean white lines as they curved into the first turn. Though her heart thumped inside her chest, she was thankful the beat remained steady. As always, she took turns shaking out one foot after the other, but at a more restrained cadence than normal. When he finally arrived, she tried to ignore the cameraman who stood directly in front of her, toting the TV camera below his waist, while another technician handled the wire snaking across the lanes behind it. With the lens pointed at her, the PA announcer's deep bass began to bounce throughout the stadium as she watched her image project up on the jumbotron positioned almost straight ahead. She found it somewhat eerie to see herself enlarged in real time. At her introduction, she acknowledged the ovation from the crowd by stepping forward with a raised arm.

The camera team left to invade Lane Two and all the subsequent lanes in turn, allowing Amber to take a last mental inventory. Stay on the heels of the runner in Lane Two to the break point and always stay linked to the pack. Take up positions on the outside to stay out of trouble and keep her options open. Keep within striking distance of at least second with two hundred to go. She had run for far too long to have a more specific strategy. Races almost never unfolded according to plan; adapting to fluid situations was the key.

After the echo of the last introduction had stilled, the camera crew vacated the track, and all eyes turned to the infield, where an elderly gentleman in slacks, a red blazer, and a white baseball-style cap stood in the pulpit of a short ladder. The buzz from the thousands died down in anticipation seconds before he raised the gun above his head.

Amber, tightening her ponytail as the adrenaline surged further, took a final look at the cloud of witnesses surrounding her. *So, this was it,* she thought. She stood at last where all paths had led her. But where did this one lead? Sucking in a last breath, she whispered a solemn vow. "For Your glory . . . "

"On your marks!" Nine women nimbly approached their lines, bent, and froze, their arms cocked. Silence. With the squeeze of a trigger, a crack resounded across the stadium.

For more information about
G. Walter Bush
and
Gifted
please visit:

www.gwalterbush.com

For more information about
AMBASSADOR INTERNATIONAL
please visit:

www.ambassador-international.com

More from Ambassador International

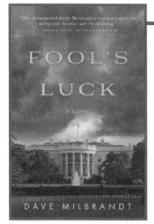

When high school teacher Myles Bradford wins the Powerball lottery, he decides to do something truly unexpected: run for President of the United States. Thrust into the spotlight, he faces attacks and false accusations from political enemies while striving to climb the ladder of success. As his attention is pulled farther away from the things that matter most, Bradford may learn that even success has its price.

Real estate tycoon Rachael Carson knows what's coming when a mob of radical government leaders threaten to take over the world's financial system. Abandoning her New York penthouse and moving to her mansion at Irish Hills, she plots to save her wealth and rescue homeless victims who fall prey to the evil dictates of an advancing world takeover. Will they survive in a world gone mad?

Leah Jung is passionate about Parkour. During her training, she unexpectedly comes face to face with world-class tracuer, Ethan Simpson. He appears to fall for her and suggests that she train with a group—an idea that grows into a vision of teaching teens Parkour while bringing them to the knowledge of the One True God Who loves them. Together with four friends, Leah brings this dream into reality. But not all is as simple as it seems.

Made in the USA
Columbia, SC
08 September 2022

66345625R00152